I0692065

Challenging Destiny

by

Cherie Colyer

This is a work of fiction. Names, characters, places, and incidents are either the product of the author's imagination or are used fictitiously, and any resemblance to actual persons living or dead, business establishments, events, or locales, is entirely coincidental.

Challenging Destiny

COPYRIGHT © 2014 by Cherie Colyer

All rights reserved. No part of this book may be used or reproduced in any manner whatsoever without written permission of the author or The Wild Rose Press, Inc. except in the case of brief quotations embodied in critical articles or reviews.
Contact Information: info@thewildrosepress.com

Cover Art by *Debbie Taylor*

The Wild Rose Press, Inc.
PO Box 708
Adams Basin, NY 14410-0708
Visit us at www.thewildrosepress.com

Publishing History
First Black Rose Edition, 2014
Print ISBN 978-1-62830-372-8
Digital ISBN 978-1-62830-373-5

Published in the United States of America

Dedication

To Pam.
Your support through the years means the world to me.

She put her hands on my waist and rose to her tiptoes. "It's a sweet thought," she said, her breath warm on my lips. "But my fate has already been sealed."

Her perfume seemed to wrap around me, filling me with the urge to pull her closer even though my brain screamed for me to step back. I wondered if this was how the people I made suggestions to felt—compelled to please me—because right then I wanted to sweep Kira up in my arms and kiss her. Although something inside of me clung to the thought that I needed to stay focused on why I was there, every other fiber of my being coaxed me to just let down my guard and enjoy being in a secluded place with a pretty girl.

Kira brushed her lips against mine.

"I'm not what I seem," she said in a husky whisper.

She kissed me before I could reply. Her lips were too hot against mine. My mind exploded with images of burning rivers and pillars made of bone. Lifeless trees reached out of the ground like the hands of the dead. Fire and brimstone rained down on the living. I could hear the screams of people I couldn't see and smelled decaying flesh. Nausea overcame me, breaking the spell I was under. I shoved Kira away, doubled over at the waist, and threw up.

"Like I said, *don't* trust me," she warned.

Praise for Cherie Colyer

author of
one of *Wovenmyst Magagine*'s Best Books of 2012
and
a SCBWI Crystal Kite finalist

~*~

"Colyer's *Embrace* grips you from page one and doesn't let go until the end."

~ *Kate Evangelista, author*

~*~

"Absolutely brilliant! Completely engaging and thrilling until the very last page."

~*Behind a Million and One Pages*

~*~

"I 100% recommend this story to any and all who enjoy a good witch/faerie read. I found it incredibly hard to put this one down and enjoyed every second of it while I was reading it. Looking forward to more work by Colyer in the future."

~*I Read Indie review, (5 Stars)*

Prologue

1732

He stood before me. Regal. Proud. No hint of the demon I knew him to be. I knelt on the cold ground behind the blacksmith's shop. Not out of respect, but because my trembling legs would no longer hold my weight.

"You will do anything?" he repeated, a hint of curiosity in his otherwise bored tone.

I forced myself to meet his gaze. He looked so normal. Like all the other men in my village. He even had a thin scar beneath his left eye. I wondered if he had cut himself in an effort to appear more human.

"If you agree to walk away—to stop pushing for this ceremony you spoke of—yes."

The man who had turned my life upside down pursed his lips as he appraised me. My heart slammed frantically against my ribs.

I could see in his perfect blue eyes that he was going to agree. My plan to save my brother and me would work.

Dry grass crunched under his expensive brown shoes as he walked slowly around me. "And when Elise comes to you, what will you say?"

At this, I raised my chin. "That I've seen the lies in her words, and I will never help her."

He came to a stop in front of me and offered a hand to help me up. I steeled my breath and took it. I was so close to putting an end to the nightmare I'd been thrust into.

"This is your will, to make a deal with me?"

I swallowed my lingering doubt about what I was doing and replied, "It is."

With a glint of something untold, he said, "Kira Rose Mercer, I accept your offer."

I breathed in deeply, relishing the victory. The fall air smelled crisper than it had a moment ago. I took a step back, ready to go home and put the last few weeks behind me.

"Not so fast." He pulled a silver dagger from his pocket.

"You—you can't harm me," I stammered, my mouth dry.

"I've no desire to hurt you." He ran the blade over his palm. A thin line of blood stained his otherwise perfect skin. "The deal must be sealed."

I had won, I reminded myself. If spilling a little blood would get him out of my life, I'd do it. I held up my hand, flinching when the cold steel sliced me.

"Now what?" I asked.

"We shake."

The moment his blood mingled with mine, I knew something was terribly wrong. Fire filled my veins, traveling swiftly through me like molten lava. He pulled me even closer.

"You should have chosen your words more carefully," he whispered gleefully into my ear. "But we will have an eternity to discuss exactly where you went wrong."

"No!" I screamed, but it was too late. I could feel myself changing in unexplainable ways. A raised red circle pierced by an arrow formed on my forearm, binding me to him forever.

Chapter One

Logan

Something was off. I can't explain how I knew, I just did. Like when you put eighty-seven octane in a car that needs ninety-three. Car starts. Gets you where you want to go. But it doesn't run right. That's what the last few weeks of my life had been like. I woke up. Got through the day. But something was different. I could feel it. It was like an unexpected chill on a blistering summer's day in July.

My younger sister sat in the passenger seat, head bobbing to the beat of the music. The carefree vibes coming from her were the only reason I didn't ask her if she felt the chill, too.

I accelerated, crossing the double yellow lines and passing a grandma in a Buick LeSabre. As I blew by the gas station, I saw her. Then the flashing blue lights. The wail of the siren screamed a moment later.

"Great," I said. "Now we're going to be even later."

Ariana looked over her shoulder before tossing a half-full bottle of water into the backseat.

I glanced at her. "This is your fault."

Her mouth fell open. "Dude, I didn't tell you to speed."

"You made us late." I eased my vintage Chevy

Camaro onto the gravel shoulder of the road and dug my wallet out of my back jean pocket. "You could make my life easier by getting up on time." With my hand flat against the center of my window—using the pressure to keep the glass in its tracks—I cranked it open. A cool fall breeze flooded the car.

"License and registration," the female officer said.

I took the registration from Ariana and handed it to the officer with my license. I could see my annoyed reflection in her dark sunglasses.

"This is the third time in a month your plates have been run," she said as she looked over my paperwork.

"Is it?" I replied, doing my best to act surprised.

Ariana leaned closer to me and whispered, "Speed this up already." I held up a hand, motioning for her to wait. She sighed and added, "Fine, but don't whine to me about how late we are."

"Shouldn't you be in school?" the officer asked, glancing at her watch.

"We're headed there now," I said at the same time Ariana blurted, "Yes! Could you please let him off with a warning and let us go?"

The officer removed her sunglasses and bent down, scanning the interior of the car with eyes the color of coal.

"You don't want to give him a ticket," Ariana added all sweet and matter-of-factly.

"I don't?" the officer asked, one blond eyebrow arched.

Ariana just kept talking. "No. You'd rather give him a warning and forget you ever stopped us."

I groaned, wishing Ariana would let me handle this. But the officer smirked, and Ariana held her gaze, an angelic smile plastered across her face.

"You have quite a bit of spunk in you," the officer commented. She chuckled as she shook her head. With one last look at my license, she handed it back to me along with the registration. "Okay, Logan. I'm going to let you go with a warning. Slow down, got it?"

"Thanks, Officer."

She looked at Ariana next. "There is a fine line between need and abuse, young lady. Not that I'm against being a little naughty myself."

The officer walked back to her car.

" 'There's a fine line…' " Ariana said in a tone that mocked the officer's. She put the registration back in the glove compartment and grabbed a piece of gum. "What the heck is that supposed to mean?"

"I don't know," I admitted. "But she obviously knew something was up. You could use a little tact when you're talking our way out of a ticket."

Ariana kicked her feet up on the dash. "Whatever. It worked. She let you go, and we'll get to school in time for me to turn in my homework, which I actually did last night."

As opposed to not doing it at all, which was the norm for her.

"If you're not careful," I said, "you're going to repeat tenth grade." Dirt and rocks kicked up behind us as I pulled back onto the road.

"That will never happen." She blew a bubble and sucked it back into her mouth with a small pop. The smell of strawberries filled the air. "I maintain a B average. So don't worry about me."

"I'm your brother." I playfully shoved her. "It's my job to worry about you, dork." Besides, it was how she maintained the B average that concerned me.

Ariana laughed and pushed me back. "And it's my job to hate it, jerk-face," she retorted, using the nickname she'd given me when she was seven.

She turned up the radio. Her foot bounced to the beat of the song. We sang along, Ariana in her bright soprano voice and me in my slightly off-key way. I couldn't help thinking about how things had finally settled down. Ariana and I were doing all right by ourselves. We had a place of our own—something we'd lived without for a long time—and friends we'd known for close to two years. We were happy.

But that chill was alive, deep in my subconscious, keeping every nerve ending in my body on full alert. I wondered if we had stayed in South Elgin, Illinois, too long. If maybe we should have moved before the school year started.

I peered in the rearview mirror, half expecting to see someone sitting in the backseat. It was a ridiculous thought, yet I still glanced over my shoulder to double-check. It was the unknown that scared the crap out of me, and for good reason. In my seventeen years, I'd seen too many good people die for it not to.

The only parking spaces left in the student parking lot were in the back, practically off school grounds in what we students had nicknamed Purgatory. It was a hell of a walk from there into school.

I parked, and we sprinted toward the entrance. I reached it first and held the door open, expecting Ariana to walk through, but she was on the sidewalk looking back toward the cars.

"Come on already," I yelled.

"I dropped my ID," she called as she took a couple

steps backward. "I'll be right there."

She darted back to the parking lot just as a primer-red Chevy Blazer rounded the corner, barreling toward her.

Chapter Two

Ariana

I'd just bent down to snatch my ID off the asphalt when the eerie sound of brakes grinding screamed to my right. The pull I felt in my stomach and the feeling of a heart pounding a gazillion beats a minute weren't mine, though. They were part of a weird sibling connection Logan and I shared—a reflection of what he felt. They alerted me to the fact that the screeching was somehow related to me crouching down in the middle of the road. I looked up in time to see the banged-up grill of an SUV coming straight at me. The driver swerved, missing me by inches and nearly hitting the parked cars to my right. He yelled something I couldn't fully hear, but the words *crazy* and *idiot* were there.

This time, the pulse banging in my ears and the trembling throughout my body were all mine. I couldn't believe I'd almost been run over by a maniac trying to get to class. He had to know he was late and there'd be no parking that close to the school. I didn't have my driver's license yet, and even I knew that.

"Ariana!" Logan called to me with forced calm.

I pocketed my ID and hurried to catch up to him. He stood in front of the glass doors looking as if he'd have liked nothing more than to pass out.

"Ever hear of looking both ways before you run

9

into the street?" He held the door open. "You gave me a heart attack."

"He was the one driving like a jackass hyped up on caffeine."

Logan shook his head and led the way to the attendance office.

I got to first period in time to hand in my homework. After the bell rang, I hurried up the stairs to the third floor. My best friend Becca had her head in her locker and her backpack opened on the floor with half its contents spewed across the light gray tile.

Becca and I were like night and day in appearance. She had eyes the color of dark chocolate. Mine were topaz like my mom's. Her hair was inky black. Mine was a rich brown. She had olive skin that became a golden bronze in the summer. I burned. But we both had a love for coffee, music, and, in eighth grade, Caleb Wright, who had moved away at the end of that year and didn't know we existed. We also shared a hatred of Kelly Miller, who Caleb did realize existed and who'd had all his attention.

"What are you doing?" I asked Becca.

"Looking for my wallet." She scooped a handful of bangs out of her eyes as she tossed her navy sweatshirt on a hook and continued her search.

I reached into the side pocket of her backpack and pulled out her bubblegum-pink wallet. "You put it there yesterday."

She sighed in relief. "What would I do without you?"

"Wander the earth lost and broke." I helped her cram everything back into her locker. "I'm not feeling art class today. Let's sneak out and grab breakfast."

"I can't. If I ditch one more class, my dad's going to take my car away."

Her dad threatened to take away her car every other week, but he never did. Still, Becca was convinced one day he'd follow through on the promise to leave her walking, and she hated physical exercise more than she hated Kelly Miller.

"I'll talk to your teacher. Tell him you had to drive me home for a minute. He'll say yes. Your dad will never know." When Becca continued to hesitate, I added, "It's my treat."

She was too easily swayed to the dark side, which I loved about her. She looped her arm around mine. After a quick stop in her second-period geometry class and her usual comment that I had the God-given talent of getting our teachers to accept whatever excuse I dished out, we hurried back downstairs to the student parking lot.

We went to our favorite coffee house. She ordered an extra-large caramel macchiato. I got an extra-large dark cherry mocha and a bagel with cream cheese and jelly to split. I rummaged around the bottom of my purse for money while we waited to hear the total. All I found were a couple crinkled singles and some loose change. I'd already talked Becca into sneaking off-campus; no way was I going to make her pay for breakfast, too.

I looked at her. She had her head down as she checked her text messages. "I got this. Want to grab some napkins?"

"Sure." She turned on her heels, fingers flying over the small keypad on her phone.

"Twelve dollars and eighty-seven cents," the

11

cashier, a good-looking guy in his early twenties, said.

I glanced over my shoulder to make sure Becca wasn't watching me. Then I pulled the singles out of my purse and waited until I had the cashier's full attention. It took a minute, which gave me time to notice the long curved scar on his left cheek. When he finally looked up, I leaned forward so I could see the brown hue in his bright blue irises and said, "Here's fifteen."

He grabbed my fingers along with the bills. "I can see through your little parlor trick," he replied in a silky voice that boiled my blood. His musk cologne, mixed with the scent of burned leaves, caught in my throat. "But I'll play along. Do you want change?"

I wanted to run, but he still had my hand in a vise grip. I settled for shaking my head no.

He smirked and inched even closer, peering at me through golden blond wisps. "I've no desire to hurt you, so there is no reason to run."

He released me, stuffed the money into the drawer, and looked over my shoulder to the next person in line. I moved to the pick-up window wondering exactly what Creepy Cashier Dude actually knew. Maybe he was like me. That would have been a first, meeting someone else who could control minds. As far as Logan and I knew, we were the only ones. I dug my cell phone from my purse, ready to text Logan, but sending a text would announce that I'd ditched class. I tapped my fingers on the phone in thought.

"What was that about?" Becca asked from beside me, a stack of napkins in hand.

I jumped, fumbling my phone in the process. "What was what?" I asked as I bent down to retrieve it.

"For starters, the cozy powwow with Hottie over there." She gestured toward the cashier, who wasn't paying us any attention. "And then you can tell me why you're so jumpy."

"He was flirting with me," I lied and grabbed our drinks, passing the latte to her. "And I didn't see you walk up. You startled me, so stop smiling like it's funny."

She rearranged her face to be more serious. "Sorry. So did you give him your number?"

"No! He's too old for me." And disturbingly able to see through my gifts. "Let's get out of here."

"No way! Thanks to you, I have a get-out-of-geometry pass, and I'm not wasting it. " She led the way to a table in the back.

Cashier Dude still hadn't looked in my direction since he'd taken my money. Grudgingly, I followed Becca. Mainly because she didn't know my secret, and my previous lie didn't explain my desire to flee the coffee shop. I should have said he'd been bothering me. Becca would have shot him her evil don't-mess-with-us glare as we headed straight for the door.

"*Sooo*, since when do you want to miss art?" Becca asked once we were seated. I made sure my back was to the counter so I didn't have to see the registers or Cashier Dude.

"I don't know." I slathered my half of the bagel with cream cheese. "Guess I'm not in the mood to draw buildings today."

"Yeah, but drawing isn't why you normally can't wait for second period. What happened to Ben Gorgeous?"

"That's not his name, and you know it." I took a

bite of bagel. "I heard him telling one of his friends he wasn't going to be here today."

Becca groaned. "That means there'll be nothing good to look at in history."

"Have you talked to him?" I asked, secretly praying she hadn't.

"For two seconds. He borrowed my notes." She squirted jelly out of one of those little packs onto her bagel. "That reminds me, did you do the assignment in English?"

"Yeah." I took a drink of dark cherry heaven. Its warmth helped steady my nerves.

"Can I copy it?"

"Sure. I'll give it to you when we get back to school. Just change the wording so Mrs. Littman can't tell."

Becca raised her cup to her lips and paused as her gaze traveled slowly from the door to the other side of the coffee shop. She set her cup back down. In a low voice, she asked, "What did you say Ben was doing today?"

I twitched a shoulder. "I didn't. He wasn't specific. Why?"

"He just walked in."

I whipped around. Meticulously dressed, wavy dark brown hair, broad shoulders, nice ass—the guy standing at the counter ordering was Ben Gregory, all right. Creepy Cashier Dude was gone, replaced by an older woman with a nice smile.

"What do you think he's doing here?" Becca whispered.

"Getting a cup of coffee," I replied, pointing out the obvious.

Ben moved to the pick-up counter. He said something to the girl making his drink. She giggled.

"Think that's his girlfriend?" Becca asked.

"No. Definitely not." He didn't lean in when he talked, and it looked as if he paid more attention to the cardboard sleeve he held than the girl.

I tucked my hair behind my ear and watched him. Maybe it was fate that had had me craving a mocha. How else do you explain Ben just showing up where I was? I knew one thing for sure: Ben and I had something in common—we both liked the same coffee house.

"I heard he's gay."

I turned my attention back to Becca. "Who said that?!"

"Laura. Think about it: he never talks to girls and dresses like he just walked out of a fashion magazine." She took a bite out of her bagel and talked through a full mouth. "And his socks match his shirt."

"Becca, that doesn't mean he's gay."

"Really. Name another guy who can pull off *that* outfit."

Ben wore a faded pink and turquoise fitted long-sleeved shirt over a periwinkle T-shirt, designer jeans, and expensive-looking leather oxfords. Not exactly your typical high school guy's attire, which around here consisted of baggie jeans, graphic tees, and gym shoes.

"Maybe that's how guys dress where he's from."

"Where's that?" Her brow rose. "Gayville?"

"Becca!" I gasped. "You're bad."

She shrugged.

"He's coming!" Becca quickly glanced down at her paper cup like the writing on it was riveting reading material.

I couldn't help it; I looked. Ben scanned the coffee shop, his gaze stopping before it reached our table. His thick brown eyebrows and long lashes helped to bring out the blue in his eyes. His face was scruffy, the same five o'clock shadow that he always seemed to have. He sat a couple of tables over.

Becca kicked me, her way of telling me to act natural. I loved her too much to point out that, unless being as giddy as a three-year-old on a sugar high was the new cool, she was acting anything but natural.

I put my elbows on the table, leaning forward so that only she could hear me. "He doesn't even know we're alive."

"Gay," she whispered as she grabbed her caramel macchiato and stood.

I rolled my eyes and followed her to the door. Could Ben be gay? Or was he like Caleb Wright and only had eyes for one girl? I glanced over my shoulder to where he sat staring at me—or past me. It was hard to tell. I was still looking behind me when I walked into someone. Mocha sprayed out of the small hole at the top of my cup.

"I'm sorry," I said, wiping droplets of milky liquid from my cheek and hair.

"No problem, it was my fault" came the silky voice of the cashier.

Without my fingers locked in his, he seemed a lot less threatening. In fact, he had the most beautiful lapis blue eyes I'd ever seen.

Curious about earlier, I asked, "How did you know?"

Before he could reply, Becca rushed back into the

coffee house. "Ariana, what's the hold-up? Ohhh!" she added when she saw us, a stupid grin on her face.

The cashier held the door open for her and me. Not able to discuss my ability in front of Becca, I let the conversation with Cashier Dude go.

Chapter Three

Logan

I bumped into John Kraft—the guy who had almost run over my sister that morning—between second and third period. The anxiety over what could have happened if John hadn't swerved quickly turned to anger, causing me to snap.

I shoved him to get his attention. "You could have killed Ariana!"

"She's the one who ran in front of me!" He pushed my hand away. "Get a grip, Ragsdale."

The fingers on my right hand curled into a fist. Ariana was the only family I had, and I'd be damned if I was going to lose her to a reckless driver. I stepped closer to John, my eyes locked on his, and growled. "Why don't you drive that piece-of-shit truck of yours into a tree?"

John reached into his pocket. I heard his keys jingle. I really hadn't meant to make the suggestion. I forced my hand to unclench and dragged my fingers through my hair. John was right; I needed to calm down before *I* killed someone.

"Is there a problem?" Dean Whitmore, who had walked out of a classroom, marched up to us.

John and I glared at each other. I reminded myself that Ariana had darted in front of his SUV. She was fine, ditching second period, which I'd known the second I'd felt the invisible tug in my gut snap.

"We're cool," I said to Whitmore and went to walk away. "Oh, and John," I added, not wanting to be responsible for hurting someone. He looked at me. "Don't drive into any trees."

With the new girl in my fourth-period foods class, it was easy to push those events out of my mind. Kira Rose sauntered in as the second bell rang. Her deep-set eyes scanned the room, pausing briefly on the empty stool at John's table—where she'd sat the day before—and then traveled over to the stool next to me. She had long, dark red curls that were always in a state of disarray, and stormy obsidian-gray eyes that seemed to absorb the room. John's chest puffed out in anticipation of Kira sitting next to him, but, that day, she walked past him and stopped in front of me.

"Is anyone sitting here?" she asked.

"No. It's all yours."

Mrs. Larson clapped her hands in excitement. "We're going to be baking oatmeal raisin cookies this morning."

Kira pulled a rubber band from her purse and gathered her hair into a low ponytail. There was a football game Friday night; I wondered if she'd want to go with me. I even contemplated taking the angst out of having to ask her by using my mind-control powers but decided I didn't want to manipulate someone into liking me.

"Mr. Ragsdale?"

I looked at Mrs. Larson.

"Are you paying attention?"

"Yeah. Oatmeal raisin cookies. Can't wait." I

rubbed my stomach as if that proved I was dying to bake cookies.

Kira hid her smile behind her hand.

"Good," Mrs. Larson continued. "As I was saying, pair off and pick a kitchen. You'll find everything you need in the refrigerator and cabinets."

I quickly stood when I saw John heading over to our table, knowing he wasn't going to ask *me* to be his partner.

"Shall we?" I said to Kira. John frowned and turned to ask someone else to partner up with him.

Kira went straight to kitchen unit three. Mrs. Larson had the recipe on the counter. We checked the list of ingredients.

"I'll grab the eggs and butter," Kira offered.

"I'll get the dry ingredients."

Just ask her if she's going to the game, I thought as she dropped two sticks of butter into the Mixmaster and turned it on. *What's the worst thing that could happen? She says no? She laughs hysterically at the idea of hanging out with me? The whole class hears?*

I decided to work my way up to mentioning the game.

"So where'd you move from?" I cracked an egg into the sink and tossed the shells into the bowl, immediately realizing my mistake. "Crap!"

Kira giggled. "Like your cookies extra crunchy?"

"Sorry." I grabbed the largest piece of shell from the bowl.

"No biggie," she said as she helped pick shell out of the butter and brown sugar. "I'm from Tucson. Ever been?"

"No." I hadn't been out of Illinois. "Do you miss

it?"

"I miss the heat. It's cold up here."

"It's actually warmer than normal this year."

"Omigod!" She visibly shivered as if a chill went though her. "I'm going to need to totally rethink my wardrobe."

I laughed. She and Ariana would get along great.

"How about your friends? I bet you miss them," I said, hoping to find out if she had a boyfriend in Arizona. We continued to add ingredients.

"Not really." She crinkled her nose. "That must make me sound like a bitch."

"No." It meant she wasn't in a long-distance relationship. With everything mixed together, we started to spoon large globs of dough onto cookie sheets. "I was thinking—"

"Hey." John stepped between us. "Do you guys have any more raisins?"

"Sure." Kira handed him the container. "Help yourself."

"Great." John gave me a sidelong look before addressing Kira. "There's a big game Friday. I was thinking…um…if you aren't doing anything, we could, you know, go together."

I cursed to myself and slid the cookie sheets into the oven next to me. First he'd tried to run over my sister, and now he was trying to steal my soon-to-be girlfriend.

Kira brushed a loose curl out of her eyes with her fingers. "I'd love to, but…" She bit her bottom lip a moment. "I just told Logan I'd hang out with him."

I paused to look at them, my hand still on the oven door. If a glare could kill, I would have dropped dead from the one John shot me. Over his shoulder, I could see Kira with her hands together as if in prayer.

Please, she mouthed.

I couldn't help feeling smug about the turn of events.

"Sorry, dude." I patted John on the shoulder. "You're ten minutes too late."

He stalked back to his kitchen unit, mumbling the whole way.

"Thanks." Kira grabbed our bowl and turned to the sink.

"No problem." As I reached around her to get the dish soap, it hit me that she might not have been serious about going to the game with me. She might have simply used me to get out of a date with John. To be sure, I added, "I was planning on going, if you want to hang out."

Her mouth twitched upward into a dazzling smile. "I'd like that."

I turned the water on and started washing the spatula to keep myself from doing something that would make me look like an idiot, like smiling stupidly or pumping my fist in the air. Out of the corner of my eye, I saw Kira watching me. No, it was more like she studied me.

"What?" I asked.

"I was just thinking I could get used to a man doing the dishes."

I smiled and flicked soap bubbles at her.

"Oh!" She reached into the sink and splashed me with a mix of suds and water. It was war. By the time Mrs. Larson intervened, we had as much water on the floor and our clothes as in the sink. We were laughing too hard to care.

"Truce?" I held out my hand.

"Truce." We shook. Kira grabbed a towel and bent down to wipe the floor. "You know something?"

I crouched and helped. "What?"

"Eternity wouldn't seem so bad if you were there."

If Kira was that fun to be around all the time, I'd have gladly spent eternity with her.

Chapter Four

Ariana

I was in the kitchen when Logan woke up Friday.

"Guess who called me last night." I took the apple juice from the refrigerator, grinning so big my cheeks actually hurt. "You'll never guess."

Logan grabbed one of our mismatched mugs from the cabinet next to the stove. "The sheriff wanting to know how we managed to persuade one of South Elgin's finest to let me off with a warning for the third time this month. Or maybe the dean wondering how you managed to snake out of second period the other day."

"You knew?"

I probably shouldn't have been surprised. Logan and I are connected by more than just blood. It's like invisible gossamer filaments give a tug on our consciousness whenever we're near each other. It had always been that way for us, but lately the distance from which he could sense me seemed to grow.

He poured coffee into the Big Brother mug I'd given him a few years ago and asked, "Why'd you leave?"

I doubted he'd want to hear I hadn't been in the mood to sit through Mrs. Murphy's discussion on the proper use of shading, so I went with the next best excuse: "I needed caffeine."

He held out the coffee pot. "Need some today?"

"No. I'm good." I was actually ready to bounce off the ceiling with excitement. "Are you going to ask me who called or not?"

"Who?" he replied, obligingly.

"It was Ben. The most gorgeous guy in school. That's who. And he asked me out." I let out a squeal. "Can you believe it!?"

"Congrats, I guess." He nudged me in the arm.

"Aw, don't get too excited now."

He grabbed a bowl and the milk on his way out of our narrow galley-style kitchen and sat down across from me at our small kitchen table. "He must be deaf, though," he added, teasingly. "My ears are still ringing from that shriek."

"Ha-ha!" I snatched a banana from the basket of fruit on the table. "Anyway, he hasn't said a word to me since he started school, until yesterday. He never really talks to any of the girls. New guy, you know. I was starting to think he was gay, but maybe he's just shy. I don't know, and I don't care. Becca is going to be sooo jealous." I peeled half the banana and took a bite. "He's from New York or Vermont, or maybe it was Philadelphia. I don't remember."

Logan ate his bowl of cereal and tried to fully wake up as I talked. He grunted and nodded a few times. I gave him credit for trying to be social. To him, holding a conversation before he finished his first cup of coffee ranked up there with going to the dentist. When he'd shoveled the last spoonful of cereal into his mouth, I scooped the bowl out from under him.

"Awake yet?" I asked. Ben's phone call wasn't the

only thing I was excited about.

"Mm." He nodded as he drank the rest of his coffee.

"Good." I opened the cabinet under the sink and pulled out a small rectangular box. I had used the comic section of the newspaper to wrap it. "Happy birthday!"

"Happy birthday to you, too." He held a small black pouch by its strings, and we exchanged gifts. "You first," he added.

I loosened the strap on the pouch and turned it over. We used to think it was cool we'd both been born on November first, exactly two years apart, and when we were young we hadn't given much thought to the strawberry marks on our left wrists. But, five years ago, when his puffy blob had turned into a double-lined, five-pointed star with symbols between the lines and even more symbols between the points of the star, we'd started to have our doubts about our birthdays being a coincidence. Those doubts had been confirmed two years later when my mark had turned into a mirror image of his. To this day, we didn't know what it meant.

I turned the pouch over. A pale pink bracelet fell into my free hand.

"Logan, it's beautiful." There were roses embossed in the soft leather and silver wings stitched on the middle like the black bracelet I'd worn since I was twelve to hide my birthmark. The coolest part about this pink bracelet was it would go with most of my clothes. I hopped up and gave Logan a hug. "Open yours now," I said.

While he tore off the paper, I switched bracelets. As soon as he had the top off the box, I said, "I picked that one because the designs etched into the surface sort of remind me of our birthmark. It brings luck to whoever carries it."

He removed an off-white talisman from the box. It was about the size of my mini-compact blush and reminded me of two oriental lily petals, but the guy at the store had cracked up laughing when I'd told him that. He said it was a phoenix, wings raised ready for flight.

I sat with one bare foot on the seat, hugging my knee as I watched Logan, who turned the talisman over, examining the markings closer. I'd gotten it from a thrift shop, but I knew Logan wouldn't care. I could tell he liked it by the way he was admiring every aspect of it.

"Ariana, this had to be expensive."

"Don't worry about it."

His gaze met mine, one eyebrow raised.

"I've been saving my babysitting money."

"I don't want you spending it on me."

"If you must know, the guy at the store wanted to haggle. It's not my fault he found my offer acceptable." Of course, no one had ever said no to one of our suggestions. Only, that was no longer true, because the guy at the coffee house had seen right through my lie.

Logan shook his head, smiling the whole time. "It's perfect. Thank you."

I hadn't told him about Creepy Cashier Dude. I'd convinced myself it was a fluke, but really I hadn't wanted to tell Logan I'd skipped class. It had been the two of us for so long that he'd taken on a semi-parental role. I didn't mind most of the time, but since he'd chewed me out for making us late that day, the last thing I'd wanted to do was confess I hadn't even stayed in school. Now that he knew, guilt consumed me. What if Creepy Cashier Dude was a big deal?

"You know," I said, casually, "one of the cashiers at the coffee house was able to see through my suggestion. Weird, huh?"

"What? What suggestion?" Logan asked.

"Well, it was my turn to treat. Becca was with me."

"I figured as much," he said, interrupting.

I flashed a smile. Becca was always my accomplice. "Well, when I went to pull out my money, I realized I only had a couple dollars, so I looked the guy in the eyes and said, 'Here's fifteen,' only, he knew I'd shorted him."

"Are you sure he knew?" Logan asked quizzically.

"Oh, yeah. He knew all right. He went as far as to say my parlor tricks wouldn't work on him. What do you think it means?"

"That you shouldn't order more than you can afford," he replied sarcastically, but I could tell he was mulling it over. After a few seconds he asked, "What did he do after he confronted you?"

"Slid my two dollars into the drawer and helped the next person in line."

"Have you seen him again?"

I shook my head. "We were bound to run into someone who'd be able to think for themselves, right?"

"I never really thought about it before, but everyone's minds are wired differently, so I guess you're right. Just promise me you'll let me know if you see him again." He waited for me to promise and then asked, "Are you going to the game tonight?"

I giggled. "You really do need your coffee in the

morning, don't you?"

"What?" He grabbed his mug and put it in the dishwasher, a puzzled expression on his face.

"I told you, I'm going with Ben." I put my glass in the dishwasher before he closed it.

"Right. Ben." Logan put the milk away. "I'm taking Kira."

"Kira, huh? Is that the girl in your foods class?"

"Yes." He slid the talisman into the front pocket of his jeans and grabbed his wallet from the counter. "Did you take my keys?"

"The girl you've been talking about in your sleep?" I pulled his keys out of my purse and gripped them tight in my hand.

"I don't talk in my sleep." Logan's cheeks flushed, though, totally giving him away.

" 'Kira, please,' " I cooed, teasing him. " 'Don't stop.' "

"I did *not* say that." He held out his hand. "Are you going to give me my keys?"

I wished mind control worked on him. Since it didn't, I put on my most innocent face and said, "I was thinking...It's my birthday, and I did just turn sixteen, and I still need a ton of hours before I can get my license, sooo..."

"No way!" He grabbed for the keys, but I moved my hand behind my back. "You are not driving my '68 Chevy!"

"Oh, come on," I begged. "Please, please, please. I promise not to hit anything." I hoped my grin didn't make me look like a cat promising not to eat the mouse.

He groaned, and I knew he was thinking about the last time he'd let me drive, and I'd mistaken a four-way stop for a two-way and had almost broadsided another car.

"I've gotten better. Please. I need the practice," I whined. "And it's not like we have another car I can drive."

"But the Camaro's my baby." He was wavering. I could tell. "I just got it painted."

"That's not a no." I knew I had him. I did a little hop of excitement and ran to my room to find socks, keys still in hand.

"It's not a yes either!" he hollered after me. "What are you doing during the two hours between school and the game? Need a ride or anything?"

I stuck my head out of my bedroom door and jiggled the keys, having fun messing with him. "I should be asking you if you need a ride."

I ducked back into my room, but not before I heard him mumble, "I'm going to regret letting you drive." Louder, he said, "Don't push it."

Within a minute, I was back and heading out the door. "Ben and I are going to grab a bite to eat before the game," I said in reply to his earlier question.

He followed. "Don't think you're driving every day. This is a birthday thing."

"We'll see."

Chapter Five

Logan

After one missed stop sign, two close calls with oncoming traffic, and a dip in a pothole, we pulled into the parking lot at school. I made sure I got my keys back and made a mental note to start looking for a second car we could afford. We were late, as usual.

"We better hurry." Ariana jogged toward the school, racing into the path of a delivery truck that seemed to appear out of nowhere.

"Watch out!" I lunged toward her, knowing I was too far behind to do anything.

The truck's tires screeched, and the back end fishtailed. Ariana turned to face the four tons of steel a moment before it was on top of her. Her eyes grew wide in terror.

"NO!" I screamed, helpless to save her.

My birthmark seared as if it were on fire. Ariana became translucent—looking very much like a hologram. The truck went right through her. It skidded to a stop some thirty feet from where she stood in the middle of the road. She was solid again, holding her wrist, mouth open in a silent scream. The driver burst out of his truck.

"My God!" A scrawny guy in a baseball cap sprinted toward Ariana, who seemed unable to move. I reached her at the same time he did. The driver's gaze bounced between Ariana and his truck. "You were…How?" He rubbed a shaky hand over his face as he drew in a ragged breath. "It's a good thing you jumped out of the way."

Ariana glanced at me. Neither of us said anything. She hadn't jumped out of the way. At the speed the guy was going, she should have been splattered across the grill like a bug.

The trucker covered his head with his arms, trembling visibly. "Man, I was sure I hit you. Are you okay?"

Ariana looked down at her torso and legs. "I think so."

"I got her." I put an arm around Ariana's shoulders and pulled her closer to me. I had no idea what to do. Hell, I didn't even know what to think. Was it magic that kept her safe? Divine intervention? Was there an unforeseen force watching over us? That didn't seem so farfetched. Something had kept us from meeting the same fate as the people we loved.

When the guy didn't leave, I looked him in the eyes. "Why don't you finish your deliveries and forget the whole thing?"

He paused, expression blank a moment.

"Yeah, yeah. I should get my deliveries done." He got back in his truck.

I steered a still dazed Ariana toward one of the benches near the school and guided her down onto it.

"How'd you do that?" I asked, forcing myself to keep it together as I checked her arms and head for any bruises. There were none.

She shrugged. "I don't know. The truck—it came

out of nowhere. I—" She stared at the parking lot. "I-I went right through it," she stammered. "Who can go through a truck?"

"I don't know." And, at the moment, I didn't care as long as she was safe. "What do you remember?"

"You screamed. Then I saw the truck coming right at me. I sort of froze. Then I felt weightless, and the truck was going through me like I was a ghost." She covered her wrist with her hand. "My birthmark...it..."

"Felt like someone rammed a hot branding iron into your skin," I said. When she nodded, I added, "I felt it, too."

"How is that possible?" Ariana's leg bounced up and down nervously. She looked like she was about to have a total breakdown, complete with screaming and freaking out. "What the hell, Logan? First John in his beat-up SUV and now the truck. Do you think someone has it out for me?"

Considering our past, it wasn't a bad question, but I didn't think we needed to be paranoid just yet.

"No, but I do think you need to start looking both ways before you race across the street." I raked my fingers through my hair. Ariana was all I had left. I couldn't fathom the thought of losing her, too. "How do you feel now?"

"Fine. Never better, actually." Ariana pinched her forearm as if testing to make sure she was solid and then asked, "Do you think we're immortal?"

She said it so innocently, like a little girl asking if fairies are real.

"What? No! We're as human as that guy in the truck." At least, I was pretty sure we could die, and I wasn't about to jump in front of a speeding train to find out if I was right.

The principal poked his head out of the door, scowling at us. "Miss Ragsdale. Mr. Ragsdale. Are you planning on joining us today?"

I was about to say *no*, but instead looked at Ariana. "Library."

She nodded and followed me into school.

One suggestive comment to the librarian that we were supposed to be there and no one bothered us. We sat at two computers entering all types of crazy questions into our browsers' search engines. We got back equally strange results; unfortunately, most of them applied to normal, everyday things.

I kept going over the morning's events in my head. Our birthmarks protected us. That much was obvious by the way they burned when Ariana was in a life-threatening situation. We had some sort of power, too. Otherwise, Ariana wouldn't have been able to go through the truck as if it were made of vapor instead of steel. I tried to remember if we'd done something special that had caused the marks to burn and Ariana to become ghost-like. Nothing came to mind.

"Here's something," Ariana said after close to two hours of searching. She slid her bracelet up her forearm to reveal her birthmark. "See how all these small markings make up the image? According to this website, it's a sigil—a type of sign believed to have occult power in astrology and magic." She switched browser windows. "And this site has pages and pages of sigils used in ceremonial magic. Get this, some of the images on this page are used to summon or ward off angels and demons."

"That's not comforting." I scanned the computer

monitor a moment. "Did you find our birthmarks?"

"Nope."

"What type of website are you on?"

She scrolled to the top of the screen. "Paganism. The other one was Wiccan. That one had lots of symbols to bring luck, make your garden grow, help with fertility, stuff like that."

I laced my fingers behind my head and leaned back in the chair, absorbing this information. "I thought paganism died centuries ago."

Ariana twitched a shoulder. "Got me."

Everything I know about it—which was what I'd learned from video games and movies—said paganism died when the Catholic Church rose to power. "Maybe we should be thinking secret societies like the Illuminati."

"Or kitchen witches."

"Nah," we said at the same time.

"The government," she suggested.

"Dad was an accountant, and Mom stayed home to take care of us." Before they died our life was apple pie. "The government had no reason to know you and I existed."

"Maybe Mom and Dad led secret lives."

After our parents' deaths, Ariana and I had theorized that they were spies and the enemy had found them, but the truth was they died in a freak accident and Ariana and I were lucky to be alive. For the sake of lightening the mood, I said, "Maybe we're mutants?"

We broke into laughter. When the librarian hushed us, Ariana closed her browser.

"This doesn't really help us," she said.

"Sure it does. We know our birthmarks are sigils

that protect us." I turned off my computer.

"We've always suspected the markings protected us. What we need to know is from whom and why." She stood and slung her backpack over her shoulder. "I just want to forget that we're different, finish out the school day, and enjoy my date with Ben." She glanced at the clock on the wall. "Lunch is in ten minutes, and I'm starving."

I fell into step with her as she headed out of the library. "Ariana, ignoring what happened today isn't going to make it go away."

"Maybe not, but neither will halting our lives waiting for answers that we have no clue how to find."

"Ariana—"

She spun to face me. "Logan, we spent the entire morning searching for answers, and like every other time we've done that we found zilch. Zip. Nada. I'm going to focus on what I can control, and right now that is school, dinner, and the football game. Want my advice?"

"Probably not." At least not when she was in a mood.

"Enjoy the rest of the day. Find Kira and ask her if she wants to grab a bite to eat before the game." She waved over her shoulder as she hurried to her locker.

****

I decided that Ariana had a point about living our lives. And Kira was a perfect distraction from all the weirdness happening around us. When I bumped into Kira in the halls, I asked her if she'd like to get something to eat after school. She said yes.

We sat in a booth in the back of the restaurant.

"So what do you do when you're not in class or

watching football?" Kira asked between bites of her oriental chicken salad. Her black long-sleeved T-shirt followed her curves, and the faded rose and thorny vines trailed from her left breast down to her waist. It was hard not to stare.

I shrugged. "I don't know: odd jobs, homework, hang out with friends."

"What sort of odd jobs?"

"I'm the handyman where we live, and I know a little about cars. I do brake jobs, oil changes, install speakers, tune-ups. Pay's good." Gave Ariana and me enough money to purchase the things we couldn't get for free. "How about you?" I took a bite out of my roast beef sandwich, wiping the back of my hand across my mouth to make sure I didn't have mayonnaise on my lips.

"Homework, mostly. I'm still trying to catch up in a couple of classes." Kira moved lettuce around her plate as she spoke. "I'll have to find a job eventually. That is, if we stay here."

I quickly swallowed what was in my mouth. "You just moved here. Your parents can't be thinking of leaving already, can they?"

"It's up to my father and his boss. Who is a huge A-hole, if you ask me—his boss, not my father." She took a sip of her soda. "I want to stay. I mean, I'm just starting to get to know you, and Jessica is really nice. She's in my algebra class."

"Tell your father you can't move." If I had to, I'd *suggest* to him he didn't want to move. Buy us more time together. "There's too much to see."

"In South Elgin?" she asked incredulously.

"Around here, anyway. There's Chicago: Navy

Pier, Wrigley Field, the Bean—"

Her eyes grew wide. "Bean?"

"Yeah, everyone has to see the Bean in Millennium Park. Then there's skiing—"

She shook her head. "You aren't going to tell me Illinois is a great place to ski, are you?"

"Well, not as great as Colorado or Vermont, I'm sure. But there is a ski resort near us. I could take you in the winter."

She grimaced. "That sounds cold."

"We'll get you a ski jacket and snow pants," I prodded and took another bite out of my sandwich.

"And strap two thin plastic panels to my feet." She bit her bottom lip. "I don't know."

I washed down the roast beef with soda. "We can go tubing if you don't want to ski."

"I can't remember the last time I did something just for fun." She popped a grape tomato into her mouth and grinned. "Maybe. If I'm still here when it snows."

"Good! It's a date."

"You're a nice guy." She regarded me through narrowed eyes as if surprised to make this revelation.

"What were you expecting?"

She smirked, leaving me to wonder if she'd suspected me to be anything more than a jerk.

Chapter Six

Ariana

It never fails: when I have plans, the clock on the wall in my eighth-period English class seems to move e-x-t-r-e-m-e-l-y s—l—o—w—l—y. Mrs. Littman sounded like an automated machine, as if she were speaking one. Word. At. A. Time. I half expected the minute hand to stop, and I'd be frozen in this very moment for the rest of my life. When the bell finally rang, I jumped, sending my textbook crashing to the floor and my pen flying toward Becca, who was on my right.

Becca burst into a fit of laughter. "Ariana, what's with you?"

I picked up my textbook. "Nothing."

Her eyebrows disappeared under her bangs as she gave me her you're-not-fooling-me expression.

"Okay. I'm nervous," I admitted.

"Nervous to have Mr. Gorgeous all to yourself." She handed me my pen. "I'd like to feel sorry for you, but I can't get there. Why you?"

My jaw dropped. "What's that supposed to mean?"

"Sorry! That came out wrong. Really." She gave me a quick hug. "It's just that I've been practically throwing myself at him. Following him around. Giving him my notes to copy and conveniently putting my phone number at the top. Does he call me? No." We got in line behind our friends who were filing out of the classroom. "I bet you didn't do any of that."

"No," I replied. And I didn't know she was doing that either.

"So he had to track down your number to call you." She sighed, not bothering to hide her jealousy. "God, what I wouldn't do for a guy to want to get to know me that much."

I really hadn't thought about how Ben had gotten my number. I was sure there hadn't been that much tracking going on, though. More like asking a few of my friends.

I was surprised to see Ben waiting for me outside the classroom. Or maybe I had told him where he could find me when he'd called last night. I couldn't remember.

"And he looks like a god," Becca whispered dreamily.

His brown hair fell neatly around his sapphire-blue eyes, making his white long-sleeved cotton shirt seem even whiter and his lightly stressed jeans even sexier. I nearly walked into Noelle, who'd stopped in front of me so she could ogle him. If Ben had noticed, he didn't let on. Becca gave her a little shove.

"Sorry." Noelle hugged her books and hurried after her friends.

"Call me tonight," Becca said.

I grabbed her arm before she could walk away. "You're not meeting us at the game?"

Becca always went to the football games. She practically had a reserved seat in her favorite section.

"Three's a crowd. Besides, you might get mad at

me if I'm drooling over your date." She hurried toward the stairs. "Call me!"

"Bye." I half waved at her back.

I was nervous about my date with Ben because I knew next to nothing about him. What if he found me boring? What if we ran out of things to talk about halfway through dinner and ended up just staring at each other? What if I realized he wasn't my type?

Okay, he'd have had to either be a complete moron or have some unforgivable habit like picking his nose for me to decide he wasn't my type on the first date. The point was, if things didn't go well with Ben at dinner, I had planned on wandering over to Becca's favorite section of the bleachers and pretending to be surprised when we bumped into her. And if dinner did go well, I would steer clear of that section so I could spend more time alone with Ben.

Ben pushed off the wall. "Hi."

"Hi," I said, casually tucking my hair behind my ear. He really did look good.

He took my books. "Is Italian food okay?"

"Yep."

Ben drove a hot silver sports car. The body kit made the car look as if it rested on the ground. Ben put my books in the trunk before opening the passenger door for me. He was definitely winning points for being a gentleman.

"Nice car," I said once he got in.

"Thanks." He started the engine. Blue Oyster Cult blared from the speakers, shaking the windows. He quickly lowered the volume. "Sorry about that."

I chuckled. " 'Don't Fear the Reaper' is a good song."

"You listen to rock?" He backed out of the parking space.

"My brother listens to it." Logan has my uncle's CD collection, which he plays on an old boombox while he works on cars. I think the CDs remind him of our dad and uncle, although he's never admitted that.

"What do you listen to?"

"Just about anything, really."

We headed north on a two-lane road as we sped past patches of trees strutting an array of bright red and golden yellow foliage. Strips of businesses broke up the peacefulness of nature. Ben tapped his finger on the steering wheel as he drove, and I wondered if he was nervous about our date, too.

We went to a small family-owned restaurant. The aroma of marinara sauce and garlic wafted through the place. Classical music played softly in the background.

We were seated right away. I ordered the linguini. He got lasagna.

"This place is great," I commented once our food arrived. "How'd you find it?"

"Driving around. I could smell the garlic from the road." He tore a piece of bread from the loaf in the center of the table. "I have a weakness for Italian."

"Me too," I confessed. The Bolognese sauce was to die for.

"Do you cook?" He dusted his pasta with fresh parmesan cheese.

"Simple stuff." I wasn't going to admit my pasta sauce came from a jar. "Burgers, tacos, an occasional stew. You?"

"I've been known to whip up a few things." He sank his fork into his lasagna, slicing off a large bite.

"My mom's a great cook. When I was little, she'd push a chair up to the counter and have me and my sister help. It's a wonder any of the vegetables made it into our dinner with how much my sister nibbled." He chuckled. "I guess I developed a love for cooking."

I couldn't remember if my mom liked to cook, let alone if she was a good cook. With a sip of iced tea, I washed down the jealousy that trickled through me.

"Do you come from a big family?" he asked.

"It's just me and my brother."

"Where are your parents?" He didn't hide the surprise in his voice.

"St. Peter's Cemetery." I stuck a noodle into my mouth. Chewed.

I hadn't meant for it to come out so cold. Ben was going to think I was heartless. It wasn't like that, though. I would love to have known my mom and dad, but I didn't. That was just part of life for me. I avoided his eyes, afraid I'd see disapproval in them.

"I didn't know." He wet his lips. Uncomfortable, I decided. Most people were when they first found out about my parents. It was like they needed a moment to decide if they should change the subject or ask what had happened. I only had to wait a few seconds to find out which way Ben would go.

"What happened, if you don't mind me asking?"

"Fire." I twirled my fork in the linguini, round and round. "Electrical short in the walls. House was ashes by the time the fire department arrived."

"I'm sorry. You must miss them."

"It was a long time ago."

His brows knitted together. "How old were you?"

"Eight." I pulled my fork from the mound of pasta

I'd created.

He took a moment to digest that news. He then asked, "Do you live with relatives?"

"We live alone."

"Since you were eight?" He looked at me with the same shocked expression I'd seen so many times before.

"No, but living with others didn't work out so well. When Logan turned sixteen, we got our own place." Talking about my parents brought back painful memories of how Logan and I had lost everyone we'd ever loved. I really didn't want to go into details about my past with Ben. I didn't want his pity either. Logan and I were used to it being us against the world, and quite honestly, we were kicking the world's butt one day at a time. "We do all right."

He nodded. Although, I noticed the muscles in his jaw twitch and the vein in his forehead bulge like my sixth-grade history teacher's used to do when he'd had it with the class.

"Do you have a big family?" I asked, hoping to get the subject off mine.

"Not really." He stuck a big forkful of lasagna into his mouth. "My dad travels a lot for his job. Mom goes with him half the time."

Proving that, just because you have parents, it doesn't mean they'll be around.

"Where's your sister?" I guessed she was older since she didn't go to our school. "Any brothers?"

He shook his head. "No brothers and my sister hasn't lived with us for awhile."

"What's she like?"

He drank half his soda, then replied, "When we

were younger, she was wild and funny and a bit of a tomboy." He looked at his plate, but it didn't appear like he really saw it. "She hated to lose, which made her determined to always do her best." He smirked. "She could really pitch a fit too, so I used to let her win." He paused as if replaying the memory of his childhood in his mind. I rested an elbow on the table and propped my chin in my hand as I waited for him to continue. "Most of all, she was passionate about everything she did, whether helping a friend or winning some stupid race."

"It sounds like you two are close."

"We used to be." He didn't meet my eyes. "Seems like a long time ago though."

I felt sorry for him. I may not remember my parents, but it hadn't been their choice to leave Logan and me. And while Logan and I had our own interests, we were very close.

We finished our dinners. Passed on dessert.

"I'm going to use the washroom before the game," I said.

He shrugged on his gray pea coat. "I'll wait for you by the door."

"*Il mio nome e* Maria," a woman's voice announced over the speaker when I entered the bathroom. "My name is Maria. *Ciao*. Hello."

I went to the bathroom as the woman continued with her Italian-to-English translations. I washed my hands in the bowl-like sink and then sent Becca a quick text letting her know I was having a good time on my date. She texted back a second later: *Jealous! I want all the juicy details tomorrow!*

I tucked my phone into my purse and went to meet Ben. He was looking out the windows at the front of the restaurant, and I was just about to tap him on the shoulder when he stiffened. I stopped behind him, realizing he was on his cell phone.

"I know the rules, Elise. No interference." He paused, listening. "How is that not interfering?" He turned and saw me. His clenched jaw relaxed.

"Ready?" I asked.

He held up a finger. "Yeah. No problem. I gotta go." He hung up.

He held my hand as we walked to the car. The breeze brushed past, mingling Ben's musk cologne with the dried leaves and mums that dotted the landscaping. I used my free hand to hold my jacket shut and block out the cold.

"Who was that?" I asked.

"My mom."

"You call your mom by her first name?"

We reached his car. Ben wrapped an arm around my back, twirling me in a semicircle until we faced each other.

"She likes to pretend she's too young to have children. How about a hot chocolate for the game?"

He was so close, if I were to have tilted my head up and forward ever so slightly, our lips would have met.

"Hot chocolate would be great," I managed to reply. "They sell it at the game."

"Perfect!"

My heart raced in anticipation of his mouth covering mine. The sounds of traffic on the main road disappeared, as did the parked cars around us. It was just Ben and me and the prospect of our first kiss.

To my disappointment, he opened the car door instead of kissing me.

We drove back to school, his fingers laced in mine. Our arrival together received a few surprised stares from some of our classmates. Noelle's "Hi, Ariana" quickly turned into an "Oh" when she saw Ben's arm around my waist. She mouthed—and not subtly, either—*Yum!* Jessica Derting's jaw dropped. John Kraft did a double take. I couldn't help feeling like I'd won a date with a prince.

Ben bought our tickets, and we got in line at the concession stand.

I sensed my brother before I saw him. I turned to face him. "Hey."

"Hey," Logan replied with a nod. He gave Ben a quick glance from head to toe. "Kira, this is my sister Ariana and her friend Ben."

He'd practically choked on the word *friend*. I glared at him, wondering what was going on behind his light brown eyes.

"Nice to meet you," Ben said as he shook Logan's hand. With a nod, he said hello to Kira.

She shifted her weight from one foot to the other. "Hi."

"How was dinner?" Logan asked. We moved a few steps forward.

"It was great," I replied. "We went to this little Italian restaurant. You'd love it. How was yours?"

Logan put an arm around Kira. "Ours was great, too."

She leaned into him. They made a cute couple. We moved to the window, and Ben ordered two hot chocolates, then looked at Logan.

"Make that four." Logan reached into his pocket and fished out some money.

"I got it," Ben said. He handed the first cup to me and the second to Kira. "We should sit together."

The smile disappeared from Logan's face, and I knew what he was thinking because double-dating with my big brother wasn't at the top of my list of things to do either.

Out of the corner of my eye, I saw Kira open her mouth and close it. When I looked at her, she said, "Sure. Why not?"

Logan shrugged and echoed her. "Why not."

I wanted to say, *Whipped already.* I also thought about saying, *No way!* But after my cold response about my parents at dinner, I was sure being the one to hate the idea of us sitting together would really make me look heartless, so I forced a smile instead.

Logan held his arm out to the side, indicating for us to lead the way. Only, once we'd taken a few steps, he grabbed my wrist. Not roughly, just enough to get me to slow down.

"I thought the new guy was a sophomore like you," Logan whispered, struggling not to sound like an overprotective brother and failing.

"I never said that," I whispered. "You better be nice."

"I'm always nice," he replied just as quietly.

But I could think of a few times when Logan's idea of nice had scared the crap out of the guy I'd been with. In eighth grade, I went out with a guy named Timmy Schultz. After Timmy had met Logan, he was afraid to hold my hand, let alone kiss me. And in ninth grade, I'd gone to the homecoming dance with Jeff Valentine. Whatever Logan had said to Jeff had left him afraid to pull me close when we danced. We'd looked like a couple out of a black-and-white movie, dancing with several inches between us. And our goodnight kiss had consisted of him giving me a peck on my cheek. All I knew was that had better not happen again tonight.

Chapter Seven

Logan

I took Kira's hand, and we followed Ariana and Ben up one of the aisles. Kira motioned for me to sit next to my sister.

"Be nice, jerk-face," Ariana hissed when she'd seen me glance at Ben, who sat on her other side.

I couldn't help chuckling. I could tell Ariana liked Ben; I didn't plan on ruining that for her. Not to mention, I wanted to make a good impression on Kira, and teasing my little sister would have had the opposite effect.

"You're such a dork," I whispered back. "Stop worrying."

"I'm watching you," she warned. Louder, she added, "If we're going to hang out, then I want to sit next to Kira."

I looked at Kira, who giggled, obviously having heard Ariana's demand. "Mind switching?" I asked.

"Not at all."

We did.

I set my cup under my seat, adjusted so that I could see around the girls, and asked Ben, "Are you a big football fan?"

He nodded. "Don't have the opportunity to watch many games, though." His gaze traveled to Ariana.

"Now, if the company here is always this great, I'll make time."

Ariana blushed. I nearly barfed up my dinner at his blatant attempt to kiss up to my sister. Kira choked out a *phfff*, which received a narrow-eyed glare from Ben.

"What about you, Kira. Big sports fan?" he asked.

"Die-hard," she replied, her chin raised in the air. Her acclaimed love for sports made her that much sexier to me.

Ariana quickly changed the subject to shopping. While she filled Kira in on the best places near us to shop, Ben and I discussed our picks for the Super Bowl. When the conversations died and Ben's attention was back on the field, Kira crinkled her nose and bumped her shoulder against mine.

"I have a confession," she whispered.

"What's that?"

She scooted closer to me. "I don't know a thing about football."

I'm sure my smile reached my eyes. "I'll teach you."

For the first half of the game, I explained the plays and fouls to her. I could likewise hear Ben explaining the game to Ariana, who asked a few dumb questions to keep him talking. "Dumb" because Ariana knew as much about football as I did.

Either Kira was a quick learner or she'd faked ignorance like Ariana. By the second half, Kira didn't need my commentary.

At the end of the game, our team had lost fourteen-to-ten. Kira and I stood.

"Ariana," I said. "I'll see you at home."

"Yeah."

Reaching over the girls, I extended my hand toward Ben. "It was nice meeting you."

"You too." He shook my hand, his mouth opening as if to say something else. He closed it with a snap. Yet when Kira and I had taken a couple of steps away, he added. "Think twice before making any deals with her."

It was said in a smooth, calm voice. Like someone giving a warning. I turned to look at him. He sat leaning forward, elbows on his knees, scrutinizing Kira.

"W-what?" Ariana stammered, her gaze bouncing between Kira and Ben.

"Nothing." Kira tried to push me toward the aisle.

"No! What did you say?" I asked over Kira's shoulder.

Ben picked up his and Ariana's cups. "You heard me correctly."

"How dare you!" Kira snapped an acid bite to her words. Ben didn't even flinch. "It's against...Urg! Have you stopped to think that I was trying? That I didn't do it on purpose? Or have you spent all this time riding your high horse thinking you're better than me?"

With surprising strength, she pushed me into the flow of people leaving the game, cussing under her breath.

"What was that about?" I asked as we got jostled by the crowd. I hadn't even realized Kira knew Ben, let alone had enough of a history for there to be animosity between them.

"He makes me so mad. You know? Acts like he knew everything. He didn't." She kicked an empty plastic cup into the heels of the people in front of us. "Just forget it, Logan."

"Kira." I grabbed her arm, forcing her to stop. People streamed by us. "What did he mean by 'don't make any deals' with you?"

She shifted her weight from one foot to the other. "Please, just let it go."

But how does one let something like that go? And how could I think about spending time with someone who kept secrets that involved my sister's new boyfriend, a guy who'd also felt the need to warn me about the girl I dated.

"No, I'm sorry, but I can't," I replied. "There's obviously something going on between you and Ben. Talk to me." When she just stared at me, cheeks reddened in anger, I added, "Look, if it's so bad you can't even tell me about it, then maybe you and I shouldn't be doing this."

"You mean seeing each other?" she asked, as if *this* could have been anything else.

I stuffed my hands in my pockets and nodded. I was probably the only idiot in our school who would be on a date with one of the most sought-after girls at South Elgin High and ruin it by demanding answers about another guy.

"Things between Ben and I aren't like *that*. I mean, we were never a couple or anything, if that's what you're thinking."

"Then how do you know him?"

"That's a long story." She spun on her heels and headed toward the parking lot before I could respond. I followed, her earlier comment bouncing around my skull.

"What didn't he know?" I asked.

She breathed in deeply, blew the air out slowly,

and completely ignored my question. "Your sister's nice."

"She can be a pain in the butt, but I love her," I replied, walking quickly to keep up with her long strides.

We reached my car. When she didn't say anything else, I asked again, "What was Ben talking about?"

"Logan, I really don't want to talk about him." She waited for me to unlock the door. When I didn't move, she rose to her tiptoes. She was so close I could feel her breath on my lips. Her endless eyes stared up into mine. "Please drop it."

I paused, questioning why I was destroying a perfect evening by talking about Ben. Yet a nagging voice in the back of my mind told me to ask again. The words made it to the tip of my tongue, but when I opened my mouth, I became sure it was nothing. I should just forget about Ben and his stupid comment.

Kira lived close to the school in a tan, split-level house with sage-green shutters. Red mums were planted between boxwood bushes lining the walk up to the small front porch.

Her smile lit up her face. "I had a good time tonight."

I took off my seatbelt and turned so I could see her. "I did, too."

It had been a while since I'd been out on a date. After Ariana's and my second set of foster parents had died, I'd put a mental wall up in my mind, not allowing myself to get close to anyone else. Losing the people who had cared about us over and over again had made me shy away from dating, but lately I'd been wondering what I was missing. Ariana, too. I'd seen her push guys away before things could get serious, and I'd never tried to stop her, but what if I should have? What if the key to having a normal life was simply to do normal things?

I'd given that subject a lot of thought before I'd considered asking Kira out, and I'd come to the conclusion that the people in my life who'd died were adults in charge of raising Ariana and me, not our friends. There was no reason to believe anything would happen to a girlfriend or, in Ariana's case, a boyfriend.

I reached over the center console and wrapped my hand around Kira's. "Maybe we could do this again."

"I'd like that." She ran her thumb over the back of my fingers. It sent a shiver through my body. I liked Kira. She was smart, easy to talk to, and she smelled amazing.

"I'd better get inside before my dad sees us sitting here," she said.

I tightened my grip on her hand and leaned closer to her. Kira sucked in a breath and held it, her lips sealed tight. For a moment, I thought I'd misread her body language that night. I thought she was going to bolt from the car screaming that she'd said she'd hang out with me again, not that she wanted to kiss me, but she didn't. Her gaze moved to my lips. I closed the distance between us, covering her mouth with mine. Her lips were warm and soft. She tasted like hot chocolate.

When our lips parted, she rested her forehead on mine. "Wow," she said.

"Yeah. Wow."

Her kiss left me wanting more. I placed my hand under her chin and lifted her mouth back to mine.

After a few seconds, she broke our kiss and whispered into my lips, "I really should go."

"Okay." But I didn't want her to. Neither of us moved.

Her free hand moved to the back of my head, and she kissed me again.

"My dad will hear your car idling." She didn't get out.

"I know." I thought about turning it off. Then I wondered if that would be too obvious and kissed her instead.

Finally, Kira pulled away and placed her hand on the door handle. "I really have to go."

With one last peck on the lips, she was out of the car and sprinting up the walk to the sage-green front door of her house.

Chapter Eight

Ariana

Ben refused to tell me what deal he'd been talking about, which totally wrecked the loving-life mood I had been in. He swore that he'd never dated Kira and that he didn't want to date her. He went as far as to call her an impatient child, which led to a whole new list of questions that he refused to answer. What was even more annoying was he wouldn't look at me, so I couldn't use mind control on him.

With most of the spectators gone, the breeze cut through my jeans, reminding me that I'd sat on the cold bleachers long enough for my butt to freeze.

I stood. "Ben, just take me home."

The silence in the car was broken only by the sound of road being eaten up in frustration. His fingers curled and uncurled around the steering wheel every few seconds; I was sure he'd rip the leather off soon. I was so upset with how the day had ended that I hadn't noticed we'd reached my apartment until we were parked in front of it.

"I'm sorry," he finally said. His shoulders slumped forward. "I ruined the evening."

I stared at my hands. Our romantic dinner seemed like it had been ages ago, and the excitement of watching the game was like a distant memory. I'd really thought I had met someone special, but what type of relationship could we have had if he kept secrets—one of which involved a deal with my brother's new girlfriend. That was just so messed up.

He brushed my hair away from my eyes with his fingers. His touch was warm. Gentle. I looked into his deep blue eyes and thought, *Yeah, you did ruin everything.*

"Can we start over?" he asked.

"You want me to forget about this evening?" I retorted, knowing there was no way I could do that.

"Well, not everything." His thumb caressed my cheek. "Just what an idiot I was after the game."

"How do you know Kira?" I fidgeted with the strap on my bracelet. I'd made eye contact; he had to answer me this time, and I dreaded the truth.

He sighed. "Through our parents. It was a long time ago. We were young. Stupid. Both of us." He paused. Maybe wondering why he'd just told me that.

It wasn't much of an answer. But there was so much remorse in his gaze that I dropped mine to the cuff of his gray pea coat. So what if he knew Kira; he'd never dated her. And he certainly hadn't looked at her the way a guy looks at a girl he likes. The way he looked at me. I wet my lips as I thought.

"Ariana, please let me make it up to you." He used a finger to tilt my chin up, forcing me to look at him. "Are you doing anything tomorrow night?"

I wasn't. Becca had her cousin's wedding to go to. That meant I would be sitting home in my favorite sweats wearing pink, fuzzy slippers, eating pizza, and watching old movies. The longer we sat there, the sillier I felt our argument was, and I found myself wondering just how Ben would make it up to me.

But then I remembered what Becca had said after she'd broken up with Chad Pickering—who she'd dated all of ten days—about letting the small stuff go too easily and him walking all over her.

"I can't this weekend," I finally replied, proud of myself that the words came out with confidence.

Ben's hand dropped to his lap as his eyes closed in what I took as disappointment—in me or in himself, I didn't know.

"Maybe next week," I added because I did want to see him again, and because I swore I could feel his rising sense of guilt at screwing up the evening, and because, well, I liked him.

But it was ridiculous to think I could feel Ben's emotions. I'd just read his body language, which screamed a guy who sincerely wanted to be given a second chance.

People deserve second chances. Don't they?

Chapter Nine

Logan

That night I awoke to a noise in our apartment. Soundlessly, I got out of bed, grabbed the metal baseball bat I kept near my door—a habit I'd picked up from my uncle—and went to look around. I pushed Ariana's bedroom door open a crack. Her room was dark. It smelled like the autumn-spice candles she always burned. She was fast asleep, curled up on her side under her thick cream comforter. A search of the family room and kitchen turned up empty. Relieved, I decided that I had to have been dreaming or had heard one of our neighbors out in the hall. I stumbled back to my room, cursing under my breath when I jammed my little toe on the edge of the doorframe.

My head had barely hit the pillow when a raspy, male voice barked, "*Trap!*"

My racing heart drowned out the rest of its words. I knew that voice, and there was never a person attached to it. My mind went numb with fear, and every muscle in my body tensed. I'd thought I was past hearing voices. I wanted to scream and would have, but I didn't want to wake Ariana.

The disembodied voice spoke again in a hurried whisper: "*Must protect.*" There was a long pause. "*Up to you.*"

And then silence. Outside, a distant horn blared and cars swooshed past the apartment complex. I sat in the shadows created by the moonlight and listened.

It didn't speak again.

What trap? Protect who? Why was it up to me? The words had been garbled so badly, I wasn't even sure I'd heard them correctly. Hearing voices freaked me out—it always had. And now I had more questions that I didn't know how to find the answers to.

A moment later, Ariana's blood-curdling scream had me out of bed and sprinting to her room.

I'm not sure what I'd expected to find when I shoved open her door: the source of the disembodied voice, a ghost, or something worse. Ariana sat hugging her pillow, her brown hair matted to the sweat on her cheeks and forehead. The candle on her nightstand washed one side of her face with its amber light.

"Nightmare," she breathed, her eyes wide open as she scanned the room.

"I gathered that." I took a seat on the edge of the bed and pushed her hair away from her eyes. "But it was just a dream."

She shook her head frantically. "It was like the ones I used to have." She squeezed the pillow nervously. "And it was bad. Really bad."

Ariana's description of her childhood nightmares flashed through my mind: our house being swallowed by a large crack in the earth; monsters with hoofed feet, the torso and arms of a man, and the face of a beast bearing down on her; her favorite toys coming to life and strangling each other. The worst of her dreams had stopped a few years ago. Her having a nightmare on the same night I'd heard the voice couldn't be good. I did

61

my best to keep my fear from showing in my expression.

"You were outside," she whispered, "surrounded by tall buildings. There were flames everywhere. Even the sky was on fire. And it smelled awful. Like the water does after they've been working on the pipes."

"Like rotten eggs?" I asked, knowing that was how she used to describe the smell when she was little.

She nodded and continued to squeeze her pillow. "There was someone there. A dark shadow. Watching. Laughing this hideous laugh. There was nowhere for you to run."

I hugged her, trying to comfort her. "It was only a dream."

"The flames—" She choked back a sob. "They...they were burning you alive, and there was nothing—" She buried her head in my chest, but I knew she'd been about to say there had been nothing she could do to save me.

I gripped her shoulders, looked her in the eyes, and repeated, "It was only a dream."

"Logan, you don't think—I mean..." She drew in a shaky breath and then blurted, "People died when I used to have these dreams. People we cared about. You don't think that's going to start again, do you?"

"No." I picked up the small stuffed St. Bernard she'd named Gabriel from her nightstand. She had a black rosary wrapped around its neck. I handed it to her. "And your dreams didn't cause those deaths."

"Logan, I'm not a child anymore." She looked at the stuffed dog as she spoke. "I know Gabriel can't protect me. And don't try to tell me that my dreams about burning teddy bears and exploding closets weren't foreshadowing the fire that killed Mom and Dad or that the psychotic toy cars weren't warning us that our aunt and uncle were about to be killed. No one's died in close to three years."

That had been when Ariana and I'd noticed a pattern: We'd move to a new foster home, become close to the family, and a tragedy would strike the parents. Then, Ariana and I would be shipped to a new home. To protect the families, Ariana and I had started to tell our caseworker that the different homes weren't working out. We had stopped allowing ourselves to get close to anyone. People stopped dying.

"No one's going to get hurt," I said, willing my words to make it true yet knowing I couldn't control the future. She looked vulnerable in the dimly lit room. "Why'd you light a candle instead of turning on the lamp?"

Ariana looked at it as if she'd just noticed it was lit. "I didn't. I must have forgotten to blow it out when I went to bed."

My mouth went dry. Her room had been dark when I'd come in earlier. If she hadn't lit the candle, who had? Ariana was upset enough. I didn't want to scare her even more by telling her the candle hadn't been lit before she'd screamed. I bent down, pretending I had an itch on my ankle, and nonchalantly checked under the bed. Nothing. I grabbed a sweater from the bedpost and proceeded to hang it in her closet. No one there either. I could tell Ariana was still dwelling on the dream, because she didn't comment on my strange behavior.

I picked up the candle next, planning on taking it out of her room. "Get some sleep."

She grabbed my arm and held on with both hands. "Don't leave me! Please."

She was trembling again. Petrified of things we couldn't see. She moved over so that I could lie down.

"I'll be right back." When she didn't let go, I turned on the light and added, "I promise."

I checked the apartment again. Ariana and I were still the only ones there. I blew out the candle, set it in the kitchen sink, and went back in her room.

She turned off her light and pulled the blanket up to her neck. I sat at the head of her bed with my back against the wall and a hand on her shoulder, like old times.

Unfortunately, old times hadn't had happy endings.

Chapter Ten

Ariana

Logan spent the night in my room. I loved him for that because I don't think I would have gotten another minute of sleep if he wasn't there. The dream had seemed so real. Like we'd really been in that desolate place, and Logan had really been burned alive. I shuddered, unable to fathom life without him. He was my rock—the one solid and strong thing that never changed no matter how bad things got.

I had coffee brewing and the apartment dusted by the time he lumbered out of bed.

"Morning," he grunted as he headed straight for the kitchen cabinet.

"Morning," I chirped back. "Thanks, you know, for staying with me last night."

"No problem."

Saturday was Chore Day. Since Logan and I couldn't afford rent we had *suggested* to the landlord he let us stay in a two bedroom apartment for free in exchange for us vacuuming the hallways in the apartment complex, and with the leaves falling and being tracked in they were more of a mess than usual. I tackled floors four through six while Logan did the lower levels. Divide and conquer had been our strategy since we'd moved in. With our abilities, we knew he'd agree. Controlling people's minds had its advantages, and that was one of them.

By late morning, our tasks were done, laundry folded, and Logan and I had the day free.

"Logan?" I sat on the floor with my back against our worn couch, a large bowl of popcorn in my lap, and my feet crossed at my ankles in front of me.

"Huh?" He flipped through a few channels on the television we'd bought at a garage sale.

"What if it's starting up again?" I couldn't look at him; I was too afraid I'd see the fear I felt reflected in his eyes. I traced the edge of the bowl with my fingertips. "What if the nightmare I had is whatever's way of warning us that something bad is going to happen?"

"It's not," he replied immediately, but there was doubt hidden in his tone.

I'd spent the morning trying to convince myself that things were fine. We were fine. But I didn't believe that. In the past, terrifying dreams had always foreshadowed the death of the people closest to us. If bad things were starting up again, who were the unseen forces after? And did I want to know the answer to that question?

I ate a couple pieces of popcorn just to do something. Logan kept clicking, paying little attention to the different programs.

"What if you're wrong?" I asked.

"I'm not." He sounded confident, but through our connection I could feel the pressure of his headache pressing against my skull as if it were my own. "Ariana, as long as we stick together, we'll be safe. That's about the only thing that never changes. And after what happened the other day with the truck, I'm sure our birthmarks protect us somehow. There's no other explanation."

"Doesn't it worry you, trusting something we don't understand to protect us from something we can't see?"

"Yeah," he admitted. "But I have to believe in something, and right now that something is that whatever marked us wants us alive."

I nodded. Alive was good.

I ran through the things I had to be thankful for while he continued to surf channels. Logan and Becca were on the top of the list. Our apartment. It was small, the neighbors above us walked as if they had bricks in their pockets, and the old lady down the hall never ran out of stories about her late husband, but the apartment was ours. And since I was making a mental list of the good things, I added our mind-control abilities, because, let's face it, Logan and I would have probably been broke and in some state home for unwanted teens, possibly even separated, without them. In a way, we'd always depended on what we didn't understand. For us, it was as natural as breathing.

I then ran through the things I regretted. I only had two. One was the nightmares and how they brought about death. They scared me. A lot. But maybe Logan could help me do something about the second regret.

"Logan, does it make me a bad person if I can't remember Mom and Dad?"

He set the remote down on the couch, leaving the television on a ghost hunter show. Two men in their twenties wore work lights on their heads as they explored a dimly lit building.

"Sure you do. We went on that trip to Wisconsin

Dells, remember? The driver of the boat let you sit on Dad's lap and drive for a while. And you and Mom used to sing while she made breakfast."

I shook my head. The only solid memory I had of our parents was two closed caskets being lowered into a hole in the ground. I couldn't remember their voices, and even their faces were fuzzy pictures in my mind. A lump formed in my throat. I sniffed back my tears. Maybe, just maybe if I had told them about the dreams I'd been having, they'd have still been alive.

"It doesn't make you a bad person," Logan said. "You were only eight when they died."

I used a finger to absentmindedly stir the popcorn. "But I haven't forgotten everything that happened before the fire. I remember you and I used to play outside on a wooden swing set, and if I had a bad dream I would sneak into your room and you'd let me sleep with you. My bedroom was purple, I think, 'cause I remember pictures of purple ponies on the wall." I looked at him. "Shouldn't I remember doing things with Mom and Dad? Being tucked in bed at night or family dinners at the table?"

He moved closer, resting a hand on my shoulder. "You are remembering things. We lived in a three-bedroom, split-level home. My room was steel blue with race cars stenciled halfway up the walls. Yours was lavender with ponies. Mom was a great cook, and no matter how busy Dad was at work, he made it home for dinner."

Logan and I had been playing out back on the swing set when the fire had broken out. I did remember that. He'd told me later that he'd heard a voice screaming for him to help our parents, but when he had run toward the house, a wall of heat had stopped him. Within seconds, flames had greedily eaten the kitchen curtains and torn through the roof. Thick black smoke had blanketed the windows. And then he'd done everything he could to hold me back, keeping me from getting any closer to the house. I remember screaming myself hoarse.

He squeezed my shoulder. "A lot has happened to us since the fire. It's a lot for someone to handle, especially a kid."

But I remembered all the other stuff: moving to new foster homes, living with different families, watching more people die.

"You were a kid, too, and you remember," I mumbled, sounding like the pouty four-year-old I babysat.

"I'm older than you."

"By only two years."

He must not have known what to say to that, because he picked up the remote. He didn't change the channel, though.

I shook the bowl of popcorn as if it was freshly popped and I was mixing in butter and salt. "Kira seems nice."

"She is," he replied, letting me change the subject.

"Are you going to see her again?"

"Sure." He reached into the bowl I held and grabbed a handful of popcorn. "We're in the same foods class."

I shook my head and moved up to the couch. "That's not what I meant."

He ate the popcorn in his hand before answering, "I'd like to, but after last night, I'm not sure I want to get close to anyone. We've been doing okay keeping it just you and me. I'm not sure if—" He ran a hand through his hair.

"You're not sure if you want to risk getting close to someone because we both know how that turns out," I said.

"Yeah," he admitted, surprising me that he did. "After last night, I can't help wondering if I'd be putting her in danger."

"Me too, with Ben."

Logan went to the kitchen and got a glass of water.

I followed, hugging the bowl of popcorn as if it could protect us from the unseen. "Funny how we both met someone we like, and the nightmares start up again."

"And the voices," he whispered, so low that I knew he hated having to tell me about them and was—despite how he always appeared to have it together—freaking out inside.

The bowl slipped from my grip. It hit the linoleum tile and shattered, sending popcorn and glass in all directions.

"Damn it!" I grabbed a towel and used it to push as much of the mess as I could into a pile. "When?"

He bent down and helped. "Last night."

I fell back on my butt so that I was sitting. I didn't want to watch anyone else die. I was afraid I wasn't strong enough to live through the death of people I cared about again. But more than anything, I was petrified the next person to be ripped from my life would be Logan. I buried my head in my knees and focused on keeping my breathing steady.

Why couldn't we have a normal life? Why

shouldn't I have a boyfriend? Or dream of a wedding on the beach in some wonderfully romantic tropical paradise? It wasn't fair that Logan and I had to be alone. I looked at him through a veil of bangs.

"Ben and I are supposed to go out again," I whimpered. I wasn't sure when, as I was playing hard to get, but that would only last a few days. Maybe until the weekend.

Wanting to continue to see Ben had to have been one of the most selfish things I'd ever considered. But I couldn't help myself. He was sweet and fun and sexy, and his touch sent my heart twirling with excitement.

Logan sighed. "Why don't we take it one day at a time? If the nightmares and voices continue, then we'll decide if I should stop seeing Kira and if you should stop seeing Ben."

I got a flattened cereal box from the recycle bin and held it on the floor like a dustpan. Logan pushed the popcorn and chunks of glass on it with the dishtowel.

"What do you want to do today?" he asked once we had the floor cleaned.

I needed to get out of the apartment. It was the only way I was going to get my mind off the dreams and the voice and those who'd died. I grabbed Logan's arm and dragged him toward the door. "We should do something reckless!"

Chapter Eleven

Logan

Ariana's idea of reckless was the thrill rides at the amusement park. We spent the afternoon riding roller coasters, swinging round and round on the giant pendulum, and eating junk food—something we hadn't done together since our aunt and uncle had died. It's funny how a day of fun can make you see life differently. Standing in line waiting to go on the rides allowed us time to talk about all the normal things in our lives: school, friends, and stuff we were saving for, like that car for Ariana. The conversation steered itself toward the good times in our past, and as we joked around, Ariana started to remember small things about our parents, like how Mom used to blast the stereo when she'd clean the house and how Dad and I would work on cars with our uncle. It gave us time to forget the voice and nightmare, at least for the time being.

On Monday, I couldn't wait for foods class. Kira was already at our table when I walked in the classroom. She looked smokin' hot in tight jeans and a frilly white camisole peeking out from under a dark red shirt. I wished we were anywhere but at school.

"Good morning," she said with a grin. She had her elbows on the table and fidgeted with a loose string on her sleeve.

"Morning." I pulled out my stool and took a seat. "How was the rest of your weekend?"

"It was nice. Went shopping, hung out with friends." She paused, her bottom lip between her teeth as she watched me. "It was almost as much fun as Friday night."

"I'm glad you had a good time. I was thinking—"

"Quiet down, everyone," Mrs. Larson said, keeping me from finishing my sentence.

Kira turned to face the front of the classroom. I sighed.

"We have a lot to cover today. We will be discussing additives in the foods we eat." Mrs. Larson wrote a page number on the board. The shuffle of textbooks being pulled out and pages flipping to the right section filled the classroom.

"Sounds fascinating," I whispered, making Kira chuckle.

Once Mrs. Larson began the lesson, I asked, "Are you doing anything after school?"

Kira made a face that looked as if she'd just sucked on a lemon. "Spending quality time"—she made air quotes when she said "quality"—"with my stepmom."

"Don't like her?"

"Kira, Logan." Mrs. Larson glared at us. "There will be a quiz on this."

"Right," Kira said.

I folded my hands on the table in an effort to appear interested.

"My stepmom's a bitch with a capital *B*," Kira whispered a few seconds later. "She makes Cinderella's stepmother look like a saint."

I'd never admit it to any of my friends, but thanks

to Ariana's love of all things princess when she was little, I'd seen Cinderella so many times I could sing along to the songs. To try and get Kira to smile again, I joked, "You don't have evil stepsisters, too, do you?"

"No! Thank God! But I really do hate to be alone with her."

"Then why hang out with her?"

"My dad insists." She rolled her eyes. "What are you doing?"

"I was going to see if you wanted to do something," I admitted.

"Oh!" Her cheeks flushed. "I totally missed that's what you were asking. It's been a long time since I've been courted."

"Courted?" It sounded even funnier coming from me. I laughed.

Her face turned bright red, her nose scrunched in embarrassment. "Sorry, one too many Brontë novels. *Wuthering Heights* is my favorite."

"Am I boring the two of you?" Mrs. Larson demanded.

"No," Kira mumbled at the same time I said, "Sorry."

I stared at a picture of a food label in our textbook while Mrs. Larson explained the different types of fats. I waited for her to turn her back to the class.

"Can't you get out of the afternoon with your wicked stepmother?" I asked. When Kira hesitated, I added, "Even Cinderella wasn't expected to spend time with hers."

"I don't know." Kira looked at me, her head tilted to the side. "Maybe if I tell my dad I'm going over to a friend's house to study. What'd you have in mind?"

I shrugged and confessed, "Not sure yet."

It was like déjà vu, only Kira said, "Let's do something reckless," instead of Ariana.

Mrs. Larson cleared her throat, and I realized that others were talking, too.

"Apparently, I'm wasting my time standing up here." She flipped her book shut with an exaggerated bang. "Since you already know everything there is to know about what they put in your food, you shouldn't have any trouble with the questions at the end of the chapter."

"But there are twenty-one of them!" John Kraft said in protest.

"Yes. Well, you better get started then." Mrs. Larson took a seat behind her desk.

The class moaned in disapproval.

"Talk about bitches." Kira nodded toward Mrs. Larson. "If I thought she had a heart, I'd ask her if we could do half."

I didn't need Mrs. Larson to have a heart. I only needed her to look at me. I could be the hero and save everyone from homework.

"Uh, Mrs. Larson," I said.

"What is it, Logan?" she replied without taking her eyes off what she was writing.

I waited. I could feel the class staring at me, wondering what I was going to say. Maybe even hoping I wouldn't do anything to upset our teacher more than she already was. After a minute, Mrs. Larson set the pen down. Her gaze met mine, her lips set in a thin line that cautioned me to tread lightly with my comment.

"Maybe you meant to say you only wanted us to do the odd numbers?"

Her expression became blank. She then rubbed her chin. "Yes, just do the odd numbers."

A chorus of *awesome* and *yes* echoed around us.

Kira tapped my hand with icy fingers. "Nice!"

"You're freezing!" I went to grab her hand, but she pulled her arm close to her chest.

"Yeah." She rubbed her hands together. "I'm having a hard time adjusting to the climate up here."

"Maybe you should wear a ski sweater or a parka or, at the very least, gloves." I shrugged out of my hooded sweatshirt.

"Ha-ha," she said, breathing into her hands to warm them.

I held out my sweatshirt. "You need it more than I do."

She glanced at my T-shirt, one eyebrow arched. "Won't you be cold?"

"I'll survive. Besides, I wouldn't want you to turn into an icicle or anything."

"Yeah." Kira pretended to shiver, shoulders scrunched up for effect. She took the sweatshirt and put it on.

She had to bunch up the sleeves so her hands could be seen. Out of the corner of my eye, I saw her breathing in deeply and hoped the sweatshirt smelled like my cologne and not B.O.

"You want to do the first five, and I'll do the last?" Kira searched through her purse for a moment. "Do you have an extra pen?"

"Sure." I handed her a black one.

"That's an interesting bracelet," she commented, pointing with the pen at my wrist.

I ran my fingers over the silver wings and made

sure the black leather was positioned to hide my birthmark.

"Ariana has a pink one like that, doesn't she?" Kira jotted down the answer to the first question, then looked at me. "They're unique."

"I suppose," I replied as if the bracelets were no big deal.

"It's a cool idea, actually," she said, then read the next question.

"Why's that?" I asked, not sure what to make of her comment.

"You know." She paused to write another answer. "It's just you and Ariana, and you guys have something to symbolize family. That's cool."

"I never thought of it like that."

"No?" She watched me a moment. "Is there another reason you wear similar bracelets?"

Ariana and I had several: To hide the birthmarks that proved we were freaks. To keep people from asking unwanted questions about said birthmarks. Most importantly, we didn't want whoever had marked us to find us. Out loud, I said, "We liked them."

She nodded, her gaze locked on my wrist. "You should consider making it a family thing. Like a ring passed down from generation to generation. Adds an air of mystery to them." She shrugged. "I'm not much of a jewelry person myself. I don't like how necklaces and bracelets stick to my skin in the heat." She cocked her head to the side thoughtfully. "I guess that's not a problem now that I'm living in chilly Illinois."

I decided to drop the conversation before she asked for a closer look at my bracelet.

At the end of the school day, Kira met me at the

double doors leading to the student parking lot, still wearing my sweatshirt.

"I thought of a plan." She grabbed my hand and led me outside.

"Where are you taking me?" I asked. Students hurried past us, several veering to the right where a line of buses waited. We went straight into the student parking lot.

"I want it to be a surprise," she replied, still pulling me forward.

We reached my car.

"But I'm driving," I said.

She leaned her back against the passenger side, making it so I couldn't unlock the door. "You could let me drive."

I stepped closer, keys in hand. Kira wasn't big. I could have picked her up and moved her out of the way if I wanted to. But I sort of liked having her trapped between me and the car.

"My '68 Chevy?" I let out a disbelieving laugh. "Not a chance."

She gazed up at me with sultry eyes that seemed to look straight into my soul. "Then I'll tell you which way to go."

Her leg brushed against mine when she shifted.

"Please," she added, running her finger down my chest, causing my heart to race.

I moved even closer to her and kissed her lips lightly. I hated not knowing where I was going, though, and knew I wasn't playing fair when I then looked into her eyes, fully intending on using mind control to get my way.

"You could just tell me."

I waited for my suggestion to sink in. *Here it comes*, I thought when her lips parted.

"I could," she agreed, shifting again so that her hip bumped mine. It was too easy, but, then again, no one could resist my powers. Or so I'd thought until she added, "But I'm not going to."

"You're not?" I repeated, confusion and shock at her refusal battling for first place. "But—"

But what? I couldn't tell her she wasn't supposed to have a mind of her own, that I had used mind control on her and she was supposed to do whatever I'd said. That's not exactly something you admit to anyone.

Even though Ariana had told me about the guy at the coffee shop, I had brushed it off as a one-time thing. I had even recreated the scene in my head: Ariana leaning over the counter, the creep breaking eye contact to stare at her chest, him thinking she was flirting with him so she could get her order for free. But now, that theory seemed less likely.

Kira and I just stood there—her looking up at me waiting to hear the rest of my sentence, and me looking at her as if she'd done something completely alien.

In my defense, being immune to my mind control did count as alien, and I didn't know what to do.

Chapter Twelve

Ariana

"What do you mean you told him you were busy?" Becca demanded. She hit the button on the clicker, unlocking the doors of her car. We got in.

"I had plans with you." I shoved my backpack on the floor under my feet.

Becca started the car. "Yeah, but we're best friends. I would have understood if you broke our plans to be with Mr. Gorgeous."

"He asked me last minute. I don't want him to think I have no life."

"But you told him no for Saturday, too."

"So?" I didn't tell Becca about the argument Ben and I'd had after the game. I felt a little guilty about keeping it from her, but I'd told Ben we'd start over. I decided the only way that would be possible is if I pretended our last date had ended before he'd made the comment about making deals with Kira.

Becca got behind the rest of the cars waiting to escape the school parking lot.

"So?" she said in an omigod-are-you-kidding-me tone. "He might ask someone else out."

"Then let him," I replied defiantly as if I couldn't care less who Ben went out with. But I did care, and now that Becca had put that bug in my head, I couldn't help wondering if I was playing a little too hard to get.

Even though our date had ended on a sour note, I couldn't stop thinking about Ben. Over the weekend, I'd had to fight the urge to call him. When Logan and I had sped over the roller coaster tracks at the amusement park, I'd found myself wondering where Ben would have taken me. In art class, it had been all I could do not to stare at him. And when he'd asked me what I was doing after school, I'd had to bite the inside of my cheek to keep from blurting out "Nothing!" like an excited child.

My fingers curled around my cell phone.

Maybe I should send him a text.

I flipped the phone open. Becca glanced at me out of the corner of her eye, a knowing smirk on her face.

"No." I put my phone away. "I'm going to let fate take its course. If he likes me, he won't ask anyone else out."

Becca shook her head but said nothing.

Logan wasn't home when we got there. Becca grabbed a couple of sodas from the fridge, and I grabbed a bag of chips off the counter. We brought everything into my room.

"How was your cousin's wedding?" I asked.

She plopped down on my bed, potato chips in hand. "It was fun."

I glanced at her skeptically. "I thought you hated her."

"I do, but I met someone." She popped a chip into her mouth.

I sat down next to her. "Why didn't you tell me sooner?"

"Because I was waiting for us to be alone."

"Well, spill!"

She moved further onto the bed, crossing her legs like a pretzel. "His name's Justin. He's in college, and he plays in a band. Alternative stuff like Linkin Park. He is sooo cute, too, with blond curls and dramatic gray eyes."

"Dramatic?" I repeated with a giggle. If I didn't know her better, I would have thought she'd made him up: an older guy who just so happened to be in a band that plays the type of music she likes and has eyes she described like a romance novel would.

She smiled dreamily. "I know. Sounds stupid, but he looks at me as if he's drinking me in. It's so intense. Can you imagine?"

I shook my head, not sure how to answer that question without upsetting her because I wasn't sure I'd want a guy who stared at me as if he wanted to consume me.

Maybe I'd read one too many books about vampires, but the thought of someone drinking me creeped me out.

"And he's such a good listener." She popped another chip into her mouth. "I've never talked that much to a guy in my life. It was amazing."

I giggled with her, happy she was in such a good mood. "Is he friends with your cousin or her new husband?"

"Neither. He was working."

"One of the band members?" I asked, thinking that was how she knew he was a musician.

"No."

I grabbed my can of soda from the nightstand. It opened with a hiss. "Then what does he do?"

"He's a waiter."

"Did he look sexy in uniform?" I waggled my eyebrows.

"You know"—she crinkled her nose—"he did."

"What college does he go to?"

Her brow furrowed. "I'm not sure."

"Is he from around here?"

"I think so."

I took a long sip of soda as I pictured Becca chatting the night away with Mystery Waiter. Logan used to hang out with a Justin who was a couple years older than him, and I wondered if it was the same guy. "What's his last name?"

"I don't know." She scooted off the bed. "Why does it matter?"

"He might have a brother or sister who goes to school with us." The Justin who Logan knew had an annoying younger brother who had liked to follow me around like a lost puppy when we'd go over to their house.

"I didn't think about that." She grabbed her English book and lay on her stomach across the bed. "I'll ask him when I see him. How much of what we went over in class do you think will be on the test?"

I put my soda down and picked up my notebook. "I marked my notes with an asterisk every time Mrs. Littman stressed something *could* be on the test."

I stared at my curvy writing, not seeing it because I really didn't want to study. "Tell me more about Justin."

"I already told you what I know." She flipped to the chapter we were studying.

It had taken her three minutes to tell me everything

she knew about this guy, and it wasn't much. My BFF warning sensors went off.

"Let's call him," I said, determined to find out more about the mystery guy who had my best friend all excited. "See what he's up to."

"If you want to see what someone is up to, call Ben."

"He's helping his dad this afternoon." When she looked at me, I added, "He asked me to come with, but I said no. Remember?" I handed her my phone. "Call Justin."

She pushed my hand away. "I can't. I don't have his number."

I let my hand, phone and all, drop into my lap. "Haven't you talked to him since the wedding?"

"He calls me."

I hopped off the bed and dug her phone out of her purse. "Let's check caller ID. Hit callback."

"He has a private number," she replied without looking up.

"And he hasn't given it to you?" I tried to hide my surprise.

"No. Ariana, what's the big deal?"

I sank back down onto the bed next to her. "People who don't tell you their last name and won't give you their number usually have something to hide."

"We just met."

"But you said you've never talked so much to a guy before, and I've seen you talk to guys, Becca. You're not exactly Miss Shy."

She shrugged. "I guess I did most of the talking."

"Does he still live with his parents?"

"I don't know." Annoyance dripped from the

words.

I knew I should have dropped it, but my mouth blurted out my thoughts before I could tell it to shut up. "You can usually tell if a guy still lives at home by his comments."

"Just let it go already." She slammed her book shut. Sat up. "Why are you trying to ruin this for me?"

"Becca, I'm not. I just—"

"You just can't believe an older guy would like me unless he's bad news."

"That's not it." There was no reason for an older guy not to like her, except maybe she was jailbait. But I wasn't going to point that out. I *was* going to say I just didn't want to see her get hurt.

"Then what is it?" she demanded.

For the life of me, I couldn't think of a reply that wouldn't upset her more. My mouth just kept opening and closing like a guppy out of water.

"Whatever." She shoved her textbook into her backpack. "I don't feel like studying."

"Okay." I pushed my notebook aside. "What do you want to do?"

She took her cell phone, which I was still holding, and stuffed it with the rest of her things in her backpack.

"I gotta go."

"Becca! Come on." I jumped off the bed to block her path to the door, but she was too quick. "Don't leave!"

"I need to—do stuff."

"Becca. Come on! Please stay."

She didn't. And it frustrated me, because if I was the one all starry-eyed over a guy who hadn't given me his phone number or his last name or any concrete details about himself, she would have been warning me that someone who seems too good to be true probably is.

Chapter Thirteen

Logan

I had always counted on Ariana's and my ability to keep us safe. If we couldn't get what we needed to survive by using our power of suggestion—or worse, if there were people who were immune to our gift—then we were vulnerable. We could lose the roof over our heads. Or not be able to get ourselves out of trouble, like speeding tickets and missed homework assignments. And if someone was able to resist our powers, did that mean they had powers of their own? Would they know they had powers? Or that we did?

I forced myself to remain calm. "Okay," I said to Kira, "you win this time. But I'm driving. You're navigating."

Kira smiled triumphantly as she moved so that I could unlock the car door. She got in.

A terrifying thought occurred to me as I slowly walked to the driver's side. What if Kira wasn't immune? What if I was losing my powers? But then, if that were the case, Mrs. Larson would never have changed the assignment in foods class to be just the odd questions.

Unless she had felt I'd asked nicely. She was sort of a pushover.

While I drove, I thought about how I had made the

suggestion to Kira. It was possible I'd been watching her lips instead of her eyes. That had to be it.

Kira was as good as a GPS, warning me when I was going to need to get in the left lane or make a right-hand turn well in advance. We made a pit stop at a gas station for two bottles of lemonade, and our final destination brought us to a remote section of a forest preserve.

"We need to work on your idea of reckless," I said as we got out of the car.

I walked around to the passenger side, grabbed Kira's hand, and pulled her closer to me. I had to know if her earlier resistance had been a fluke. Her gaze met mine. This time, I made sure I stared directly into her gray eyes. "What's so special about this place?"

She smiled. "It intrigues me."

That didn't help me. I tried again. "Tell me what intrigues you."

I meant to hold her gaze, but I couldn't help noticing how the tip of her tongue traced her upper lip as she thought or how her thigh rubbed against mine when she shifted. I placed my finger under her chin and lifted her face until our eyes met. "How about we go to the mall or drive to the lake? We're halfway there now."

She did that thing where she bit the side of her lip as she thought. "No. I want to stay here."

I dropped my hand. Surprise, intrigue, and trepidation all pushed to be in the front of the line.

Kira gave me a quick kiss before she smiled deviously and stepped away from the car. A dark shadow flickered behind her eyes. I shook my head, sure I had imagined it, and followed her as she stepped onto an overgrown path leading deeper into the trees.

"*Are you sure you want to follow?*" asked the gruff voice I'd heard in my room the other night. A warm breath brushed the back of my neck when it spoke. I spun around, fully expecting to see someone standing behind me. No one was there.

"Coming?" Kira stopped to wait for me. The sweatshirt had slipped off one shoulder, and she tucked her wavy red hair behind her ear. She looked beautiful and dangerous all at once.

I stepped forward, pausing again when the disembodied voice whispered, "*Not your smartest move.*"

Under my breath, I hissed, "Then show yourself, because I don't trust what I can't see."

I ignored the voice when it *tsked* at me and let Kira lead me deeper into the forest until the trees thinned. She flopped down in the middle of the grove and patted the ground next to her.

I sat. The grass was patchy and more yellow than green, the wild flowers were plentiful and wilted, and the elder tree a few yards behind Kira was enormous and dead. Its branches seemed to reach toward us.

"How'd you find this place?" I asked, still looking around. The bark on the maples closest to the elder tree had turned black. A part of me—probably my common sense—wanted to run from this place, but another part felt oddly at ease.

"I heard a few people at school talking about it my first week here." Kira twisted the top off one of the lemonades and poured a fourth of it into the grass.

"What is this place?" I held the cap she handed me and watched her curiously.

"They called it Satan's Portal, claiming that the Devil himself has been here, but I'm not superstitious like that." She studied me, brow furrowed. "Are you?"

Superstition is very much like coincidence in that it shouldn't be taken lightly. Was it a coincidence Ariana and I were born on the same day two years apart? Or that we could sense when the other was near? Or even that we were born with birthmarks as detailed as the most intricate tattoo? I didn't think so. I had stopped believing in coincidence years ago. I also didn't believe humans were the only beings who walked this earth. That meant I knew enough to be cautious of the unknown. That *didn't* mean I believed what a bunch of high school students said about a patch of forest obviously deprived of sunlight.

I shook my head. "No, I'm not superstitious."

"Good." Kira pulled a bottle of alcohol out of her purse and poured it into the lemonade.

I now understood what was supposed to make our afternoon reckless. "Vodka?"

"You only live once. Right?" She held out her hand. "Cap."

I handed it to her. She screwed it back on and shook the bottle, then took a drink and held it out to me.

I went to grab it but paused. My hesitation wasn't because I had never had a drink or that I didn't feel I could hold my liquor, because I had and I could. It was because I didn't like how alcohol caused me to let my guard down, and seeing as I was with someone who could resist my charm—that being the ability to put ideas in her head—I wasn't sure that was a good idea.

Yet I wanted to know what made Kira special. If alcohol made me let go of my inhibitions, it was sure to do the same to her. She had to weigh thirty or forty pounds less than me, so she'd feel the effects of the vodka long before I would. All I had to do was keep my focus on the end goal, which was to find out what made her tick.

What had the voice said just before it *tsked* at me? *Not your smartest move.*

I laughed inwardly as I took the bottle, sure that the voice would disapprove of me drinking more than it disapproved of me spending an afternoon in the forest with a hot girl.

I was right to think Kira would feel the effects of the vodka before I did; it didn't hurt that I barely sipped while she gulped. We were almost finished with the second bottle of lemonade, which was half alcohol, when Kira became a giggly drunk.

"People here are sooo different from what I'm used to," she said, serious for a moment. "Happy and friendly." She shrugged. "The heat back home makes everyone crabby." She burst into laughter again.

Nothing Kira said about her family or her old friends hinted that she thought she was special in any way. She was the younger of two children. Her father was a second-level manager for a telecommunications company. Her mom worked at an animal hospital. She'd had boyfriends, but no one she'd liked enough to miss. She was comfortably normal, and I started to feel guilty about tricking her into thinking I was drinking more than I was.

Kira crawled closer to me, toppling over once on the way. She came to a stop, her nose a few inches from mine.

"Logan, do you think you're pretty? Oops." She

covered her mouth with her hand as she giggled. "I mean, do you think *I'm* pretty?"

"Yeah." I ran my fingers through her hair. "Irresistible is more like it."

Her expression became somber again. Her dark eyes held mine. "Then why aren't we kissing?"

From the moment she had walked into my fourth-period classroom, all I'd been able to think about was kissing her. My fingers brushed her cheek. She leaned into my hand.

"Your hand's cool, and you smell"—she breathed in deeper—"you smell good. Like the mountains or maybe the valley. I've never been to either."

"You're drunk."

"Yep. Kiss me." She puckered her lips.

"I would love to. Really." I moved my hand to her shoulder. "But not like this. Not when it will feel like I'm taking advantage of you."

"You're not taking advan"—she hiccupped—"advantage of me."

"Says the girl who isn't going to remember much about this afternoon come morning." I looked her in the eyes. "You need a cup of coffee." Maybe the whole pot.

"I don't want coffee." She fisted a handful of my T-shirt and pulled me closer to her. "I want you."

Man, was the feeling mutual, and she was practically begging for it. I wrapped an arm around her back. The wind picked up, blowing her fiery red curls around her face. The tip of her tongue traced her upper lip, and I had to quickly glance away. I'd hate myself in the morning if I let things between us go too far while she was that messed up. I stood before I could change my mind, holding onto her as I did. "This isn't a good idea. Not right now, anyway."

"I can't even seduce a guy right." She snorted and stumbled away from me toward the elder tree. "I brought you here. I got you drunk. I'm coming on to you. And you don't think this is a good idea." She threw her hands into the air. "For Asmodeus's sake, out of all the jerks in the world, I get a nice guy."

"What? Who?" I'd really let her drink too much.

"Who what?" she asked, tripping over nothing as she took a step closer.

I bent down to pick up her purse. She was right in front of me again, swaying. I wrapped an arm around her waist to steady her.

"One kiss?" She craned her neck to bring her lips to mine.

Her perfume was intoxicating, a mind-blowing blend of wild roses and lilies. I couldn't resist her any longer. I let her purse fall back to the ground and covered her mouth with mine. She tasted as good as she smelled. Her lips were hot, almost too hot. Her fingers twisted around my hair.

My hands wandered down her back, stopping just below the pockets of her jeans. Cupping her butt, I lifted her up so that I wouldn't have to lean over. Her legs wrapped around my hips.

After several long seconds, I broke our kiss, slid my hands to her waist, and placed her back on her feet. She released her grip on my hair and hid her face in my chest.

She mumbled something that sounded a lot like "This would be easier if you were a jerk." And sniffed.

Holding onto her shoulders, I took a step back. "Are you crying?"

"No!" She turned, hiding her face and wiping at her eyes. I dumped the rest of our lemonade-vodka mixture into a patch of yellowing grass, thankful that I hadn't really been drinking and was okay to drive, then emptied the bottle of vodka before I grabbed her purse.

She swayed as she watched me.

"Come on." I wrapped my arm around her again. "Let's get caffeine into you."

"I don't want caffeine."

I looked into her eyes. "Yes, you do want a cup of coffee."

"I'm not drinking it."

She mumbled that several times on the way back to the car. I drove through the drive-thru at the nearest fast-food restaurant on the way to her house and bought a coffee and a cola. Kira tossed both out the window.

At her house, I had to help her up the walk and find her keys in her purse. A raven landed on the mailbox, and its caw startled Kira. She turned to see what had made the noise and almost toppled over sideways. I tightened my grip on her waist.

Just as I stuck the key in the lock, the front door swung open. A man I assumed was her father stood in the doorway. He was big, like ex-professional-wrestler big, and he didn't look happy when he saw Kira.

She stumbled over the threshold and threw up all over his sock-covered feet.

He told me to leave, but before I did, I met his glare and said, "Kira ate something that didn't agree with her. You'll want to bring her upstairs and let her sleep. No need to punish her. Or hate me, for that matter."

I didn't know if my suggestion would work on him

since none of the ones I'd made to Kira that afternoon had had any effect on her whatsoever. But then he paused, his back a little straighter and his eyes serious. He said, "I'm sure she's just tired. Thanks for bringing her home."

His reaction confirmed I wasn't losing my gift, which had me so relieved that I almost yelled "Yes!" at the top of my lungs. But as I walked back to my car, I wondered what made Kira special?

Chapter Fourteen

Ariana

It took a pint of triple-caramel-crunch ice cream, an enormous bag of colorful candy-coated chocolate gems, my English notes, and a LOT of groveling before Becca would talk to me again after our disagreement. It was totally worth it. And something I'd said must have sunken into that thick skull of hers, because she found out Justin's last name—Calvert—and that he was a student at the college near us. He played in a local band. I couldn't remember its name, but they played at places around the Chicago suburbs. Oh, and she got his number.

I took a little of her advice, too, and stopped saying no to Ben. We were going to hang out after school.

That morning in art class, we painted with acrylics. The day's subject was a banana, an apple, and a bunch of grapes. The lesson taught me one thing: I am not the next Cezanne or Picasso. My bowl was lopsided and my fruit one-dimensional. Ben chose the easel next to mine, but he wouldn't let me see his canvas.

As promised, we started our relationship over. Only, instead of him not talking to me, like he had done before he'd asked me to the football game, he was friendly.

I stepped back from my painting, pretending I

wanted to get a better look at my work. I watched Ben instead. He eyed his canvas, added a stroke of purple, squinted, and then dabbed his brush in the white on his palette. I moved toward him, hoping to sneak a peek at his painting. He cracked a smile and turned his easel so that I couldn't see it.

"Oh, come on!" I slid even closer to him. "I'll let you see mine."

Ben caught me around my waist before I could take more than a step. "It's not finished."

"Yours can't be worse than mine." I craned my neck but still couldn't see what he had painted.

Laughing, Ben picked me up and set me down in front of my easel. He kept his arms locked around my body, pinning my arms to my sides. He had me so close to him, I could have easily kissed his neck. His chin. His lips. He smelled incredible, like the ocean and soap.

"What are you talking about?" He studied my painting. "It's good. Very Jackson Pollock."

I twisted in his arms so that I could see, too. My painting looked very second grade to me. "Who's Pollock?"

"An artist from the Forties."

"Ben?" Mrs. Murphy said.

Ben and I untangled ourselves and faced her. She pursed her lips as she examined his painting.

Mrs. Murphy frowned. "You were supposed to draw the fruit."

He moved next to her. "The fruit's there."

This time when I went to look, Ben let me.

He had painted a picture of me painting. The bowl of fruit we were supposed to paint was there in the background, sketched in light gray. My mouth fell open.

Mrs. Murphy nodded. "It's very good. You're talented."

I gawked at him.

He stuffed his hands in the front pockets of his jeans and scuffed the toe of his fancy black boot against the tile. "Do you like it?"

What wasn't there to like? He'd managed to capture how the fluorescent lights caught the auburn highlights in my hair and the extremely serious look in my eye as I'd painted. He'd included the daisies on the sleeve of my shirt and the smear of color that was the paint on my palette. There was even a streak of purple on the cheek of the painted-me. I touched my own cheek with my fingertips. Sure enough, there was something crusty and dry there. I rubbed at it with my sleeve.

"It's beautiful," I said.

He smirked. "So are you."

****

After school, Ben took me to this trolley museum not far from the high school. We boarded the brick-red and white trolley for a round-trip journey along the banks of the Fox River.

"You find the most interesting places," I said.

"It is pretty cool." We took a seat in the middle of the trolley. "I couldn't believe that they still ran."

I'd never been on a trolley. It looked a lot like the buses near Woodfield Mall, only the trolley was limited to the tracks, powered by electricity, and the bench seats were wood instead of vinyl. The dark water of the river flowed lazily downstream, keeping pace with us.

"Do anything fun since the game?" I asked, curious

98

how he'd spent his free time.

"Not too much. Helped out at church Sunday morning." He had his arm resting on the back of the seat behind me, his fingers playing absentmindedly with a few strands of my hair. "Do you go?"

I shook my head. We'd had foster parents who had been into the whole church scene. Mrs. Johnson had even lit candles for our parents, explaining that it was a way to honor them, but when you've seen as much death as I had, you start to question if there is a God.

"I'm not very religious," I replied.

Ben's arm slipped down so that it was around my shoulder. His thumb moved gently back and forth over my biceps, leaving my skin all tingly. "My parents do a lot with the church. That's why they travel so much. They study the neighborhoods around a church and help them create programs their community needs. Dad got me my job. Pay's not great." He shrugged. "But it's fun."

"Are you an altar boy?" I tried to picture Ben in a long white robe.

He shook his head. "I entertain the younger children while their parents attend mass. We sneak in the religious stuff."

"That's nice." He liked kids. Total plus in my book. Not that I knew for sure if I wanted kids, and I was getting way ahead of myself with Ben. It was only our second date. First date if starting over meant the other time hadn't counted. "I babysit. Have a few regulars who recommend me to their friends. I think it's because I don't let the kids veg out the whole time in front of the TV. We play games, read books, stuff like that."

"It's rewarding, isn't it? Knowing you're making a difference in someone's life."

I'd never really thought about it that way, but I guess I did make a difference in the kids' lives. I'd even taught them a few things, like how to do cartwheels, blow bubbles with bubble gum, and make peanut butter and jelly sandwiches so that the bread doesn't get mushy.

The evening ended with Chicago-style hotdogs, fresh-cut fries, and milkshakes at this small fifties-era diner that had faded pictures of Marilyn Monroe, the cast of Happy Days, and various other TV shows pinned to the walls and ceiling.

I didn't want the day to be over, but the bright half-moon against an inky sky let us know it was getting very late.

Once at home, Ben walked me to the entrance of my apartment complex. At the door, he took my hands in his. I had to tilt my head back to see his eyes.

"How'd I do?" he asked. "Am I forgiven for being such an idiot the other day?"

"Yeah." I'd forgiven him days ago.

Someone exited the building, their shoes making a clipping noise against the cement as they hurried down the steps. The air was cool and dry and scented with the aroma of spruce and burning wood from the fireplaces in nearby homes.

Ben stepped closer, taking my hands and wrapping them behind me. His beautiful blue eyes watched my lips. I was sure he could feel my heartbeat quicken.

I tilted my head up. His lips met mine. Softly. Just a taste at first. Then his hands cupped my face. His kiss was like hot fudge, whipped cream, and dark cherries, warm and sweet with just the right amount of desire.

My hands moved to his hips as I got lost in the moment. Mrs. Harker, my neighbor, shuffled past us, but not before getting out a whimsical "Get a room!" first.

Ben rested his forehead against mine.

"Thanks for a great time today," I said, sorry it was about to end.

"Thank you for coming." He put a finger under my chin and brushed my lips with his. "Maybe we can do it again?"

I smiled. "I'd like that."

I felt like I was on cloud nine when I shut the door to the apartment. I'd had a really good time with Ben. We were seeing each other again, and life was wonderful for me. Logan, on the other hand, looked miserable. He sat on the couch brooding, eyes staring at the television with a faraway expression like he wasn't really seeing it.

I sank down next to him. "You okay?"

His solemn gaze met mine, and his fingertips messaged his temple. "I need to tell you something that you're not going to like."

Chapter Fifteen

Logan

Ariana took the news about Kira being immune to my powers better than I had expected. I'd been ready for her to want me to replay every moment of my date with Kira over and over. Instead, she listened quietly, nodded occasionally, and then rambled on for a good five minutes about how, after Coffee Shop Dude, we shouldn't be so surprised. She went as far as to say I was reading too much into the whole situation. She might have convinced me that was true if she had looked me in the eyes when she spoke and hadn't said "right" every other sentence.

Kira missed several days of school. I called her but got voicemail each time. I started to question if the suggestion I'd made to her dad the other night had worked after all. But then I doubted he'd keep her home from school as punishment for getting hammered.

Thursday, she strolled into foods class deep in conversation with Elaina Preble. They took a seat at one of the tables in the front of the classroom. Kira avoided looking in my direction. Elaina caught me watching them and promptly turned her head so that she could hide behind a curtain of hair.

I couldn't believe Kira was giving me the cold shoulder for not taking advantage of her when she'd been drunk. I got the feeling she'd wanted me to be a jerk. What girl *hopes* she'll meet a loser? I didn't get it.

I tapped my pen against my workbook, frustrated. Screw her. I didn't need an alcoholic girlfriend anyway.

The bell announcing the beginning of class rang.

Maybe she wasn't avoiding me because I was a nice guy. Maybe she didn't remember what had happened in the forest. Maybe she thought we *had* done something and she regretted it.

I got up, snatched my things off the table, and marched up to Kira and Elaina.

"Kira, we need to talk."

She frowned. "We're good, Logan. Let's just forget the other day. Okay?"

"I can't." I bent close. "You need to know nothing happened."

She glanced from me to Elaina.

"Logan, give her time," Elaina said.

"I have. Days." I set my books on the table and looked Elaina in the eyes. "You want to switch seats with me."

A dazed expression passed quickly over her face. Then she grabbed her things. "Why don't you have a seat?"

"Thanks." I lowered myself onto the stool she vacated.

Kira pulled the sleeves of her white sweater over her hands. She opened her mouth, but instead of saying anything, she let out a soft sigh.

"I called you," I said.

"Yeah. Sorry I didn't call you back." She bit her bottom lip and then added, "I was busy. Um... helping my stepmom."

"Did she trap you in a tall tower, leaving you to be rescued by singing mice?" I joked.

"Only Disney fairytales have happy endings, Logan."

"Right." So much for getting her to smile. I felt awful about letting her think I'd been drinking when I really hadn't. It was my fault she'd gotten wasted. If I'd been honest with her, our date would have ended with us making out instead of her throwing up on her father. "I wanted to make sure you knew that we only kissed."

"I remember our date. No need to remind me that I made a fool of myself."

"Is that what you think? Kira…" I reached for her hand, but she dropped it to her lap. "With how much we'd drunk, I didn't want you to hate me for letting things go too far."

"It was a kiss, Logan."

That would have led to more, because no way did I want to *just* kiss her and no way that was all that was on her mind at the time. But maybe she didn't remember how forward she had been. Since she was talking to me, I wasn't going to push.

"Did you get in a lot of trouble with your dad?" I asked instead.

"No, he seemed to think I ate something that upset my stomach."

I would have told her *you're welcome* because it was my suggestion that kept her from getting grounded, but she didn't know that. Mrs. Larson began the day's lesson. Kira turned her attention to the front of the classroom.

Mrs. Larson went over the day's project, which included chocolate and strawberries the size of small plums. We were told to pair up.

"Are you doing anything after school?" I asked as we stood.

She shook her head. "Look, Logan, you're nice, and I like you, but I think we're better off as friends. You know?"

"Quick." Elaina stopped next to Kira, a pleading look in her eyes. "Partner up with me before John asks me."

Kira looked at me, faking a smile before she grabbed Elaina's wrist. "Come on."

It took a moment for me to fully understand what had just happened.

I got stuck dipping strawberries into creamy milk chocolate with John Kraft, who didn't look any happier than I was about being partners. I felt as if I'd been punched in the gut. Since when did not taking advantage of a girl get you dumped? My shock turned into anger. Nice guys really did finish last.

By the end of class, my anger had transformed itself into acceptance. I reasoned that fate was warning me not to get involved with anyone right now.

I did think fate blew.

It took a couple of weeks for the awkwardness that hung in the air between Kira and me to dissolve into a good working relationship. It wouldn't have been so bad not having a girlfriend if it hadn't been for how well Ariana had hit it off with Ben. I was both happy for her and jealous of her at the same time.

And I kept hearing the voice: at home, at school, and once when I was driving. It had become as familiar and as annoying as an unwanted friend, and it no longer startled me when it spoke. This voice was different than the ones I used to hear when I was younger. It spoke in a rushed whisper, as if afraid it would be overheard. Its words were often clipped or garbled, and the advice—if that's what it was—made little sense: *"Don't listen," "Keep your guard up," "Watch out."* I never got an entire sentence. It had yet to take me up on my offer and show itself, and I stuck by what I had said before, that I don't trust what I can't see.

Ariana's nightmares steadily increased until she was afraid to fall asleep. We started camping out in the family room, falling asleep to late-night TV. Being near each other seemed to stifle the dreams. I think it was all too much for her, the dreams and the voices and knowing that people could be immune to our power of suggestion. It took a toll on her. She became quiet and spent a lot of time staring at nothing.

I wanted answers. I couldn't shake the feeling that if we could find information on our birthmarks, we would find the answer to why we were different. We might even find out what it meant for our future.

Saturday, after our chores were done, I drew three of the symbols from our birthmarks onto a sheet of paper along with a few unrelated symbols Ariana had found on the Internet—we hoped by having random images we wouldn't attract unwanted attention to ourselves when we asked for help. We then went to a used bookstore in Chicago that specialized in mythology and lore of all types.

The store was located on a seedy block between a pawnshop and a liquor store. The stench of day-old garbage wafted out of overflowing dumpsters in the alley. Ariana walked next to me, her eyes roaming the shabby buildings.

"I don't like this neighborhood," she whispered as we walked by a homeless man crouched down in front of a laundromat.

"Spare some change," the man said, his grubby glove-covered hand held out toward us.

I dug in my pocket and gave him a dollar, then put my hand on Ariana's back and hurried her forward into the bookstore.

A blast of heat assaulted us as we entered. With it came the musty smell of old books. The store was long and narrow with shelves lining the walls from floor to ceiling. Metal bookcases packed the available space in the middle, and fluorescent lights hummed above us. Ariana picked up a small tan book, read the cover, and set it back down.

A man with thick gray hair and bifocals sat behind the counter. He looked up from the newspaper he was reading. "May I help you?"

"Yeah," I replied. "We were hoping to find a couple of books on symbolism."

The man stood and stepped from behind the counter. His nametag read *Ted, Owner*. "What type of symbols are you looking for?"

I pulled the piece of paper I'd drawn on out of my back pocket and handed it to him.

He studied it a moment. His bushy eyebrows pulled together to look like one long, hairy caterpillar.

"This one..." Ted pointed to the arrow with a line through it. "Is the zodiac sign for Sagittarius."

Ariana and I already knew that one—it was one of the symbols that formed a circle around the star—but since it was a common symbol, we decided to include it anyway. We also knew it was often used to symbolize war. Seeing as the people who had loved us had died violent deaths, we were pretty sure it had less to do with horoscopes and more to do with destruction.

"This one is Celtic, I believe." He pointed to one Ariana had found on the Internet. "I've never seen the other ones, though."

He walked over to one of the bookcases in the middle of the store. We followed.

"Here." He handed me back the sheet of paper and began pulling books off the shelves. "These symbols aren't from one belief or system. What are you studying?"

"It's for extra credit," Ariana said, taking a thin black book from him. "For art."

He glanced down at her, quizzically. "They have you finding the meaning of random symbols for art?"

"It's for artistic inspiration," she replied without missing a beat. I was impressed at how quickly she improvised. She went on in a tone that emanated intrigue. "It's interesting, really. There were a few symbols grouped together. A star with, like, ten symbols around it. I haven't found the significance in that yet."

"That sounds like a sigil—a magical symbol, if you will. People use them much like talismans." Ted checked the bindings of a few books, then handed one to me. "This one should explain them."

Ariana and I held five books between us when Ted was done with his search.

"Take a look at those and see if they help." Ted led us to a cluttered table in the back of the store. "You can look through them here. Leave them when you're done. I'll put 'em away."

He went back to his stool behind the counter at the front of the store.

Ariana and I took a few minutes to flip through our choices. Each of the books had its benefits. We would need time to actually read them to know which would be the most helpful.

I checked how much cash I had on me. "What do you have?"

Ariana handed me a five and a single. I added it to the pile. Together, we had enough money to purchase three of the books. I grabbed the entire pile.

"Come on," I said and led the way to the front of the store.

Ted looked surprised when I set the books on the counter. "You want all of these?"

I nodded.

"But you can copy down the meaning of the symbols without spending a dime."

The guy was a nice old man, and I respected the fact he was trying to save us money even if it meant he lost the sale. But we needed to know more than a brief description, and there were other symbols, ones I hadn't drawn on the paper, that we also needed to find. Ariana and I exchanged glances.

"My sister finds the whole subject of symbolism interesting and wanted to read up on it." She smiled as if to confirm what I said was true. "A friend of mine mentioned you had a sale going on," I added. Ted looked up at me. "Buy three, get two free."

I felt a little bad about using my powers on him. His mouth formed a thin line as my suggestion took hold of his thoughts. He nodded. "Right. Good time to buy, really. We don't run many sales."

"These would be free," Ariana added, picking up the books we couldn't afford.

He slid the two books she handed him into a bag and rang the others up.

****

Back at home, Ariana lounged on an overstuffed chair in our family room, her legs dangling over one of the arms. She checked her wrist every now and then, comparing a picture in one of the books to her birthmark.

"Nothing else matches," she complained after a couple of hours searching. "There's always an extra line or a missing curve or something."

We'd been excited to find the markings within the star in a contemporary copy of the *Lesser Key of Solomon.* The symbols represented two very different classes of angels: the ones in Grace and the Fallen. In plain English, you had your angels (in Grace) and your demons (the Fallen). There were five supreme beings represented in our birthmarks.

The websites we'd found the other day had said sigils were often used in ceremonial magic to ward off or summon higher powers, and I wondered which ours did. Having a hotline to an angel would be sort of cool. Not so much if it did the same for a demon. Not to mention, I wanted to stick with my belief that demons didn't exist and that Lucifer was as made-up as the Tooth Fairy and Santa Claus.

I set the book I'd been reading on the couch next to me and pinched the bridge of my nose, trying to fight off the headache that edged closer and closer to the back of my eyes. "The symbols around the star form a circle. That has to be important."

"Or whoever branded us thought the circle helped to organize them. There doesn't have to be a meaning."

I sighed, preferring to think everything had a purpose. "Let's just say—for argument's sake—that it means unity. That the symbols are meant to work together."

"Okay." She turned the page in the book she was reading and replied without looking at me. "I'm not so sure that's a comforting thought."

"Why not?"

"Well…" She let the word drag on a moment. "We know what three of the symbols that form the circle mean. The cross thingy with a loop at the top symbolizes eternal life, and the squiggly line with a dot symbolizes a passage, but the arrow means war. Add the symbols in the star—"

"The angels, both in Grace and Fallen," I said, trying to follow her train of thought.

"Yeah. Those." She looked at me as if it were obvious. I stared back at her with an expression that I'd probably give an alien if I ever met one. She sighed and added, "So if our birthmark is a sigil binding the different images together, then it might very well mean that you and I are destined to find ourselves in the middle of a war between Heaven and Hell for eternity."

"That's crazy." I cringed at her interpretation of the information we'd found and was secretly amazed at how her mind worked.

"Trust me, I'm trying to come up with another theory." She hugged the book in her hands. "Like maybe we've been tasked with a journey. You know, a large manila envelope—or maybe it will be a small plain white one—is going to arrive in our mail slot, and it will provide instructions on a voyage we're to embark on. Which direction we take—passage, get it?—will depend on if our souls go to Heaven or Hell on Judgment Day."

I barely followed that one. Several more minutes passed in silence as we read.

I wished we knew someone we trusted enough to show them our wrists, someone who might know scripture or who had studied symbolism. I couldn't help believing our parents would have been able to shed some light on the subject or at least have known to whom to turn for help. I cradled my head in my hands. With everything that had happened recently I felt our time was short; like it or not, we would be forced to face our future unprepared.

"Logan, I'm scared that what's coming is going to be worse than anything we've ever seen. I mean, a couple months ago I wasn't having nightmares about you being burned alive, and you weren't hearing a voice telling you to watch your back or whatever it's trying to say. And now there are people close to us whose minds we can't control. What the heck does it all mean?" Her voice was a little higher, annoyed and frantic at the same time.

Those were questions that had plagued my mind for a few weeks now, ever since Ariana had had that first nightmare. I wondered if it was because we were dating people. Well, Ariana was. My relationship with Kira had been short-lived. But Ariana's dreams weren't about Ben. They were about me.

"We'll figure it out," I said, willing my voice to sound reassuring. "You've had dreams before, and I've always heard voices. Like you said before, we were bound to meet someone who wouldn't feel the pull of our words. We just didn't have to think about it until Ki—" I paused. Ariana had said there were *people* close to us, not *someone.* I looked at her questioningly. "Have you seen the guy from the coffee shop again?"

She twisted the book she held, tearing the binding. "No. Ben's immune, too."

My mouth went dry, and everything inside of me turned to ice. Kira was one thing, but Ben too? "Are you sure?" I asked, praying she was wrong.

She nodded. "Yeah. I suggested we ditch eighth period, and he wasn't having it. I even begged a little. He said he didn't want to be a bad influence on me and I should think about my attendance. Ha! Like you and I haven't been late enough times to ruin any chance of having good attendance."

"You shouldn't ditch," I replied robotically, like *that* was our biggest problem.

I rubbed my temple to ease the pressure threatening to burst through my skull. The feeling that something wasn't right—that life was off somehow—had started a couple weeks into the school year, around the time Kira and Ben had shown up.

"Why didn't you tell me sooner?" I asked.

She shrugged. "I was hoping it was a fluke. I've tested it enough now. It wasn't."

I sank back onto the couch. My hands folded into fists as I tried not to show the fear and panic coursing through me.

"It could be a coincidence," she mumbled, still bending the book as she spoke.

I took it from her before she tore it in two. "I don't believe in coincidences."

"I know. Me neither."

The voice I'd been hearing told me to protect someone—I believed that someone was Ariana—but how could I protect her from the unknown? Maybe I'd been wrong to think we could get involved with someone. Maybe the answer was to get away from Ben and Kira. If it had all started with hanging out with them, then maybe it would all stop if we didn't see them anymore.

"We'll get out of South Elgin. Move somewhere no one knows us," I said.

"*Can't run,*" the voice replied calmly. Its words were clear for the first time. "*They'll find you.*"

"Can't run." Ariana sobbed out the words. "They'll find us."

I stared at her openmouthed. "You heard it, too?"

Ariana brought her knees to her chest, hugging them as she trembled and nodded. There was only one other time we'd both heard the voice. We'd been exiting the grocery store, and it had practically screamed one word: "*Stop!*" Seconds later, an armored truck had slammed into our aunt and uncle, killing them.

"Who will find us?" I yelled to the air around us. "Damn you! If you want to help, then show yourself!"

There was no answer. There never was.

Chapter Sixteen

Ariana

Logan and I arrived at school with time to spare on Monday. We parked in one of the spaces closest to the student entrance.

"Don't let Ben see you're upset, okay?" He waited for my nod of agreement and then added, "We could be wrong. It's possible our gifts don't work on people we're dating."

"Puh-lease." I looked at him, eyes narrowed in disbelief. "You can't tell me you believe that."

I knew Logan too well. He'd say anything if he thought it spared me unnecessary stress and worry. It was nice, when I was ten.

We got out of the car. He adjusted his pace to match mine.

"Well, we've never liked someone until now," he said lamely. "Besides, there's no point in Ben finding out that we're different if he doesn't know anything."

I could work with the last bit. I slung my backpack over my shoulder, its weight reminding me that I needed to clean it out. "I won't say anything to Ben, but only because, under that I'm-not-afraid-of-anything exterior you've been strutting, I can tell you're just as freaked out as I am."

"Thank you."

"What are you going to do while I'm being all Susie-knows-nothing with Ben?"

"I don't know. I was thinking about asking Kira what she knows about us."

"Really? Just like that?" I stepped in front of him, making him stop walking. "Are you going to ask her why she doesn't do what you tell her to or ask her why you're hearing voices? Either way, she'll think you're mad. As in crazy."

"I have a hunch that she knows something." He walked around me. I had to jog to catch up.

"A hunch? Are you serious? Our lives are falling apart, and you're going to follow a *hunch*."

He held the door open. "Kira's been avoiding me ever since our last date, but, the thing is, we were having a good time. It doesn't make sense, unless she's hiding something."

He followed me inside.

I wasn't so sure I agreed with his reasoning. Kira could have been avoiding him because she was embarrassed about her behavior. Then again, Logan had said she would talk to him in class, so she couldn't be *that* abashed. Maybe she was afraid of being rejected again. But she had to know that wouldn't happen, not with him being so sweet to her. There was still a flaw in his plan, though.

"If she's avoiding you, how are you going to ask her?"

I could tell by his clenched jaw that he didn't know. The warning bell rang, giving him an excuse to leave without answering.

In art class, I should have won an award for my performance as Clueless Supporting Actress. I attempted to use my powers to get Ben to draw the delicate Carolina roses Mrs. Murphy had instructed us to draw. He mumbled something about roses and thorns and drew a bouquet of wild lilies instead. He otherwise didn't do anything unusual to let on that he knew what I'd tried to do.

Halfway through the morning, I sent Logan a text asking him how it was going.

Haven't seen her, was the reply I got.

I sent another text after lunch.

This time he sent, *Don't think she's here.*

Which I knew wasn't true because I had literally run into her on my way to fourth period. Now that I thought about it, she should have been on the other side of the school heading to her foods class. After seventh period, I saw her talking with a couple girls I recognized as Jessica Derting and Elaina Preble, both juniors. I decided to take matters into my own hands.

"Can we talk?" I said, interrupting their conversation.

Her friends exchanged looks. Kira adjusted her purse to be higher up on her shoulder.

"Um—" She glanced longingly down the hall as if trying to think of an excuse to say no.

"Please. Two minutes."

She sighed. To her friends, she said, "I'll catch up to you guys later."

"Sure," Elaina said. She and Jessica disappeared into the crowd of students making their way to eighth period.

"Did Logan put you up to this?" Kira asked with a look that would have wilted the leaves on the healthiest of plants.

"No. He doesn't know I'm here." I ushered her into the nearest bathroom, which to my mistake was the boys' bathroom. A freshman quickly zipped his pants and bolted out the door without washing his hands.

"Oh!" Kira covered her nose and went to leave. "Really? We can't just chat in the hall?"

I blocked her path. No way was I going to give Kira a chance to change her mind about talking to me.

"Two minutes," I reminded her. As I clicked the lock to keep others from entering—I really didn't want anyone else to find me in the boys' bathroom—I made a mental note to double-check the sign on the door next time I decided I needed a private place to chat. "I need to ask you something."

Her expression became guarded. "Look, your brother's really nice. I assume he told you, you know, that we were drinking and all. I may have had a little too much. Most guys would have taken advantage of a situation like that. He's special. Any girl would be lucky to date him."

Logan had told me that she'd come on to him. He'd admitted it was tempting to just let whatever was going to happen, happen. He'd also said that he just couldn't do it. It was the whole wanting-someone-to-like-us-for-ourselves moral we shared. Letting things go further with Kira when she was drunk wasn't too different from using mind control to tell a girl she wanted to go out with him. We didn't do things like that.

Kira bit her lower lip and fidgeted with the strap of her purse. I decided she'd meant what she'd said. She really did think Logan was special. If she hadn't crushed his spirits, I might have backed off. But Logan hadn't been quite the same since their date. In one afternoon, she'd managed to have him questioning his actions. Now was not the time for Logan to doubt himself. Not when there were unknown entities warning us that the bad times were about to start again. Between the two of us, Logan was always the strong one. He was the reason I had made it through the loss of our parents and the only reason I hadn't crawled inside myself after our aunt and uncle had died, too. I had to find out what was up with her, for Logan's sake.

"Any girl, but not you?" I asked, hoping she'd say something that would help me tell if she knew she was different from other people.

Someone banged on the door from the outside.

"It's out of order," I yelled loudly enough to be heard in the hallway.

The guy cursed and moved on.

Kira shifted her weight from one foot to the other nervously under my unrelenting stare. "He's a really nice guy." She let out a shaky laugh. "God knows I'm not used to that. It's just, well, he's not my type."

"What type of guys are you used to?" Maybe that was her secret. Maybe she'd gone out with some real losers and didn't know how to behave around someone who showed her the respect she deserved.

Her gaze turned steely. "Trust me. You don't want to meet them." She paced away from me. "It's better that Logan and I aren't a couple. No one can blame me if he realized he doesn't want to hang out with me, which is what I'm going to say when asked."

"Who's going to ask you why you and Logan aren't going out?"

"Logan and I can be civil," she went on, ignoring my question. "Talk in class. No harm in that. Right?"

She stopped next to me.

"I guess." I really had no idea what she was talking about. I already knew she was the one avoiding Logan, so why make a big deal over who didn't want to date whom. And why would anyone care if she and Logan were friends?

"Tell Logan we really are okay." She reached for the lock.

"You're the one who's been avoiding him."

"No." She shook her head, her voice trembling. "It was his idea."

She was adamant about it. Like her life depended on it. Like Logan's life depended on it. A chill traveled swiftly through me.

"Kira, what's going on?"

"Nothing." She grabbed the door handle.

I put my hand flat against its cold surface, holding it shut. "I want to know what you're hiding."

She tugged. I didn't move, though, and the door didn't open.

"Please," she whispered. Her eyes brimmed with tears. "Just let me go."

"*Don't*," a voice warned. I jumped, and my back slammed against the door. I looked around. It was still Kira, me, and a bunch of urinals. How the heck had Logan stood hearing voices for so long? I'd have gone insane. Thank God, Kira thought I'd moved to make sure she couldn't escape my interrogation. "*Push her for the truth*."

"Cut the crap," I demanded, forcing myself to look at her and not for the owner of the disembodied voice. "It's not a coincidence that you're here, is it?"

"Please, Ariana. Tell Logan to forget he ever met

me." She blinked, causing tears to spill down her cheeks. "I can't do this anymore. I just can't."

I got the feeling she wasn't talking about her and Logan. She was petrified of something. So scared she was afraid to be seen alone with him. It was all the proof I needed that she knew she was different. Just how that affected us, however, I didn't know. I reached next to me, waving my hand over the sensor on the paper towel dispenser. It churned out a brown sheet, which I tore off and handed to her. She wiped the tears from her cheeks.

"It's not a coincidence that Ben's here either, is it?" I managed to ask, not wanting to hear the answer but needing to. Kira didn't reply, but I knew it was true.

I felt betrayed. I had trusted Ben. Let myself like him. Really like him. I had told him things about me and Logan and my friends that I hadn't told anyone else. I should have known he was too good to be true.

Kira pressed her lips together and studied the floor next to us. Someone else tried to get in the bathroom, and I told him to go away.

"Kira, please tell me what's going on," I begged.

"I can't." She grabbed the handle with both hands. "Move."

I backed up enough to let her open the door.

"I'm sorry. I wouldn't wish this on my worst enemy," she whispered just before dashing into the hall.

"*Wait!*" the disembodied voice screamed in my head when I went to follow.

My hand—still gripping the handle—trembled. Why wait? Was I in danger? Was this warning similar to the one I'd heard moments before my aunt and uncle had been killed?

"Logan." His name barely escaped my lips. He had to be okay. I burst out of the bathroom and glanced to my left and then my right. The hum of the fluorescent lights seemed deafening in the quiet hall. A tall man with golden blond hair rounded the far corner. Not wanting to run into any teachers, I quickly went the other way, rummaging in my purse for my phone. My fingers flew over the keypad.

You okay? I texted, then hit send and prayed I would get a reply.

Chapter Seventeen

Logan

The worst part of living in an apartment and working on cars to earn cash is no garage. It meant I worked in the back corner of a parking lot.

That afternoon turned out to be chilly. Gray storm clouds blanketed the sky. It was a race against Mother Nature: me trying to get Jim Baker's brakes changed while it was still dry out and Mother Nature adding even more gray clouds to the already dark sky, preparing to drown me. To add to the excitement, Ariana was outside doing her version of helping me, which included a lot of talking and the occasional handing me a tool or part.

"But Kira's reaction wasn't the worst part," she said from her seat on the tire I had removed. "I heard the voice." She told me its vague warnings.

I slid a new rotor onto the front driver's side of the Pontiac Grand Prix. "Is that why you sent the text?"

"Yeah. I checked on Becca, too."

Why the voice had wanted Ariana to wait only added one more question to our ever growing list. I pointed to the brake-pad box next to her feet. She handed it to me.

When Ariana had first told me she'd talked to Kira, I wasn't happy. I wanted to be the one to confront her. I wanted to see the look in her eyes when I told her I knew something was up. But mostly, I wanted to know if I had imagined her feelings for me. As soon as Ariana had told me that Kira had been fighting back tears, I was actually glad Ariana had gotten to her first. I hated to see a girl cry, and it was always worse when I knew I was the reason.

I checked that the rotor and pad were secure. "I'll need your seat."

Ariana got up, and I rolled the tire over to the car and lifted it in place. She handed me the lug nuts. Thunder rumbled in the distance.

"Logan, what are we going to do?"

I had no idea what we were supposed to do. It wasn't like our powers had come with an instruction manual or our birthmarks had arrived with a card telling us their meaning. But there was one thing that had always seemed to work for us.

I spun the cross wrench, hand-tightening the lug nuts one at a time. "We give it a week," I said. "If we don't find anything, we'll move."

"I like it here," Ariana protested as she tossed my tools into my metal toolbox. "My best friend is here."

"I know." I picked up the old rotors and put them in a box to be brought back to the auto-part store. "But not staying in one place for too long worked to keep people safe before."

"The voice said we *can't* run." Ariana leaned against my car, arms folded over her chest.

"Screw the voice."

She scowled, jaw clenched and eyes glassy like she was fighting back tears. I seemed to have that effect on girls lately.

"That's only if we don't figure something else out," I said, backpedaling. I put the box of parts in the Grand Prix and my tools in my trunk. "Okay?"

"So we'll stay?"

"We'll try." I slammed my trunk shut. Large drops of rain fell, pelting the ground and the cars. Ariana and I made a break for the doors to the apartment.

The next day, we ran late for school again. Between my sister's inability to be ready on time and the new storm clouds pushing in from the north, I was in a foul mood.

"I swear, Ariana." I floored the accelerator and blew through a yellow light. "I'm going to start laying out your clothes at night like Mom used to do if you don't figure out a way to get organized."

"Mom used to lay out my clothes?"

I took a right into the school parking lot and parked in Purgatory. "Yes. And you were never late. Seriously, how many times do you think we can sign in after the bell without the school doing something about it?"

"You're eighteen, and I'm in your care. What can they do?"

As we sprinted to the doors, a shiver went through me, and my birthmark warmed. Not a searing pain like the time Ariana had gone through the truck. This was subtle, like the brush of a hand on my arm. My first instinct was to grab Ariana and run back to the car, but Ariana didn't slow her pace. That told me I was the only one who felt it.

I glanced around. A black Eclipse with limo-tinted windows idled about a hundred yards from the doors. I can't explain how, but I had a good idea who would be driving. Ariana didn't notice the car. After we signed in—ignoring the disapproving looks from the lady in the attendance office—Ariana went to her first-period class, and I walked back outside. The car had moved closer to the doors.

The passenger window lowered. I bent down. "Ditching?" I asked, not at all surprised to see Kira.

"Get in," she replied, her tone businesslike.

I grabbed the handle but didn't open the door. What if this was the trap I'd been warned about? "I thought you didn't want anything to do with me," I asked, stalling. "What changed your mind?"

She glanced around us, then said, "I did a lot of thinking last night, and I realized things would have been different for me if I had known the truth. My life might have gone in a totally different direction, and you might just be my only chance to set things right. Come on, get in."

I ran a hand through my hair and hoped I was doing the right thing as I got in.

Kira had her red hair gathered in a low ponytail. A few loose curls framed her face, and her sweet-smelling perfume hung heavy in the confines of the car, making my head swim.

"The first thing you need to know is that you shouldn't trust me," she said. "You shouldn't trust anyone."

"I don't," I replied, watching her for a reaction, but she remained as still as a statue. "But I'm running out of options, and I need answers."

She nodded as if my response was the right one. There was a calm resolve in her expression as we drove off, and she promised to answer my questions once we were away from school.

We ended up back at the forest preserve.

"You really like this place." I leaned against the elder tree in the grove.

"It's private." She picked a small purple wildflower from the ground and twirled it between her fingers. "We can talk freely here, but we should hurry. I don't want to be gone too long."

I took that to mean *I don't want to be alone with you longer than I have to be.*

I didn't know what to make of Kira's cloak-and-dagger routine. She must have been involved in some pretty messed up stuff to be that worried about talking to me. Then again, my birthmark was pretty messed up in itself. I adjusted my bracelet nervously and swallowed the lump in my throat as I reminded myself I had promised Ariana we'd stay in South Elgin. That meant we had to know what we were up against. There was a part of me—maybe my inner snot-nosed nine-year-old who wished he could remain naive forever—that didn't want to know.

Kira went on. "I can't tell you everything. There's not enough time, and there are things I'm bound not to say."

"Bound how?" I asked. "Like you swore an oath or something?"

Her head titled to the side. "Something like that. I think a good place to start would be your birthmark. How much do you know about it?"

"What do you know about it?" I was sure she'd never seen it, and I had to consciously keep myself from grabbing my wrist.

Kira continued. "I know you wear the bracelet to cover it. That's not a bad idea, but it won't hide you from your destiny. You had to have guessed as much or you wouldn't be here. What you don't know is it's the mark of the Chosen. I'd tell you that's a good thing, but it's not."

"Chosen for what?"

"A war that has been brewing for more than two millennia. You've been given a starring role, actually." Kira almost looked sorry to be the one to tell me this.

"Whose war?" I looked over my shoulder, half expecting to see an army waiting with a spare uniform. The trees that surrounded us seemed to be closing in, but we were still alone. "And why us?"

"You need to know what I am before I can answer your first question. As far as why, you and your sister match the children in a prophecy that's almost as old as man. It speaks of a brother and sister who are born on November first exactly two years apart. Only Fate herself can make that happen, and she doesn't do it often."

I grabbed fistfuls of hair at the back of my head. I knew our birthmarks had to be bad. I'd seen too much death to think otherwise. But I hadn't imagined someone would one day tell me that Ariana and I had been chosen for a war, and I still didn't know whose war we were talking about. To be honest, I didn't care.

"Ariana and I are not going to be a part of it."

"Yeah, I hope that goes better for you than it did for me." She rested a hand on my arm. "Logan, you're dealing with forces that have waited for you and Ariana not only to be born, but to become old enough to choose to do your part."

"That's easy. Ariana and I are not getting in the middle of a war that has nothing to do with us." We'd drop off the grid if we had to. Ditch our cell phones. Start over. Given our options, I knew Ariana would be packing as fast as I was.

"My boss isn't going to take no for an answer, and it doesn't matter where you go, he'll find you." Kira indicated with a nod toward my wrist. "Your birthmark is better than any tracking device."

"Someone could be trailing me right now?" And then an even scarier thought occurred to me. "They could be following Ariana? Is Ben in on this?" I spun around, ready to race back to the car. "Kira, so help me, if getting me out here was a diversion—"

Kira caught my arm. "It's not! I swear! Ben and I don't talk, so he has no idea we're here."

"But he knows about all this? He knows Ariana and I are Chosen?"

"Yes."

"Jesus Christ, Kira!" I had to warn Ariana. I pulled my phone from my pocket, quickly sent a text to my sister, and then asked Kira, "Who do you work for?"

"A—" Kira coughed. "The—" The next words out of her mouth were spoken as if she were gargling. "Ugh! I'm forbidden to tell you his name in answer to a direct question."

"Forbidden, as in mind control? Like you have to do what he says?"

"Yes."

If Kira's boss had the same power of suggestion I did, and if he used that ability to force people to do bad things, we were all screwed. I paced in a circle. What if he brainwashed my parents into letting him into our house so that he could brand me and then two years later came back for Ariana? What if he was strong enough to brainwash *us*? "How many people are under his control?"

"A lot, but I'm the only one he's sent here. So far, anyway."

"And you're scared of him?"

"I'd be crazy not to be."

I agreed with her there. I had the feeling she needed help. That maybe it wasn't my sister who was in danger after all. Maybe Kira was the one the disembodied voice wanted me to protect. I put my hands on her shoulders and looked into her eyes. "Kira, if we trust each other, we can help each other. We'll find a way out of this. You. Me. Ariana."

She studied me a moment. "You mean that, don't you?"

"Yes." She seemed to need me as much as I needed her.

She put her hands on my waist and rose to her tiptoes. "It's a sweet thought," she said, her breath warm on my lips. "But my fate has already been sealed."

Her perfume seemed to wrap around me, filling me with the urge to pull her closer even though my brain screamed for me to step back. I wondered if this was how the people I made suggestions to felt—compelled to please me—because right then I wanted to sweep Kira up in my arms and kiss her. Although something inside of me clung to the thought that I needed to stay focused on why I was there, every other fiber of my being coaxed me to just let down my guard and enjoy being in a secluded place with a pretty girl.

Kira brushed her lips against mine.

"I'm not what I seem," she said in a husky whisper.

She kissed me before I could reply. Her lips were too hot against mine. My mind exploded with images of burning rivers and pillars made of bone. Lifeless trees reached out of the ground like the hands of the dead. Fire and brimstone rained down on the living. I could hear the screams of people I couldn't see and smelled decaying flesh. Nausea overcame me, breaking the spell I was under. I shoved Kira away, doubled over at the waist, and threw up.

"Like I said, *don't* trust me," she warned.

Chapter Eighteen

Ariana

It wasn't until the end of second period that I realized Logan wasn't at school. Mr. Omigod-we're-late-again had some explaining to do. I figured if he could ditch, then so could I. And what fun would it have been if I didn't convince my best friend that she wanted to enjoy the beautiful fall day, too? Becca and I sat on the hood of her car, our backs against the windshield, eating chocolate gems in her driveway.

"Are you going to tell me what's up with you and Ben?" she asked me as she waved to her next-door neighbor.

I didn't know what was up yet; that was part of the problem. I flipped my cell phone open and reread Logan's text: *With Kira. It's bad. Stay away from Ben.* That's all he'd said. No explanation why. No hint that Ben was dangerous. No inkling that he had an ulterior motive. Nothing.

Ben had been next to me when I got the message. He couldn't see my phone, but I'm pretty sure he could tell that whatever it said had upset me, because I suddenly had to go. Logan didn't spook easily, so I took his warning seriously. My plan was to avoid Ben until Logan and I talked.

"Nothing's up," I replied to Becca.

"Ariana, this is me you're talking to. You've gone from Ben-this and Ben-that to Ben-who."

"We're fine," I insisted.

She glared at me, eyes narrowed disbelievingly.

"Honest." I held a hand up as if swearing I was telling the truth, the whole truth, and nothing but the truth.

She grabbed a few pieces of candy and tossed the brown ones into the grass. "That's why you pretended not to hear him call your name when we were leaving school?"

I scrunched up my nose. "Was it that obvious?"

"You have better hearing than I do." She held the bag of candy out to me.

I reached in and took a few pieces. How could I explain to Kira that I knew Ben was different without telling her my secret? "There's something odd about him," I finally said with a shrug.

"You know what your problem is?" She took off her sweatshirt, balling it up to use as a pillow.

I looked at my friend and frowned. "What?"

"You think too much."

I belted out a laugh.

"Well, you do." Chocolate crunched between her teeth. "He's cute, smart, and he's totally into you. What's so odd about that?"

I watched a large puffy cloud drift lazily across the sky as I spoke. "That's just it. *Why* is he totally into me? And how is it he always seems to know exactly where to find me or that I prefer the hot chocolate at the deli to the hot chocolate at the coffee house?"

"Everyone knows the hot chocolate at the deli is better. And maybe he's paid attention to your schedule, so that's how he knows where to find you. *And* he asked you out because you're the prettiest and nicest person in school." She chucked a few more brown pieces of candy into the grass.

"You're only saying that because we're friends."

"Best friends," she corrected me. "And I'm saying it because I believe it's true."

I nudged her shoulder with mine. "You know I love ya."

"I love ya too."

We broke into a fit of giggles. I hadn't completely given up on dating Ben. Logan could be overreacting; I'd find out when I saw him.

"Are you still seeing Mystery Waiter Guy?" I took the bag of candy from her.

At the mention of Justin, Becca checked her phone. She rested it on her stomach as she let out a sigh and replied, "You know, I think I could spend an entire day kissing him."

I nodded. A few days ago, I would have said the same thing about Ben.

She continued, "He bought me flowers the other day. Did I tell you? A mixed bouquet."

"Cool." I was really happy for her, but my mind drifted back to Ben. Whatever Logan had found out couldn't be *that* bad. Ben had been nothing but nice to me—sweet and caring, easy to talk to, a perfect gentleman. Not exactly your typical creep. Kira had probably told Logan that her and Ben's parents knew each other. Maybe they were part of a cult or some other group that taught their members how to protect themselves from people like Logan and me who had the ability to get into their heads. That had to be it.

"Justin wants to meet you."

Hearing this pulled me out of my own thoughts and back to our conversation. "Me? Why?"

"Probably because I'm always talking about you." She sat up and looked at me. "I know! We should double-date."

"If we don't break up." I was only seventy-five percent sure whatever it was Logan would tell me wouldn't be that bad. There was still the other twenty-five percent that kept reminding me that Logan doesn't scare easily.

"Ariana, you always do this." Becca pointed her phone at me as she described my dating habits in less than twenty-five words. "You start hanging out with a guy, things get a little serious, and you come up with some excuse to break it off."

I hadn't realized I was so transparent, but I had no intention of actually admitting she was right.

I hit her leg with the back of my hand. "I don't do that!"

"Yes, you do." Her expression softened. "You and Ben make a cute couple. Don't push him away before you really get to know him."

Maybe Becca was right, maybe I did push guys away, but I had a very good reason. People who got too close to Logan and me tended to die. And Ben had a secret; I just knew he did. What I didn't know was if it was a totally awesome, I'm-going-to-be-thrilled secret or an I-never-want-to-speak-to-you-again secret.

"We'll see," I replied, which she clearly took for a yes because she squealed, "Yay! Our double-date will be epic!"

I shook my head, not bothering to stress that my

answer was a very *iffy* maybe. She lay back against the windshield. The puffy cloud was gone, leaving a pale blue void in its wake.

She tossed another piece of candy into the grass.

From behind us we heard, "Have something against the brown ones?"

Startled, we sat up. For a moment, I thought it was Becca's dad. But instead, Ben stood off to my left with his hands stuffed in his pockets.

"They're boring," Becca replied. "I only eat the bright colors."

"How'd you know where we were?" I asked, surprised to see him.

He studied the blacktop instead of answering.

"Did you follow us?" I demanded, thinking this was one more time he'd known exactly where to find me. Seeing him shifted my warning meter from 75/25 to 25/75 in favor of the nagging little voice.

His gaze met mine. "Don't be mad. I..." He kicked a pebble into the street. "I-I wanted to know if I'd done something to upset you."

The words *You have a sixth sense when it comes to my whereabouts* stopped at the tip of my tongue. I would wait until I talked to Logan before questioning Ben. I shook my head. "No."

"Ariana," Becca whispered. "Give him a break." When I didn't say anything, she looked at Ben and said, "I was just going to drive her home. Unless you wouldn't mind doing it. That would totally save me from having to race there and back before my mom gets home." She faked a cough. "I'll have to play sick, you know."

I gave her a piercing look. "We still have—"

She elbowed me and looked expectantly at Ben.

"If she'll let me," he said and held out a hand.

"You're such a traitor," I hissed at Becca under my breath. Maybe I should have showed her Logan's text. Maybe then she wouldn't have pushed me off on Ben. Maybe she'd have been protective of me and told Ben to take a hike. Only problem with that was she'd have wanted to know why Logan was texting me cryptic warnings about the guy I was seeing.

Whatever Logan had to say couldn't be that bad, I reminded myself.

Becca hopped off the hood, ignoring me. "Thanks, Ben! You're a lifesaver."

Ben and I walked side by side to his car, which was parked in front of her house. He watched me but didn't try to take my hand like he normally would.

"Please tell me what I did," Ben asked once we were on our way to my apartment.

"You didn't do anything." I played with the radio to keep my hands busy.

"Then what is it?" He waited a few seconds, his finger tapping the steering wheel. "Yesterday you were excited to see me. Today you can barely look at me."

I left the radio on 101.9 and sat back. He was right. I couldn't look at him. I was too afraid that, if I did, I'd forget he wasn't just another teenager trying to make it through high school and that he was somehow connected to all the weirdness in my life. Not knowing what that connection was drove me nuts.

"Ariana, something happened or you would have kissed me hello."

He was right. Before I could stop myself, I blurted out, "Why me?"

His brow furrowed. "I don't understand."

"Why did you ask me out? You had girls practically throwing their number at you." Becca being one of them. "Yet you tracked mine down and called me. Why?"

"Because I wanted to get to know you." He gave me a sidelong glance, like that was obvious.

"Where do you live?"

"Off Dunham."

"And you just happened to move here at the same time as Kira?"

"I guess." He stopped at a red light and looked at me, his eyes narrowed. "Is it really that big a deal?"

I crossed my arms over my chest. It wouldn't have been if either Kira or Ben could be manipulated with mind control.

"Our parents were close once. Mine might have told hers how great the area was. I can ask them if it would make you feel better."

That made sense. Ben did tell me their parents used to hang out together. I rolled my eyes, feeling a little silly for snapping at him about a choice his father and mother would have made. "That's not necessary," I relented.

The light changed. A couple minutes later, we were parked in front of my apartment complex. He got out and walked around the car to open my door. I stood without taking the hand he extended.

"Ariana." His fingers trailed down my arm. "I think you're special. That's why I asked you out and not someone else. You're smart and funny and sensitive all wrapped up in a person who cares about the people around her. I keep asking you out because I like hanging out with you."

I so wanted to believe that he was telling the truth. That he was standing in front of me right this minute because he wanted to be with me. But my conversation with Kira had pretty much confirmed that his being here wasn't a coincidence. Where he lived might have been his parents' choice, but there was more to the story than he had told me. A small piece of me broke when I'd found that out. Like a hairline fracture in my heart. I couldn't let myself have feelings for him without knowing the truth. Could I?

Chapter Nineteen

Logan

I spit the last of the puke from my mouth and walked unsteadily away from Kira, not keeping my back to her for long. I stopped in the middle of the grass. My lips burned from our kiss. The horrible screams still echoed in my ears.

I raked my hands through my hair, grabbed the back of my head, and closed my eyes, letting out a bewildered, "What the hell?"

Instead of seeing darkness, I saw flesh and bone twisted and melded together to form a throne as if closing my eyes had restarted the sick images I'd seen when Kira had kissed me. The stench of sulfur and burning flesh stung my nostrils, and I dropped to my knees and threw up again. I didn't know what was happening to me.

Kira took a seat several feet away, sitting cross-legged. She pulled a bottle of vodka from her purse and held it out. "It'll soften the shock of finding out the truth."

I looked up at her. My head felt heavy like a bowling ball. "Alcohol? Are you serious?"

"Trust me, you'll want some." She took a swig from the bottle and scooted closer to me.

"You told me not to trust you." My throat felt raw.

My stomach tightened and heaved, but I had nothing left to throw up. Kira placed a hand on my shoulder. I swatted it away; I didn't have enough strength to do much more. Her kiss seemed to have been laced with poison.

"I can make it stop—the visions, the hurling, the loss of strength—if you'd let me." She raised her hand. "Don't move."

I wanted to move. More than anything. But my stomach cramped, making even flinching impossible.

Kira combed her fingers through my hair, brushing it away from my face. With her touch came a soothing calm that settled my stomach and ceased the screams in my head. It did nothing for the fear clawing through me, though.

"Sorry, I'm new at this, but I still should have anticipated your reaction to that type of mind manipulation." Kira wrapped her arms around my back. "Let me help you up."

"I don't need your help." I jerked my shoulder and crawled away from her. She followed, taking a seat on the ground a couple of feet from where I had collapsed in the grass. Every muscle in my body ached. "Who are you?" Given what I'd just seen, I added, "*What* are you?"

"The second guess is more accurate, but I'm not allowed to answer that question." This time when she held the bottle out to me, I sat up and snatched it from her. "But if you were to guess, there's nothing keeping me from telling you if you're right or wrong. Why don't we play a game? Twenty Questions?"

"Great, guess what type of freak your girlfriend is." I took a long pull from the bottle, ignoring the burn of the vodka hitting the back of my throat.

Kira frowned. "Under the circumstances, I won't take that personally." She nudged me with her foot. "You can do this. I'll even give you a hint. Your birthmark is made up of several smaller markings. Do you know the meaning of the symbols inside the star?"

I looked at her. The elder tree was several feet behind her; its branches reached out like the talons of a hawk ready to grab its prey. "First, tell me how you know so much about it."

She pulled the sleeve of her sweater up to the crook of her elbow, revealing a birthmark similar to mine on the inside of her left wrist. Above it, raised red skin formed a circle pierced by an arrow. "I was born on All Saints Day also. I was once Chosen, like you are now. But things didn't go as...my boss had planned. I'm something else now." Her gaze fell to my wrist. "Now you answer my question."

I set the bottle on the grass between us. "They represent angels." I paused, eyes narrowed. "You aren't going to tell me you're an angel, are you?" I was pretty sure angels didn't carry vodka in their purses or skip school.

Her lips quirked upward into an amused smirk. "No, I'm not an angel."

"Then what are you?"

"I thought we established that I can't come right out and tell you that. Here's another clue; if I were an angel, I'd live in Heaven, right?"

"Yeah, I guess. You tell me."

"What if my home was in a place that is the opposite of paradise?" she asked.

I shook my head, trying to understand her vague

hints. "Tucson can't be that bad."

"Come on, Logan." She bounced her knuckles against her forehead. "I'm not talking about the continental United States. I showed you pictures of my home when I kissed you. Think. The opposite of Heaven would be—"

"Hell," I replied automatically. "You think you're the Devil?"

"No, but you're getting closer. Keep guessing."

"Fine. If you're from Hell and you're not the Devil, then you're a demon." I couldn't keep the sarcasm out of my voice.

"Yes!" Kira screamed, startling me and causing me to knock over the bottle of vodka. I quickly set it upright on the grass. "I'm a demon." She giggled with malevolent glee. "Look, now that you know, I can say it. Demon. Ha! Won't Hell be pissed off when they find out I found a way around their gag order?"

"You're pulling my leg, right?"

"You were willing to believe in angels just a minute ago."

"Well, yeah, angels are good."

She leaned forward. "If you're so sure I'm not a demon, kiss me." Her words brushed my lips. Warm. Daring.

"That's okay." I wasn't certain what she was, but I did know I didn't want to see body parts or smell the awful odors again. Mind games, I reminded myself. Kira's "boss" must have told her she was the spawn of the Devil; I had to remember that she believed it was true. "Why are you helping me? That is what you're doing, right?"

"Yeah." Kira smiled a sad little smile as she ran her

hand over the grass absentmindedly. The blades turned brown under her touch.

My blood froze at the sight of the dying grass. *She's human*, I repeated in my head, then ticked off all my proof: beautiful, whimsical laugh, soft skin, amazing lips. Even if demons existed, they wouldn't look like gorgeous sixteen-year-old girls. They'd be big and red and have horns and a spiked tail, maybe even hoofed feet.

I racked my brain for a logical explanation of how she could turn grass brown with one touch or how she'd managed to make me see the things I had when we'd kissed. Some sort of drug could have made me hallucinate. Maybe something in her lip gloss? But then again, Kira was always biting her bottom lip. The drug would affect her, too. Magic? More like a trick of the eye.

"Maybe you were right, and we can help each other." A tear slid down her cheek. "You know, I was human once."

I believed she was still human, and this boss she'd mentioned had done one heck of a number on her: suggesting she's a demon, not allowing her to talk about him, continuing to control her mind. It was cruel. He had to be strong, too, or my powers would work. I'd be able to tell Kira that everything was fine and she'd believe me. If I could get her to talk about him, maybe I could find a way to get through to her, help her realize how absurd her claim actually was.

"What happened?" I asked, determined to fix her.

"I made a deal with a demon to save my brother and lost my soul in the process."

"Where's your brother now?"

"I lost him the moment we sealed the deal." Her expression turned steely. "Ironic, isn't it?"

"Kira, you didn't lose your soul, and I'm sure you didn't lose your brother either. Don't you see your boss has messed with your head? He's controlling your mind."

She huffed out a shaky, "Ha!"

"Seriously, Kira, who did this to you?" And was this what Ariana and I had to look forward to? I cupped her chin in my hands and looked into her eyes. "I can't help you if I don't know who you're so scared of. Tell me, Kira. Who did this to you?"

She shook her head. "I can't. He'll punish me."

"Was it Ben?" Maybe he wasn't as wonderful as he led everyone to believe.

She shook her head again.

With all my energy focused on my ability to control minds, I said, "Kira, tell me his name."

She placed her hands on mine. "Mind control won't work on me, Logan. I'm immune, and so is he."

That didn't surprise me, but I had to try.

"Then tell me because you trust me," I said before she could pull away.

She worried her bottom lip between her teeth a moment and nodding. "As—" she choked on the word. "I can't. I'm sorry."

Because she's forbidden, I scoffed to myself. But I'd be damned if I would let this person brainwash Ariana or me. I brushed Kira's hair away from her eyes. "We'll just call him your boss for now. How about our birthmarks? Can you tell me what they mean? Why did he mark us?"

"This is where he really screwed up, because he

145

didn't forbid me to tell you why you and Ariana are so important to him." She sat a little straighter. "It's an ancient prophecy—demon bible school, if you will. God gets angry at a group of angels so He has them cast out of heaven one by one. But the condemned get wind of what's happening, and one soon-to-be-vanquished angel gets smart. He does a spell that creates a gateway to Earth, one that can be opened at a later date when he can free all of his brothers and sisters. The key to the door was to be a special child, born on All Saints Day, but the angels stepped in before the spell was completed and added a caveat."

"Siblings."

"Not just any siblings, a brother and sister born exactly two years apart. One who will have the fires of Hell running through their veins and the other to have the light of Heaven." She twisted the strap of her purse around her fingers as she spoke. "Logan, those in Hell want revenge."

"You mean a war between Heaven and Hell? Like angels versus demons?"

"Exactly."

"No way." I stood, rubbed the back of my neck. "Do you realize how bizarre this sounds? Angels and demons? Kira, this boss of yours is lying to you. He's using you for God knows what."

"Refusing to believe isn't going to change what you are. It's not going to make everything go away."

Exasperated, I kicked a rock across the ground. "I've heard enough."

It was obvious that Kira couldn't really help me. Not with her head filled with nonsense. I figured I'd hitchhike back to school if I had to. I made it within a few feet off the path when fire sprang up from the ground like a geyser. The flames spread out on both sides, blocking my way.

I glanced over my shoulder. Kira stood several feet behind me, fire running through her hair. Real fire. Yet she was unscathed.

"You wanted proof." Her gaze was fierce. "Is this good enough for you?"

I took a few steps away from the fire near me and managed to nod.

The flames behind me and in Kira's hair subsided. "We don't have much time before my boss or the demons who work for him realize our bat signals"—she held up her wrist—"have disappeared."

"The whole tracking system thing you mentioned earlier?" I asked, not liking the idea of higher beings, as Kira called them, knowing Ariana's or my every move.

"Yeah."

"Can't run," I mumbled, repeating what the voice had said to Ariana and me when that thought had first occurred to me. I stalked over to the bottle of vodka and picked it up. My hand shook as I brought it to my lips. Angels and demons were real. I would have preferred to find out Ariana and I had been marked by a covert part of the government who'd snuck into our bedrooms on the eve of our twelfth birthdays and branded us. And why the heck, if angels and demons were walking around Earth, weren't the angels on my side?

"Damn it!" I threw the bottle across the grove, feeling helpless. If Kira wasn't a girl, I would have punched her just to make myself feel like there was something I could do.

Kira rested her hand on my arm. "I'm sorry. I

really am. But there's no going back. You have to move forward, and I have a plan."

A dark storm cloud slid across the sky, stretching and contorting into what looked like the face of Satan, horns and pointed beard included. My pulse quickened. I took several deep breaths, forcing myself to calm down. There had to be a way out of this.

"A plan. Great." I paced back and forth. *You need her*, I reminded myself. *Hear her out*. "Our being Chosen is truly a coincidence?"

"Yes. My boss isn't allowed to help with the conception of the children—forcing the Chosen to be born would be cheating, breaking the rules. The Chosen have roles to play. Yours is to open the door to the gateway. Although, I was supposed to tell you that you're the key to keeping peace between the Fallen and those in Grace."

I stopped pacing and looked at her. She was sitting again. "If I open the door, then what does Ariana do? Reinforce the lock?"

"That's how I understand it. There's a ceremony that has to be performed. If you participate in it, it will be Hell on Earth, and if Ariana does it, all the creatures of our nightmares will remain locked in the pit."

"What type of ceremony?"

"I don't have all the details, but I do know there's an altar, some candles and herbs, and an incantation that has to be recited by one of the Chosen."

"But you know for sure that I would tip the balance toward evil and Ariana would tip it toward good."

"That's what the prophecy says."

A hint of hope coursed through me that I might not have to meet any more demons. "So Ariana performs this ceremony, secures the lock, and we're out of it?"

Kira's eyes grew wide. "No! Weren't you listening? You'll be in the middle of it. By agreeing to the ceremony, she's agreeing to join the angels. That means you'll be tethered to a demon, and not a lowly one like me. There is no going back to your old life. She still starts the war. The battle is still fought on Earth. People still die."

Chapter Twenty

Ariana

I stood between the open car door and Ben. A depressing song of lost love pushed around me, escaping the confines of the car. Ben slid his hand down my arm.

"You are special," he whispered, the words caressing my skin as they found their way to my ears. "May I kiss you?"

Inside, I screamed, *No!*

I closed my eyes, trying to clear my head. Something I couldn't do when I was gazing into his endless blue eyes. *He didn't just ask you out because he thought you were special*, I reminded myself. *He and Kira are here for a reason.* I needed to know what that reason was.

But when I opened my eyes, my head betrayed me with a slight nod to say yes.

Our lips met. He kissed me softly, as if he was afraid I'd push him away. I would have sworn I heard birds singing and smelled fresh-cut lilies. He pulled me closer, and I got lost in the moment. Every fiber of my being told me that life could be perfect if I trusted him.

"Kashmir" by Led Zeppelin blared out of my jacket pocket, snapping me out of the trance I was in. I broke our kiss. "I have to get this."

I offered Ben an apologetic smile as I flipped my phone open to read the message.

That's staying away from Ben? It was from Logan.

Now that I wasn't locking lips with Ben, I could feel the familiar tug in my gut. I looked toward the far end of the parking lot. Logan was just getting out of his car.

Ben's gaze followed mine. "He doesn't look happy."

"He's been having a rough day." I tucked my phone back in my pocket.

"Call me?" Ben asked.

I nodded. Ben got in his car and left.

"I would get mad at you." Logan's fingers wrapped around his keys. "But I get it now."

"Get what?" I asked, trailing so close behind him that I stepped on the heel of his shoe. "Logan!"

"You will not believe what I learned." That was all Logan would say until we were in the privacy of our apartment. He went straight for the bottle of whiskey we kept hidden under the sink.

"I take it Kira is no longer avoiding you?" I grabbed two glasses and put a couple ice cubes in each one.

"At least not today." His hand trembled as he poured the caramel-colored liquid. He made his a double.

"What did she say?"

"Oh, nothing out of the ordinary." He downed his drink, poured himself another, and added, "Just that she's a demon sent from Hell to find me."

"A wh-what?" I followed him into the family room. "Were you guys drinking again?"

He sank down onto the couch. "Told you you weren't going to believe me. When I called her a liar, she lit up like a torch. Pretty much made me a believer."

I sat next to him. A picture of Fire Starter from the movie *Hell Boy* came to mind. By how upset Logan was, I knew he wasn't exaggerating. "She was on fire, like a walking inferno?"

"Just her hair."

"A demon?" I asked, making sure I'd heard him right the first time.

He nodded and told me everything he'd learned from Kira.

"Oh my God." It made sense if I thought about it. The symbols on our wrists represented angels, some who had fallen, who had become demons. When we'd discovered their meaning, I'd never considered we were literally marked by angels or demons. "And Ben, he's a—" I couldn't get myself to finish my sentence. Ben couldn't be evil.

"I don't know what he is." Logan got up and grabbed our laptop.

"Didn't you ask?" If I'd been making out with a demon, I wanted to know.

"I was preoccupied trying to swallow the fact that the girl I like is a real, fire-producing demon." Logan sat on the edge of the couch, the laptop on the coffee table in front of him. "Ben's not the Devil, if that makes you feel better," he added as he waited for it to boot up.

"Not really." I took a sip of my drink and immediately scrunched up my nose. Normally if I drank whiskey, it was diluted with a lot of soda. Although, after hearing what we were up against, I wished Logan had poured me a double.

Ben couldn't be a monster. He didn't have horns, I reasoned to myself. I had run my fingers through his silky hair more than once, so I would have noticed if he did. He was generous and good and sweet. Seriously, the guy didn't even swear. No way was he from Hell. He was pure, like an angel. Only, he didn't have wings—I was pretty sure the lumps would show through his shirts. Nor did he have a halo or even an ethereal glow about him. That had to mean he wasn't an angel. I really wanted—no, needed—to believe he was just a guy who happened to have a mind that wasn't easily swayed by my suggestions.

I rested my hand on Logan's forearm to see if he was warm. A fever might explain the delusional comment. He felt normal. I thought about checking his forehead but figured he'd swat my hand away.

"Just because Kira's not mortal, doesn't mean Ben isn't, too."

"You can't believe that." When I didn't reply, he glanced up at me. "They're both new here, neither can be controlled by our suggestions, the dreams, the voice—should I go on?"

"No." I hated when he got all logical, mainly because he was right. "Kira really lit up like a torch?" I asked.

"Yes! And I'm a little freaked out right now." He was more than a *little* freaked out. I believed him, though. He pointed to the coffee table. "Grab one of the books. See if you find anything on prophecies."

We spent the next couple of hours scouring the Internet and the books we had bought in Chicago for anything to back Kira's story. We didn't find much.

When my stomach growled, Logan ordered us a sausage-onion pizza. Thirty minutes later, the buzzer rang. Logan went to meet the delivery guy while I moved our things to the kitchen table and got out plates and a knife.

Logan tossed his wallet on the table before grabbing a slice. As he searched the Internet for information on prophecies, I studied my arm. Our birthmarks were just as weird as demons being real. And demons certainly went along with the whole fire theme of my nightmares. But there was one part of Kira's story I didn't get.

"Tell me something—" I plucked a piece of sausage off my cheesy goodness and popped it in my mouth. "If the daughter is supposed to have the light of Heaven running through her veins and the son is supposed to have the fires of Hell running through his, how did Kira end up a demon?"

"She wasn't specific on who was good and who was bad." Logan sprinkled red pepper on his slice. "It was more like a son and daughter are born, one with the light and one with the fire."

"Ah-ha." I rubbed my wrist. "And they can find us because we have these markings."

"Yeah." Logan ate while he surfed the web. "Something to do with the symbols and our signature."

"Right. Supersonic auras." I wondered how that worked. Did they have to be within so many feet/yards/miles from us to feel our signatures, or could they zero in on our whereabouts by thinking about us? Did the whole demon-tracking ability only work because we'd been marked?

I took a bite out of my pizza. Logan continued his

search.

"What if we got rid of our birthmarks?"

"They aren't tattoos. It's not like we can go somewhere and ask for them to be removed." Logan leaned even closer to the screen on the laptop.

"Maybe we just have to alter them."

But he was apparently too engrossed in the article he'd found to hear me.

I grabbed the knife from the table and skimmed the tip of the blade over my wrist. If we couldn't be tracked, this would be over. We'd be safe.

I gripped the black handle tighter, sucked in a deep breath, and dragged the point over my skin, leaving a thin line of blood in its wake. It stung something fierce. I bit my lips to keep from letting out a cry.

I can do this, I told myself. I closed my eyes and sliced another thin line to form an X. This time I did yelp.

The knife was out of my hand before I could work up the courage to do it again.

"Are you nuts?" Logan pressed a thick stack of napkins against my wrist. The bloody knife was tossed onto the table. "What are you doing?"

I was queasy—definitely in pain—but I wasn't nuts.

"If we don't have these things, then they can't track us," I managed to say. My arm throbbed.

"These 'things' also protect us." He turned the blood-soaked napkins over so that the clean ones were against my arm. "Besides, removing the brand doesn't change the fact that we match the siblings in the prophecy. From what I've been able to find on prophecies, that pretty much means we're screwed. We have to find a way to outsmart them."

I brayed out a sharp laugh. "Outsmart demons? How?"

"I'm working on that." He examined my wrist, then indicated with a nod for me to look at what I'd done.

I prepared myself for the worst: deep gashes that would leave ugly scars, gore, possibly a view of ligaments or something. I glanced quickly and then ran to the sink to wash the red smears from my skin. The cold water didn't sting like it normally would when I cleaned an open wound.

"No way!" I exclaimed. The cuts were already healing. Thin red lines remained as if I'd been merely scratched by a branch or maybe someone's fingernails, then they faded as well. "How's this possible?"

Logan studied my birthmark. "I guess they don't want us messing with it."

"Well, we don't want it on our skin. Shouldn't we get a choice?" It was a rhetorical question. Kira had already made it perfectly clear that we didn't.

By the time I stalked from our small galley kitchen back to the table a few feet away, even the faint red lines of the X were gone. If there was ever a time Logan and I were to believe in miracles, it was now because there was definitely divine intervention involved in healing my wrist.

I listened to the soft hum of the computer as I thought. I really didn't know what to think about Kira. There was her sudden change of heart, going from not talking to wanting to tell Logan everything. Then the whole demon-boss thing. If it were true, why risk being sent back to Hell for someone she barely knew? From what I could tell, the only thing she was gaining from helping us was a clear conscience. It wouldn't change what she'd become. And, if she had some elaborate trap waiting for us, how did telling Logan about the prophecy help her?

Unless she'd lied.

Then there was the possibility that she was following her boss's orders, and everything she did tell Logan was part of his plan to get us to cooperate.

I could tell Logan wanted to trust Kira, but she was a demon. I was sure there was more to this prophecy than what she'd shared with him. Probably more than what her boss had allowed her to learn. Logan and I needed to be able to read between the lines.

Then it hit me. "Even if Kira is trying to help us, she gets her information from demons."

"Yeah?" Logan replied, quizzically.

"What if her boss knew she'd disobey him? He'd take precautions to make sure he didn't lose. He'd lie to Kira."

Logan cocked his head to the side. "Go on."

"What if the war *is* avoided if I complete the ceremony?"

Chapter Twenty-One

Logan

I didn't know what to expect from Kira the next day. Would she be more relaxed, relieved she finally had someone to confide in? Apprehensive, worried that her boss would find out she'd talked to me? She might have changed her mind again and decided not to help me after all. No matter what mood she was in, I had to know she was all right, that she wasn't being punished for going against her boss's orders.

I had no luck running into her between classes. If the whole celestial tracking system thing was true and she didn't want to see me, then she'd know which hall to avoid. So when she ditched fourth period, I was sure I wouldn't get any more help from her. Either her boss had dragged her back to the pit, or she felt she'd made a mistake telling me what she had.

At the end of the day, I was shocked to see her digging around the top of her locker. She didn't seem to know I was there; maybe the whole birthmark-tracking story was to scare me into thinking I couldn't run.

I stood quietly behind her waiting to see if she'd sense my presence.

"Hi, Logan," she finally said. She didn't even turn around. I made a mental note: tracking thing, true.

Over her right shoulder, I whispered, "How do you

know?"

"How do I know what?" She grabbed her geometry notebook.

"That if Ariana does her part, she starts the war."

Kira spun around, her eyes wide. "Are you crazy? This is not the place to talk about that."

"What if that's what this boss of yours wants you to believe?" I whispered. "What if he lied?"

"Elise told me that," she replied in a low voice. "Not my boss."

"Who?"

"The angel who approached me when I was human."

"You know an angel?" I asked.

"Hey, Kira!" We turned to see her friend Elaina hurrying toward us.

"Knew," Kira whispered. "Close your mouth."

I did. Though I couldn't help thinking that I'd love to see her friends list: Lilith—crazy demon bitch; Clarence—angel first-class; Cain—CEO of the Underworld.

"Hi, Elaina," Kira said.

"Are you going to Jessica's?" she asked.

Kira brushed her red curls away from her eyes and smiled. "Wouldn't miss it. She said four o'clock, right?"

"Yep. I have the top you lent me. I'll bring it." Elaina waved and headed toward the stairs. "See you there!"

Kira shoved her notebook into her backpack and slammed her locker shut. "Look, Logan, yesterday was the time to talk about this. In the forest. Not today in the crowded halls at school."

I held my wrist up, though my birthmark was safely hidden behind my bracelet. "Yesterday, I was too busy coming to grips with finding out that I'd been marked by demons to think through everything we discussed."

She gave me a knowing look and said, "You mean you had time to talk things through with your sister and you guys are hoping I'm wrong about Ariana's role in all of this, but I'm not." She scanned the crowded hall. "Look, this really isn't the place to have this discussion, not to mention Elaina and Jessica are waiting for me. I promise we'll talk later."

"I'll walk you to your car." I took her backpack from her. "What did this angel, Elise, say?"

She folded her arms over her chest. "You're not going to drop this conversation until later when we can talk in private, are you?"

"Nope."

"Fine, but we need to look like a happy couple walking out of school in case I'm being watched."

I inclined my head and held my hand out in front of me to let her know I was okay with that. We walked slowly.

She spoke quietly. "First thing you should know is an angel can't lie, but don't let that fool you into thinking you can trust everything they say. They're experts on omitting important details." When I nodded, she went on. "Elise didn't sugar coat my role in all this. The purpose of the Chosen is to start the war. Reciting the incantation needed to fulfill the prophecy is like screaming *charge* on a battlefield. But if I was the one to agree to my role, read a few words, then I'd make the Angels in Grace more powerful."

160

"Giving Heaven the upper hand," I said.

"Yes. Elise went as far as to say that while she couldn't promise no innocent blood would be shed, she could promise I'd be saving lives."

"Why'd you say no?" Her tone had implied she believed the whole saving-lives thing.

"Because Elise made it clear that by agreeing to do my part in the ceremony, I was entering into an agreement with her, and I couldn't go back to my old life and neither could my brother. When I asked what would happen to him, she changed the subject." Kira stopped to look at me. A red flush of anger crept into her cheeks. "Like I wouldn't notice she didn't answer the question."

We walked toward the parking lot. My feet dragged as if I had the weight of the world on my shoulders. I had assumed Kira's role was the same as mine since she was now a demon, but if an angel had approached her, that couldn't be right. She must have been destined to help them.

"So what happened? How'd you end up in Hell?"

She shuddered at the memory. "I was so scared of what might happen to my brother that I went to the guy who is now my boss swearing I'd refuse to do as Elise asked if he stopped pursuing my brother's help. He agreed. To this day, I'm not sure why, unless he knew he wasn't going to get my brother to go through with the ceremony. Let's face it: you don't have to be an expert on the subject of celestial beings to know demons are bad."

"You didn't tell your brother what you were doing?"

"No." She pulled her keys out of her purse. With a

quick chirp, her doors unlocked.

"Since neither of you said yes, the war was avoided. That seems like a good plan," I admitted, waiting to hear how it had backfired on her.

"That's what I thought, but my boss failed to mention that the price of the deal would be my soul."

"And your brother just gave up on you?" No way would I let my little sister spend eternity alone in Hell. The demons would have to go through me to take Ariana, and if it came down to it, they would have to drag me to the pit right along with her.

"He swore he'd do whatever it took to set things right, only he gave up. Not that I blame him. It's not like he could have broken into Hell and busted me out." Something in her tone made me think that was, nonetheless, exactly what she had expected him to do.

She'd been naïve, believing she could make a deal with a demon. Trusting one would be like holding a metal rod with both hands during a thunderstorm and trusting Mother Nature not to strike. Either way, you were playing with fire.

"You said you had to agree to help. Why didn't they just force you to do your part?"

She took her backpack from me, tossing it on the passenger seat. "There are rules that have to be followed. A Chosen has to choose to help."

That wasn't going to happen. I would never be a part of something that hurt others, prophecy or not. I watched a squirrel scurry up a maple tree next to the school, disappearing into a knot in the trunk. I wished I could hide that easily.

At least the demons were governed by a strict code of ethics. Or maybe it would be more accurate to say they were limited in what they could do by moral standards they couldn't deviate from. Per the prophecy, the order of things was important: the first born must be a son, and he must be born on November first, a daughter must arrive precisely two years later, one of us has to agree to do our part, and then participate in a ceremony that no doubt was worse than Kira let on. Then what?

"So what happens to us if the ceremony is performed?"

Kira glanced around us, waving at Elaina as she drove by. "Worst case, a supernatural battle of epic proportions with you, me, and Ariana in the middle of it."

"Do you mean pitted against each other or hiding just out of sight while the two sides fight?"

"No idea. I didn't get that far when I was Chosen. Look, Logan. It's really not a good idea to be standing in the middle of the school parking lot talking about this." She slipped her arms around my neck. "Even if we look like we are talking about fun, exciting non-demon stuff. Besides, I promised Jessica and Elaina I'd hang out with them."

I wrapped my arms around her waist, trapping her. "You said you'd help me."

"And I will. If only to be able to do this"—she snuggled close to me—"for the rest of my existence."

She tilted her head up and kissed me. I went to push her away, but she whispered, "Don't," as I raised my hands. Instead of shoving her, I cupped her face and kissed her back.

When our lips parted, I rested my forehead on hers; my heart pounded, and I knew I was at her mercy. "You don't need to make eye contact to control someone's thoughts," I said.

It wasn't a question. She'd spoken one word— *don't*—and my mind went from *What the hell are you doing kissing a demon!* to *Who cares what she is?* If she could control my thoughts, what would stop her from telling me to say yes to my role in the prophecy?

"My 'don't' was for you not to push me away." She smirked, a gleam of happiness in her eyes, and got in her car. "I didn't force you to kiss me back. You did that all on your own."

Chapter Twenty-Two

Ariana

Becca got her way. No surprise there. But my agreeing to a double-date was for totally selfish reasons. She already had plans with Justin, and I didn't want to be alone with Ben. We ended up at the movies watching a madman go after unsuspecting campers. The movie was all bad acting and fake gore. My thoughts kept drifting to other things.

I was having a hard time with the whole angel-demon conspiracy Kira had dumped on Logan and he'd, in turn, dumped on me. The bitter realization that I had finally let myself get close to someone and he'd turned out not to be human had me fighting back the urge to laugh hysterically. I couldn't decide if the whole situation pissed me off or depressed me.

My fingers traced the edge of the wings on my bracelet. It was funny—in a very ironic way—that out of all the symbols at the leather shop, we had chosen wings. It wasn't because we believed in angels or anything like that. To Logan, wings represented simpler times. Of when we had parents. A family. He'd gotten the idea from a picture that my aunt had had on her mantel. In the picture, I was seven and Logan was nine. It was Halloween. Logan dressed as a super hero. I was a pixie—silver dragonfly-like wings and all. I had insisted on wearing those wings everywhere I'd gone for the next few weeks, telling anyone who'd listen that I was an angel. I chuckled at the memory and wondered what had happened to that picture.

Maybe Logan and I had been given our powers as a way to test what type of people we were. I was suddenly very thankful that Logan had insisted we work for what we had. I decided vacuuming the hallways in the apartment complex was a fair trade for our two-bedroom home. After all, we did save our landlord some money. Right?

I wondered if suggesting one's way into major discounts was a sin. After running through the Ten Commandments in my head, I decided it wasn't. We didn't outright steal, and we never bartered with someone we knew needed the money. That had to count for something.

An ominous melody echoed through the theater as a girl in the movie slowly crept up the stairs of an old, abandoned farmhouse. She was already stupid for entering the decrepit building. Going straight for the stairs made her an idiot—like being stuck on the second floor was going to be a good idea. When she pushed opened the door to the room at the end of the hall, a gloved hand grabbed her wrist. Becca jumped, sending popcorn flying everywhere. We both broke into a fit of the giggles.

Needless to say, the actress didn't make it to the next scene alive.

"I need to use the bathroom," Becca said after the movie. She looked at me meaningfully, and I quickly said I did, too.

"This was fun." Becca led the way past a few

women who were washing their hands, set her purse on the counter, and rummaged through it.

"It was," I agreed dutifully. "Justin seems nice."

A movie probably wasn't the best place to go when you'd just met someone. Because Becca and I had sat next to each other, I don't think Ben and Justin had said more than ten words to each other.

"Isn't he great?" she beamed.

I returned her smile before grabbing my lip gloss from my purse.

Justin had this bad-boy look to him: ruffled, dark blond hair, studded earrings, leather jacket, and loose-fitting jeans that he'd worn enough to completely fray the hem. The look worked for him, and he appeared to be really nice to Becca.

I looked at the pink lip gloss in my hand, decided I didn't want to make my lips more enticing, and dropped it back into my purse without using it.

"Want to grab a bite to eat?" I asked, not ready to be alone with Ben yet. Part of the problem was I didn't know what to say to him. *Heard you're immortal.* Something less direct. *How old are you, exactly?* Light humor? *Logan nabbed himself a demon. Pretty hot, huh?* Or maybe I should cut to the gritty details. *Spill. Demon or angel?*

My flippant attitude was really nerves. If Ben realized I knew he wasn't normal, would the sweet-guy act be tossed out the window? Would I be in danger?

"Can't," Becca replied, bringing me back to our conversation. She brushed a shimmering rose onto her cheeks. "Justin has an early class tomorrow, and he already told me he has a ton of reading to do."

Ben and Justin were waiting for us in the lobby. I

couldn't help noticing they weren't talking. Ben had his arms folded over his chest, his jaw clenched. Justin leaned against the wall, watching a spot on the floor between them.

"Is everything okay?" I asked when we joined them.

"Yeah." Ben slid an arm around my waist. It felt right. It shouldn't have, not if he wasn't human, but I leaned into him regardless. He *felt* human. Warm. Strong. Solid.

Ben gave a squeeze, pulling me even closer.

Justin took Becca's hand. To Ben and me, he said, "It was nice to meet you."

"You too." Out of the corner of my eye, I saw a nerve in Ben's temple pulse, getting the impression that he didn't agree.

"I'll call you later." Becca lunged forward and hugged me, her face on the opposite side of where Ben was. "I knew we'd all get along," she whispered excitedly.

I wasn't so sure she was right, but I hugged her back anyway, glad she was so happy.

She stepped back, wrapped an arm around Justin, and they left.

"Want to grab a burger?" Ben asked when we reached his car.

I breathed in deeply. I had to confront him at some point.

"Sure." I tucked my hair behind my ear and slid into the passenger seat.

Ben got in and started the car. In the dimming light of dusk, he looked extremely sexy. The red lights from the dashboard made his eyes an even deeper shade of blue and gave his skin a rosy glow. He drove with his left hand on the steering wheel and his right on the stick shift.

"Movie was…" Ben paused as if searching for the right word.

"Awful," I offered.

He nodded. "Yes."

We both laughed.

"How many times can a bunch of teens end up at a camp with a psychopath?" he joked.

"I know." I shifted so that I could see him better. "Becca's really into horror films. We see them all at the theater."

He slowed down and flipped on his turn signal. "I don't think I've seen Justin around school."

"He's in college."

Ben nodded again. "Becca should be careful. Take things slow."

"Why, do you know something about Justin that we don't?" I asked, thinking about their cold behavior toward each other at the theater.

"No, but guys aren't always what they seem. Becca's good. I'd hate to see her get hurt."

"Are you sure there's nothing else?" I asked. If Ben was superhuman, maybe he could sense if a person had bad intensions. "Becca's my best friend. If you know something, anything, I want to know."

"We didn't really talk." He glanced at me. "I'm just speaking from a guy's point of view."

I nodded, replaying everything I knew about Justin in my head and trying to pick out any nugget of negative information. The worst thing I could think of was him encouraging Becca to get her eyebrow pierced.

But was that really so bad? It seemed to pale in comparison to possibly dating a creature from Hell like I was.

Ben tapped his index finger against the steering wheel as he waited for traffic to clear so that he could take a left into a strip mall. His sleeve slid partially up his wrist. The light of the dashboard made his pale skin a sunburned red. Poking out from under the cotton fabric of his cuff were several scars. White lines. Curves. Markings that looked an awful lot like my birthmark.

I tilted my head to get a better look as the car rolled forward. He turned the wheel, and I couldn't see his wrist anymore. We parked in front of a small mom-and-pop restaurant that had everything from burgers to fried pizza puffs.

He cut the engine and went to get out.

"Wait!" I reached over and grabbed his left arm. When I went to yank up his sleeve, he placed a hand over mine with lightning-fast speed.

"I want to see it." Was I right? Had he been marked, too? If he had, would he let me see his wrist? My heart hammered in my chest, and I fought to keep from trembling as I waited for his reply.

"There's nothing to see." But it was too late for him to deny it; I'd already felt his muscles tense and seen the look of shock in his eyes.

"Don't lie to me." I tried to lift his hand from mine.

He looked at me appraisingly, but he didn't yank his arm away. I took that as a sign I was still safe with him, at least for the time being.

"I just saw it," I blurted. This was the moment of truth. "When you turned the wheel."

After what seemed like a very long time, he pulled up his sleeve.

My fingers lingered over his wrist. His birthmark was very similar to mine. Same double-lined star, only he didn't have as many symbols between the points or between the lines. Over the star, as if superimposed, there was a cross.

My eyes filled with tears, and I hated myself for being so irrational. I had already known he wasn't here to finish high school. I'd known that meant he wasn't human, but seeing the symbols on his wrist made the whole nightmare real. The only thing keeping me from screaming was the cross. He had to be one of the good guys. There might still be hope for Logan and me.

His eyes narrowed, questioningly. "You don't seem surprised to see it."

"The sigil is the mark of a Chosen," I replied, remembering every word Logan had said the previous night. "How many of us are there?"

"How do you know—" His fingers closed around my arm. "Kira." The rest of his words were spoken in a language I didn't recognized.

"How many, Ben?"

"There have been four sets of siblings." He mumbled something else I couldn't understand.

"Which are you from?"

"Doesn't matter. What does matter is I'm here to protect you."

"No, you're not," I growled through my teeth, and fear of what I'd learned and what was to come bubbled over all at once. "You're here because of the prophecy. You want to talk me into participating in a ceremony, claiming that I'll be saving a bunch of people, but that's crap. It starts a war."

Ben turned several shades paler. His grip on my arm tightened. "Kira told you that?"

"She told Logan. You're hurting me!" I tugged, trying to break free.

"What else did she say?"

"I don't remember!" I tried to pry his fingers from my arm, but it was no use.

"Think!" His eyes flared with anger. His abrupt mood change seemed to suck the air right out of the car. For the first time since I'd met Ben, I didn't see a hottie. I saw a monster.

"Um." I swept my free hand through my hair, trying to remember. No one walking in or out of the different stores noticed us sitting in the car. I hoped if I answered him, he'd calm down and let me go. "Kira—she's a demon, and she's supposed to tell Logan he'd be helping keep the peace or something like that, but it's a lie. There's no going back, whatever that means. And she wasn't supposed to tell him any of that, but she did. Seriously, Ben, you're hurting me."

My gaze dropped to his hand wrapped around my arm. He loosened his grip but didn't let go. With his eyes closed, he took several slow breaths.

"Is it true?" I asked, my voice trembling. "Is Kira really a demon, and are Logan and I really expected to start some war between Heaven and Hell?"

He looked at me, his gaze gentle and kind again. "Yes."

"What does that make you?" I'd had all that time in the movies to think about this. Kira had said that a brother and sister were born, one with the fires of Hell running through their veins and one with the light of

Heaven. If Kira was here on behalf of Hell, then Ben had to be here on behalf of Heaven. "Are you a-an angel?"

"Humans can't become angels." He let go of my arm.

I slid my hand to my lap, my fingers curled around my purse, ready to bolt from the car.

"If you want to go, I won't stop you." Ben watched me as if he could read my mind. After a moment, he added, "It's not me you should be afraid of."

A non-human boyfriend with an ironclad grip was definitely something a girl should be scared of, but I pushed that thought to the back burner. Curious about his earlier comment, I asked, "Why can't a human become an angel?"

Logan and I had attended the funeral of our first set of foster parents. I remembered relatives telling their son that his mom and dad were now angels in Heaven.

"Because humans have souls. Angels don't." I cocked my head to the side, confused. He explained, "It was one of the things God gave mankind when he created it. It was to offer man—a weaker being than an angel—a way to be forgiven for his sins."

"You're a demon, then, like Kira." No wonder Ben's kisses were so hot.

"Quite the opposite. I'm a Blessed."

"What does that mean?"

"A servant of the Angels in Grace," he explained.

"And before you became a Blessed, you were a Chosen?" I asked, making sure I understood.

He nodded.

"What happened? How did you escape your role in the prophecy and become what you are, and what happened to your sister?"

"You don't—" He snapped his mouth shut and gave a slight shake of his head before answering. "My sister and I learned the hard way that you can't fight destiny. Some might even go as far as to say we committed suicide."

Logan and I were going to fight it, but I wasn't about to tell Ben that. I looked at my pink bracelet, picturing the sigil hidden beneath it. "Do you serve one of the angels represented in my birthmark?"

"Maybe. I haven't seen yours to know for sure." He reached over the center console and took my left hand in his. With the cream strap that held my bracelet tight around my wrist pinched between his thumb and finger, he asked, "May I?"

I nodded. He removed my bracelet.

We compared our birthmarks. He had a total of three angels within the double lines of the star; I had five. Only two of them were the same.

"Do you know why they're different?" I asked.

"No." He ran his thumb over the sensitive skin of my wrist, awakening every nerve from my forearm to my toes. "If I had to guess, I'd say different angels watch over you than did for me."

I traced the superimposed cross on his wrist, feeling how the thin salmon-colored lines were slightly raised. "What is this?"

"The marking of a Blessed. It binds me to the angels."

"How did you know you could trust them?"

"Angels are good, Ariana. They protect mankind."

I forced myself to meet his gaze. "Can I trust you?"

"I was sent here to help you accept your destiny,

but, more than that, I'm here to keep you safe. Even from sleepy truck drivers who aren't paying attention to things around them."

The grill of the delivery truck popped into my mind. "My ghost act…that was your doing?"

He nodded. "Either way, you wouldn't have died, but you would have felt the impact. Broken several ribs, probably bled internally, but you would have healed."

"Um…" What does one say when they meet their Guardian Angel—or Blessed, in this case? "Thank you."

He smirked and inclined his head in a silent *You're welcome.*

One good deed, though, didn't change the fact that Ben hadn't been honest with me. He had gigantic, overwhelming, life-changing secrets. Not to mention, he wasn't human and had only noticed me because of what I was, not who I was.

"Why didn't you just tell me who you are?" I asked, giving him a chance to come clean. "Why ask me out?"

"Would you have believed me?"

The answer was easy: no. But right then, that was so not the point. Ben was there because of the prophecy. He had asked me out because it suited his cause. I was special only because I was a Chosen. It wasn't fair. Just when things had started to look up, my world fell apart. This week's info dump left me numb all over.

"Ben, this is too much for me." I slid my bracelet back over my birthmark. He tied it in place without me asking. "Please. If I really can trust you—if you're not here to hurt me—take me home."

Chapter Twenty-Three

Logan

I tossed and turned most of the night. The little time I'd spent asleep had been cut short by my sister's exasperated, "Dude! Snore any louder and you'll wake the entire building." I'd almost pointed out that she did have a perfectly good bedroom she could sleep in if she didn't like my snoring, but her dreams had turned to nightmares the second we weren't in the same room. She'd wake screaming, and I'd be up anyway.

I couldn't stop thinking about Kira and our kiss. She was right. I had kissed her back because I'd wanted to. I liked the feel of her in my arms. The taste of her kisses. But when I was near her, I had to remind myself she was a demon. She could burn me alive in the blink of an eye.

To help drill that fact into my brain, I went over what I knew so far. There had to be a way to avoid the war. Kira had done it, but Ariana and I couldn't make the same mistakes she'd made. Whatever we did had to keep us human.

I refused to believe that the prophecy didn't offer clues on how to stop the war—a small piece of information that would tell me what to do, if I could only find a copy of it, which proved to be impossible. It was as elusive as the damn disembodied voice I'd been hearing.

I watched Ariana sleeping on the couch, curled up on her side hugging her cream comforter. In the moonlight, she looked almost angelic. I realized she and Kira were a lot alike: pretty, smart, and caring. It gave me some comfort knowing that Ariana's destiny brought her to Heaven.

Heaven was good. Right? A paradise. And angels were good. People prayed to them in times of need. Right? Yet, Kira didn't believe that. She'd run from the safety of an angel into the hands of a demon. Did I even have that right? Her boss was in charge of demons; he had to have ultimate power or else those under him wouldn't be afraid to rebel.

I sighed and kicked off the covers. Ariana grunted in her sleep and rolled over to her other side.

Kira's words replayed in my mind: *one soon-to-be-vanquished angel gets smart*.

"No way!" I shot off the floor where I'd been trying to sleep and ran to our small kitchen table, sure I'd figured out who Kira's boss was, and woke our laptop from sleep mode. I searched under *demons*. As I read, my heart raced, threatening to burst out of my chest and hide under the couch.

****

The next day in foods class, Mrs. Larson thought it would be fun to mix chemistry with cooking. Each team was given a thermometer, two fondue pots, and a few other items with the goal of understanding the difference between heating a liquid like water versus something more solid like cheese. I was just looking forward to eating small chunks of bread dipped in gooey, warm cheddar and brie.

I scooted closer to Kira, hoping to get a better understanding of her demonic powers. "Can you make the water boil without the burner?"

"That would screw up the experiment." She used a lighter with a long neck to start the burners under our pots.

I dropped our cheese cubes into the one closest to me. "I'll take that as a yes. Why'd you do it?"

"Logan." My name oozed with annoyance. She poured water into the empty pot. "I'm not going to just start lighting fires. Come on. Get serious."

I waited for her to look at me. "I meant, why did you make the deal with a Fallen Angel?"

Her expression went blank. "How'd you figure out what my boss is?"

"Something you said the other day." I stirred the chunks of cheese with my fork. "But I can't figure out why you would make a deal with him. Why didn't you just tell Elise—an angel who I assume stands for all things good—to get lost?"

"I told you, people like Elise and my boss don't take no for an answer."

"Not good enough." I checked the temperature of the water and then the cheese, although it hadn't all melted yet. "You told me that a Chosen is protected. If that's true, then something had to have happened to make you run from the safety of an Angel in Grace to beg for help from a Fallen Angel."

She pulled her sleeves over her hands. Her jaw muscles clenched. I waited. The cheese was the consistency of rice pudding by the time she answered.

"Elise stressed that once I made a choice we'd need to complete the ceremony quickly, because my yes would lift some of the bonds that the Fallen had to abide by. But no way could I start a war that would be fought on Earth and risk the lives of innocent people. Not to mention she only guaranteed my safety, not my brother's.

"So my brother came up with this plan. He was going to tell the Fallen Angel he'd do it. My brother figured the Fallen would drop his guard during the ceremony. Be at his weakest, you know? My brother's plan was to wait for the opportune time, when the Fallen had his back turned or was preoccupied in some other way, and then he'd kill him. If he failed, he'd just refuse to go through with the ceremony."

It was a reckless plan, I thought, one of a desperate man. Almost as reckless as running to a Fallen Angel and striking up a deal of your own like Kira had done. It did spark my curiosity.

"You can kill an angel?"

"I'm sure there's a way. Everything has a weakness, but my brother didn't know how. Not really."

I jabbed a piece of sourdough bread with a fondue fork and handed it to Kira. She swirled it around in the cheese.

"What was he going to do?" I asked, wanting to know if it was something I could try if the need arose.

"Stab him with a silver candlestick we'd found in the trash. Or maybe bash his brains in with it." She shrugged. "I'm not really sure, but he didn't know what he was doing either. And it wouldn't have worked. Elise had already told me there was no option available to me or my brother that would allow us to defeat an angel, Fallen or in Grace."

"I still don't get why you made the deal," I admitted.

Kira shook her head. "Don't you see the flaw in my brother's plan? It started with him saying, 'Yes, I'll do it.' Those four little words lift the bonds that keep the Chosen safe."

My eyes widened in realization. "After that, the Fallen could hurt him or you."

Kira blew out the flame under our pot of water. She then wrote down how long it had taken for our cheese to melt and how hot it was.

"My brother was set on going through with his plan anyway." Kira stabbed a piece of bread with her fork, then another and another. "I was petrified of what the Fallen Angel would do to him once he found out my brother had not only lied, but was also trying to kill him. I went to the Fallen begging him to leave. In return, I told him I'd do whatever he asked. Refuse to help Elise. Never speak to another angel. Anything."

"Miss Rose." Kira and I looked up to see Mrs. Larson standing next to our table. "Take it easy on my fondue fork."

"Sorry." Kira set it down. When Mrs. Larson walked away, Kira added, "You know the rest."

The images of mangled bones flashed through my head. I really wished Kira had never shown me them. I blew out the fire under the second fondue pot, no longer hungry.

"If I understand correctly, then a demon is a damned soul that serves Fallen Angels."

She nodded. "We're the lucky ones, if you can believe that."

We walked to the sink. I scooped the rest of our

cheese into the garbage can as Kira filled the sink with soapy water. I mulled over what she'd just told me in my head, checking off each *don't*. Don't trick an angel. Don't try to kill an angel. Don't say you will do your part in the prophecy thinking you can change your mind later.

Shit, there were more *don't*s than there were *do*s.

Kira did say that everyone had a weakness, though. Maybe that was what I needed to focus on. I dropped the fondue pot into the sudsy water.

"This boss of yours, does he have a name?" I asked, thinking that if I knew his name I could find out more about him.

She sighed. "Logan, I'm—"

"Forbidden," I said. I grabbed a clean towel and dried the things Kira had washed. "Maybe if I guessed?"

She snorted out a laugh. "There are, like, hundreds of Fallen Angels, Logan."

I frowned, not finding my idea funny. "I'll say them all."

She put the second fondue pot in the drying rack and pulled the stopper out of the drain. "No. And I'll tell you why. Names have power, and his has the power to send me right back to the pit, and I don't think I can survive another day, let alone a decade, down there. I'm sorry. I'm just not strong enough to go through that again."

She walked over to Elaina's sink, making it obvious she was done with our conversation. And I still didn't know anything about the plan Kira had mentioned in the forest. That should have been my first question.

The bell rang a few minutes later. I reasoned with myself that I needed time to analyze everything I'd learned in the last couple of days and then I'd ask Kira what she had in mind, but, the truth was, I wanted an excuse to see her later. That had to make me one sick son of a bitch, knowing what Kira was and still wanting to hang out with her. I didn't care, though. If I was going to go to Hell—like the prophecy indicated—I might as well do something to deserve my fate.

Chapter Twenty-Four

Ariana

"What do you mean Justin wants you to move to California?" I asked as Becca and I made our way through the lunch line in the cafeteria.

Becca grabbed a plate of fries. "He applied to the Musicians Institute, and he asked me to come with him."

With all the stuff going on with demons and Blesseds and angels and prophecies and destinies, I needed things with my best friend to remain unchanged. I needed her here where I could see her. Not three thousand miles away.

"But you have two more years of high school." I took a carton of milk for myself and handed one to her.

"I can finish up there."

"You don't play an instrument."

"Ariana, I don't have to play an instrument to be with him."

I personally thought she had lost her mind. Justin must be one heck of a kisser to have her ready to follow him to another state. Unless—"You slept with him, didn't you?"

"Shh!" She pulled me closer. "I don't want everyone to know."

"Ohmigod, Becca. When?" I lowered my voice

even more. "He must be good."

"Ariana!" Her cheeks flushed. "He is, and he loves me," she whispered, all giggles now.

We paid and found an empty table near the windows. Now I knew she was crazy, but isn't that what love is all about, following each other to the ends of the world?

"Will your parents let you move?" I already knew the answer to that question. There was no way her parents would let their only child run off to California with a musician.

"Probably not." She nibbled on a fry. "Justin still has to get accepted and find an apartment if he does. No point in telling them until it's official. And no squealing to them either! This remains between you and me, got it?"

I sighed in defeat and listened to her babble on about her plans. I figured there was no point in telling Becca she was being an idiot. Once she got an idea in her head, she ran with it, no turning back. Besides, perhaps their relationship wouldn't last through the end of this winter, let alone the end of the school year. Not to mention, she'd be broke, and Becca enjoyed her double caramel macchiatos and shopping too much to survive without Daddy's credit card. I kept the subject off guys for the rest of the lunch hour.

At the end of seventh period, my cell vibrated.

Kira and I are hanging out after school. Do you need a ride home? The text was from Logan.

No, I texted back. *Going to see what else I can get out of Ben.*

Logan and I had talked the previous night, so I wasn't surprised he'd made plans with Kira. Our main focus was on staying human. That meant finding out as much as we could about our roles in the prophecy so that we didn't make the same mistake Kira and Ben had. Logan and I pinkie-swore—our most sacred of all promises and something we'd been doing since we were little—that we would stick together. A united front. Whatever we did, we'd do it as one. Logan was even convinced that Kira was the person the disembodied voice kept telling him to protect. I could tell he cared about her, even if he wouldn't admit it out loud.

After school, Ben and I hung out on the bleachers, half-watching the football team practice.

"I'm curious…" I kicked a boot-covered foot up on the bleacher in front of me. "If you were just another eighteen-year-old trying to make it through your senior year, would you still talk to me?"

I don't know why it was important for me to know the answer to that question, but it was. Maybe I'd have felt less used.

"Would it bother you if I didn't?" Ben straddled the bleacher, his full attention on me.

I shrugged like it was no big deal.

His finger traced the outline of my palm. Slow. Soft. "I was sent here to protect you. I could have done that from afar. I chose to get to know you."

I grinned. His gaze wandered back to the field.

"Were you Kira's guardian angel, too? Is that how you know her?" I could feel his fingers slipping away. I closed my hand around his. "I'm sorry. I don't mean to pry. It's, well, you're the one who made it obvious you know each other, and it would make sense if you'd protected her when she was human."

"I didn't do a good job, did I?" That vein in his temple twitched, and his jaw clenched as if he were biting back words.

I sat up straighter. "You had feelings for her."

"I cared about her, yes."

"Like you care about me?"

"Not exactly. I didn't kiss her or anything like that."

"But you feel guilty about what happened to her."

"She made her choice." His hand became chilly, like ice. The cold pierced my skin, forcing me to let go of his fingers. He turned away from me, toward the players on the field.

"Logan told me what she did. She made a deal with this demon-boss of hers. She did it to save her brother," I said, hoping to reason with him. "You had to have been friends at one time. How can you just turn your back on her now?"

"I'm not turning my back on her," he shot back.

"You're not helping her either."

He was silent for several long minutes. When he finally answered, he remained focused on the drills the players ran. "What do you think a demon might do if he saw Kira talking to me?"

Torture her popped into my head. "I-I didn't think about that." I tucked a stray strand of hair behind my ear and decided to change the subject. "Why isn't Heaven trying to avoid the war?"

"How do you avoid a war that the other side wants so badly?" He breathed in deeply, then heaved out a sigh. "If it were an option, the Angels in Grace would probably just kill the Chosen as soon as the girl is born, but they are bound to the rules of the prophecy, so they can't."

My mouth fell open in shock.

"I'm sorry. Two lives versus the lives of thousands, maybe millions, would be a sacrifice they could accept. Neither of us would be here now." He rested his elbows on his knees. "You can make a difference, though. You can make the world a better place."

"You can't guarantee that."

He faced me again. His fingers traveled along my cheek, combed through my hair. "I've seen it."

He kissed me. Somehow, the air smelled cleaner. His musk cologne mixed with fresh cedar and the soft aroma of roses. My eyes were closed, but I could see our school. The jocks were sitting with the geeks from the math club. In a flash I saw the city, the same seedy block Logan and I had walked to get to the bookstore. Only, there were no bums sitting on the sidewalks or trash overflowing in dumpsters. Another flash, and I was in some third-world country, but there was enough food for everyone. Yet another flash, and I saw children on a playground, all kids playing happily together and their parents sitting side by side on benches.

I pulled away in awe. "Is that really what life would be like?"

"It could be."

"I still don't get how me doing the ceremony is a bad thing. Logan said I'd be reinforcing the gates to Hell. So how does that blow some divine trumpet that tells Heaven and Hell the battle has begun?"

"The difference is in the size of Hell's army."

"What do you mean?" I asked.

"The only reason the Fallen haven't already attacked those in Grace is because there are more

Angels in Grace than there are Fallen and more than half of the Fallen are trapped in Hell. Only a few have been able to claw their way out as Kira's boss has done." Ben paused. "If you read the spell, the door remains closed. The Fallen wouldn't have their full numbers, plus they would have to fight without the aid of the demons they've created."

A knot formed in my stomach. "And if Logan performs it, he opens the doors."

"Releasing all of Hell's fury."

Chapter Twenty-Five

Logan

Kira and I went to the mall after school. We strolled around for a while, browsing through a few stores. Neither one of us bought anything. Our conversation was kept to simple things: school, music, and cars mostly.

"Have you always been into American muscle?" Kira asked as we walked. Rap music flooded out of a hip-hop clothing store.

"Yeah." I shoved my hands into the front pockets of my jeans. "The Camaro was my dad's. He used to keep it in my uncle's garage. We'd go over there on weekends to work on it."

She gathered her hair in her hands, moving it off her shoulders and letting it fall in a sheet down her back, which revealed a long, slender neck perfect for kissing. I forced myself to look away. *She can roast you alive,* I reminded myself.

"How'd you manage to keep it after your uncle passed?" she asked.

"How do you know he's dead?"

"Besides the fact you and Ariana live alone?" She fixed me with a pointed stare. "News about the Chosen traveled fast in Hell. When something happened up here, a demon would report it back to my boss down there. Since he didn't let me too far out of his sight, I was kept well-informed."

"And you still thought I'd be a jerk?" I asked, remembering her comment from our second date.

"Hoped was more like it. So how is it the Camaro didn't get sold along with everything else?"

"I convinced our caseworker to have it moved to storage along with all of my uncle's tools."

Kira nodded; her lips tugged upward into a knowing smile. "And you convinced the guy at the store-it-yourself place to give you a great price on the storage unit."

"Something like that."

We reached the food court. The aroma of rich butter, sugar, and cinnamon overpowered the food at the other restaurants.

Kira looped her arm through mine. "Let's split a cinnamon roll. My treat."

A few minutes later, we sat at one of the small, café-style black tables, away from the other shoppers.

"I love these things." Kira tore a strip of sticky pastry and ate it, licking the extra icing off her fingers one at a time. She paused, her thumb between her teeth as her gaze met mine. I never realized how long her eyelashes were. Her cheeks flushed, and she looked away.

I tried to slow my heart, which beat a hundred miles a minute. *Burned alive. Not the way you want to die.* Yet I couldn't look away when she wrapped her lips around the straw of her soda. I decided to change the subject to something that would remind me Kira was trouble.

"Can demons come and go as they please?"

Kira looked around, checking to make sure no one was listening. "No. Definitely not."

"How'd you get out?"

"On my boss's back."

"Really?" I asked, intrigued. "Piggyback?"

"It was that or let him carry me out like some hero carrying a child from a burning building." She grimaced. "No way was I going to give him the satisfaction of seeing how truly happy I was to be getting out of that place. So, yeah, piggyback. And no sarcastic comments on it being fun or romantic or anything like that."

I held up a hand to stop her. "I wasn't going to go there."

She frowned like she didn't believe me. "Some demons claw their way out of Hell. I've no clue how they do it."

"So Fallen Angels can come and go as they please?"

"Enough of them can."

"Are we the only lucky ones to be the Chosen?"

"Eat, before it's gone." Kira pushed the plate closer to me. "From what I understand, my brother and I were the third set of siblings to fit the prophecy. The first two killed themselves. Double suicide, from what I heard."

"Wait. A Chosen's protected." After Ariana's stunt with the knife the other night, I knew we couldn't hurt ourselves. "How'd they manage to kill themselves?"

"They didn't have these little get-out-of-death markings." Kira wiggled her wrist as she said it. "You and I have the Underworld to thank for them. Anyway, the brother of the second set said yes, found out afterward that the angel he was talking to was a Fallen one, and rammed a dagger into his own gut." She demonstrated with an imaginary knife to her midsection. "The Angel in Grace convinced the sister to take her revenge out on Hell by performing the ceremony."

"So this war has been fought once already?" I asked, wondering if maybe that was what the Crusades or maybe World War I had really been about.

"No. Get this." Kira leaned in. "With the brother dead, the ceremony didn't work. But as long as Hell couldn't rise, Heaven was happy."

I watched two brothers, no older than seven or eight, fighting over the last onion ring at the table behind Kira. I wondered if it were the last onion ring in the world, would they still fight or would one of them sacrifice their own wants for the other? "So as long as one of the siblings commits suicide, Heaven wins."

"Yep. I don't think any of the angels knew that until the spell failed. The Fallen were smart. They weren't going to risk a repeat performance, so they marked the Chosen, protecting them."

I added *Kill yourself* to the *don't* list. Although I wasn't sure if I was brave enough to ram anything into my stomach anyway.

"What about our ability to manipulate people's minds? Who do I have to thank for that?"

"The Fallen—it's a side effect of the sigil"—she wiggled her forearm—"a combination of being touched by a higher power and the angelic symbols. Comes in handy, so I guess that's the upside to what we are."

Just then, a woman in a dark red suit caught my eye. She clutched a smart phone, her fingers flying over the screen at a speed that would have impressed even

Ariana.

"How do you know all this?" I asked Kira.

"Some souls in the pit aren't all that bad. The record-keeper, for one."

"There's a record-keeper?" I pictured a wise old skeleton of a man with a quill and an endless scroll. "Is there something that links the Chosen? Besides our birthdays, I mean?"

"Not that he's said." She drew a figure eight in the icing on the plate as she spoke. "My parents were from Charing Cross, London. They came to America in the early seventeen hundreds. The Chosen before us were from Egypt and Greece."

"You don't sound English. You know, 'bloke,' 'arse,' 'brilliant.' Stuff like that."

She laughed. "It was more like 'sir,' and 'ma'am' when I was there."

"Don't tell me I've kissed an old lady," I teased. In a more serious tone, I asked, "How old are you?"

"Sweet sixteen and I'm not telling you how long I've been that."

"Fair enough. Did your parents die when you were young, like mine?" I took a drink of my soda. It was obvious that the higher powers didn't like Ariana and me to have any steady adults in our lives.

"No." She continued tracing her finger through the icing. "Mine never knew what happened to me. They died in their forties. Back then, that was a long life."

"Then why did mine have to die?"

She averted her eyes, concentrating on wiping the icing from her finger. "I'm sorry about your parents. Watching them die, that must have been terrible."

I reached across the table. "Kira, what aren't you

telling me?"

As painful as the memories of the fire were, I had to know the truth about why my parents had been ripped from my life. Only, Kira no longer seemed to be listening to me. The rosy color drained from her cheeks, and her hand trembled under mine.

Chapter Twenty-Six

Ariana

The defensive line took turns running into the cushioned wooden dummies. Coach Jackson stood in the center, yelling for them to strike harder, and a few of their groupies huddled together on the other side of the bleachers. At the far end of the field, past the football team, the cheerleaders set up to practice their routines. For everyone else, it was just another day.

Ben hadn't said a word since he'd shown me what would have been if hatred didn't exist, what could be if I agreed to help him. I let my head fall back. The sun felt comforting, beating down from the heavens on the unseasonably warm fall afternoon. Yet I couldn't stop shaking. Could life really be as it was in the images Ben had shown me?

He draped his wool pea coat over my shoulders. "Being a Blessed isn't so bad."

I let out a skeptical "Ha!" Being a Blessed meant giving up my humanity and leaving everything I knew and loved behind. It meant starting a war and letting innocent people die so Heaven and Hell could settle a millennia-old argument.

"No." I shook my head, like that was going to help reinforce my decision. Yet, if my sacrifice could bring world peace, shouldn't I do it?

"Someone will say yes." He sat next to me with his head bowed.

"You didn't."

He gave me a sidelong glance. "Not a day goes by that I don't regret my decision."

"Kira said no," I continued to argue, all the while reminding myself that Logan and I were a united front. We agreed that neither of us would do it. We'd find a way out of our roles.

"When you see her, ask her how that worked out for her." There was a bitter bite to his words.

"I won't do it." And I was ninety-nine percent sure I meant it.

"Logan will."

"No, he won't." I knew my brother. He would never be a part of something that resulted in the death of even his worst enemy. There had been a mistake. We were not the right siblings for this task.

Ben picked at a snag in his jeans. "I've been in his shoes. He might not want to, but when push comes to shove, he'll say yes."

Ben sat as still as a statue as he watched the field. It may have been the way the afternoon sun reflected off the metal bleachers, but he appeared to have a fine white light around him, an angelic glow. He spoke softly. "Logan will do it."

"You don't know him," I insisted.

"The Fallen will use you to get to him."

"But they can't hurt a Chosen."

"They can't *kill* a Chosen. They can kidnap you. Keep you somewhere you'd wish for death. They probably would have done it already if I wasn't here."

I gasped, hand over my mouth to keep from

screaming in terror.

"Do you think Logan will continue to refuse to do his part in the prophecy knowing that a demon is holding you against your will?" Ben looked me in the eye. "He'll say yes. I know because I would do anything to save my sister."

A tear slid down my cheek. I couldn't let Logan go to Hell for me. I wouldn't allow it.

"I'm sorry," Ben whispered, "for what will happen and for the part I'll play in it."

My mouth opened, void of any words. I'd never seen Ben so defeated. Something had changed since the last time we'd been together. I could almost taste it in the air, bitter and acidic. Life was never going to be the same, no matter what Logan and I did.

Chapter Twenty-Seven

Logan

The food court at the mall seemed to become deathly quiet.

"What is it?" I said and glanced around Kira and me.

I recognized a group of people from school. Ariana's best friend Becca was there. She and a guy in a black Linkin Park T-shirt held hands. On the other side of us, the woman in the red suit had been joined by a woman with bronze skin and short blonde hair. They looked away as soon as I looked at them, but it was obvious by their behavior they had been watching us. The second woman looked familiar.

Kira kept her eyes locked on mine. "How long have they been there?"

"Not long, I don't think." I held Kira's gaze, but my focus was on my peripheral vision and the women, trying to place where I'd seen the blonde before.

"They from back home?" I asked, looking down to show I wasn't talking about Tucson.

She nodded.

"Let's get out of here." I stood, pulling Kira up with me.

"Do you think they heard us?" Kira whispered after we'd left the food court. "I'm worse than dead if they did. Damn it! I know better than this. Never talk in the open. Crap!"

I glanced over my shoulder. "They're not following us. We're fine. You're fine."

"They don't need to walk behind us to follow us, Logan." She rubbed her temple. "We are so not fine! I'm going to be fried alive!" She threw out her hands, accidently knocking several items off a mall vendor cart.

A mother pulled her son closer to her as she walked by us.

"Kira, calm down," I whispered. "Where can we go?"

She inhaled a shaky breath. "The forest."

"Kira, I'm not driving to a secluded forest with demons on our ass."

"It's safe there. The area's protected." She grabbed my hand. "Come on, I'll show you why."

I couldn't help feeling that I had crossed some invisible line that screamed I shouldn't trust my own judgment when I accepted without question Kira's word that the forest was safer than being in the middle of a crowded mall. For all I knew, the Fallen could have been waiting for us. I could have been walking into the trap I'd been warned about.

By the time we pulled into the remote parking lot, the color was back in Kira's cheeks, and she had stopped trembling. She practically sprinted to the grove. There was no ambush waiting for us.

"Why do you like this place so much?" I leaned against the massive, dead elder tree. Its branches loomed ominously above us, the grass near it was now completely yellow, and more of the surrounding trees were turning black.

Kira rested a hand on my shoulder, and my vision heightened like someone had peeled a fuzzy film from over my eyes and I was seeing the forest around us for the first time.

Everything—the grass, the wildflowers, the feathers on a black bird some twenty feet in front of me—seemed unnaturally three dimensional. The foliage around us became a deeper shade of green than it had been a moment ago. I could see the veins running through each leaf as if I were looking at them through a magnifying glass. Drawn on the rough bark of several oak trees were symbols I hadn't seen before, and the ground around us was marked with white lines, some straight and some curved.

"The markings hide us from demons," Kira explained. "This is my quiet place for when I don't want to be found. Only a demon with the right access will be able to find it." She removed her hand from my shoulder, and the images around me disappeared. Everything else faded back to its normal muted colors.

"What about angels?"

"I threw in a few symbols to keep them out, too."

"A safe haven." I nodded in approval. I took my talisman out of my pocket and turned it over and over in my hand as I talked; the repetitive action helped calm my nerves.

"He must know—my boss—that I'm not following orders." She paced aimlessly. "Why else would he send Jazlyn and Tess here?" She paused. "Unless he's getting antsy. I hope that's it."

"Kira…" I knew I should have been just as worried about the other demons as she was, but I didn't see how their being there changed anything. It didn't make me more Chosen, and it wasn't going to make me change my mind and help them. "You said we're safe here. Is that true?"

"Yeah." She plopped down on the ground. "But we can't stay here forever."

"I know." But it bought us some time. I sat next to her. "It's killing me, knowing that you have answers about my parents' death and me completely in the dark."

"I only know pieces." She picked up a handful of acorns from the ground around her. "You've always been watched, by both Heaven and Hell. Every couple of months a demon who was topside would report in. From what I heard, for eight years nothing changed. You and Ariana were healthy. You lived in the same house. Your dad worked at the same place."

"That would be about right." We had a pretty average life.

"One day the demon said he couldn't get close to the children. The house was covered in angelic symbols."

"Like the ones you have in this clearing?" I looked around me, unable to see them now.

"Similar, yes." Kira whipped an acorn at an oak across from us. It hit and ricocheted to the right. "It pissed off the higher-ups. They didn't know if your parents had found out about the prophecy or what. My boss sent Tess to assess the situation."

"You mean burn down the house with my parents inside."

Kira shook her head. "She was instructed to find out what your parents knew, remove the markings, and leave. Tess talked to your father. He didn't know anything. She tried to remove the symbols but couldn't. Not with her powers or the fires of Hell. Not even with soap and water. So she got creative." Kira paused. "You sure you want to hear this?"

"No." I breathed in deeply. "But I need to."

Kira tossed another acorn, missing her target this time. "Tess decided if she couldn't wipe the house clean or burn it down, she'd get your father to do it. She tricked him into believing that the markings were demonic."

"Wait, he trusted a stranger?"

"Tess is the queen of deceit. I'm sure she had him believing she was a specialist from the church sent to save the world from demonic possession or something creative like that. What matters is she managed to convince your father that his only hope of shaking the demons after his family was to destroy everything."

"Could my father see the symbols?"

"No more than you could see the ones here without help, I'm sure."

"I don't get it. Why would my father start the fire while he was still in the house?"

"He probably thought he could get out." Kira's voice dropped to a whisper, like she didn't want to tell me what had happened next. "Only now that your parents knew about angels and demons, they were a liability. Tess fueled the flame with more oxygen, causing the house to burn faster."

My hands froze, the talisman flat in my palm. "What were the angels doing while all this was going on?"

Kira scrunched up her nose. "Trying to get you or

your sister to go inside the house, probably hoping the fire would negate the protective power of your birthmark."

"Son of a—"

She placed a hand on my knee. "I'm so sorry, Logan."

Eight years had passed since the day of that fire. Eight. I remembered the wall of heat that had kept me from trying to save my parents. Ariana's piercing screams still haunted my dreams. Hatred seared through me. Not just for the demon, Tess, who had trapped my parents in the house, but for the angels who had done nothing to save them.

"Hey, where'd you get that?" Kira asked, indicating the talisman with a nod.

"Ariana gave it to me for my birthday. Why?"

"May I see it?" I handed it to her. She ran a finger over the etchings. I only half-listened to her as she examined it. "I've heard of these, although I had my doubts that they existed. These markings are Nordic, carved into the bone of a Fallen Angel by the Archangel Michael."

"Wait!" I said, forgetting about the past for a moment. "Did you just say that talisman is made out of the bone of an angel?" I asked.

"Yeah." She giggled for the first time since we had seen the demons. "Do you have any idea what this can do?"

I shook my head, still trying to process that I'd been carrying the bone of an angel in my pocket.

She pinched the round center between her thumb and forefinger. A thin silver rod three times the length of the phoenix shot up between the tips of its wings.

Kira's lips tugged upward into a devious smirk. "This can kill a demon."

She held it out to me.

I touched the sharp point of the dagger gingerly. "It looks fragile."

"It's stronger than any metal known to man. It was carved in the image of the angels. Hold your finger on the body."

I did. The spear retracted. Looking at the talisman more closely, it did look more like an angel, its wings high over its head, than a bird.

"And it can kill demons?" I asked, amazed.

"It's not easy. You'd have to stab them through the heart, and it's not like they're going to line up and stand there while you do it. But slice one with this and it will sting, might even slow one down."

"I could kill Tess?"

"Logan"—she put her hands around mine—"I know you want revenge, but killing Tess is something that is easier said than done, and creating immortal enemies is not a smart idea. Trust me on that. But we can do the next best thing."

I turned the talisman over in my hand, contemplating just how hard it would be to stab a demon through the heart with the small dagger. If the archangels had truly intended this to be a weapon that could kill a demon, why make it so insignificant? Why not forge a sword? As much as I hated to admit it, Kira was right, I had little to no chance of killing Tess with the thing.

"What did you have in mind?" I asked.

"We send Tess, my boss, and the others to the deepest depths of Hell. Cage them in a part of the pit they can't escape from."

"I'm listening." Waiting to hear the catch.

"I found this incantation."

And there it was.

"Let me guess, I'm supposed to read it during some mysterious ceremony. You must think I'm an idiot."

"This is different." Her eyes pleaded with me to trust her, yet one of the first things she had said to me was not to trust her.

I rubbed the back of my neck, trying to ease the tension building there. A black bird landed on the branch of a maple. Its beady little eyes fixed on us. "I don't like the looks of that thing."

"It's just a bird."

I was beginning to think nothing was as it seemed, and being watched by a raven creeped me out. It made me question just how protected we were in the grove.

"I feel like a sitting duck."

"No one can find us here."

I wasn't so sure about that. I walked out of her safe zone. She followed.

"Logan, it's not the ceremony that opens the gates of Hell." She spoke urgently. "It's a few phrases spoken within a circle made of salt."

"Why don't you do it yourself?"

She stepped in front of me, forcing me to stop. "The spell sends everyone who isn't human back to Hell. That includes me. If I do it, I'll be trapped in a cage with a really pissed off Fallen Angel and his demon pets."

"And the Angels in Grace? How do we get around them?"

"We trap them. If we're lucky, it will take weeks,

maybe months, before the other angels realize something is wrong. It will give us time to find a way to truly disappear."

A branch snapped behind us. We spun around. Kira grabbed my hand. Another snap. Then a deer leaped across the path. I exhaled, relieved it wasn't the women from the mall or Kira's boss.

Yet Kira's nails dug into the palm of my hand. "Something's not right."

I listened. The forest seemed to listen, too. Dead silence answered.

"Come on." I pulled her forward.

We made it thirty feet. Maybe. Kira stopped.

"Another demon's here. They know." She turned, taking a couple steps back toward the clearing before stopping again. Tears streaked her cheeks. "I'll be begging for death when my boss is done with me."

"Kira," I whispered, keeping my voice low even though I couldn't see anyone. "Are you sure someone's here?"

"Yes! I can feel them."

"The symbols in the grove—" I grabbed her arms to get her to look at me. "Kira, are you sure they work?"

"Yes!" She glanced around us. "But we aren't in the grove, are we?"

If the grove really was a safe haven, then there was hope that whoever was here hadn't overheard our conversation. They wouldn't know how much Kira had shared with me or what direction we had come from.

"Act natural and follow my lead."

Kira bit her bottom lip.

I wiped her tears with the sleeve of my sweatshirt.

"Kira, trust me."

I pulled her forward in a playful manner. At the first sight of the gunmetal-blue paint of my car, I stopped and wrapped my arms around Kira's waist.

"One happy couple coming right up," I whispered into her ear. "Giggle."

She did, although it sounded more like the disbelieving titter a girl makes when she can't believe what she's about to do than a girl having a good time.

I grabbed her ass, pulling her even closer. "If you don't stop trembling, the demon is going to know we're acting."

Kira nodded. I laughed. She giggled again. We stumbled out of the clearing, and sitting there on the hood of a new black Mustang was the guy I'd seen at the mall with Becca. I was too shocked at seeing him to say anything.

"What are you two doing?" he asked.

I forced myself to snap out of my stupor. I stood behind Kira, arms around her. "Tell me you're not one of those losers who come to the forest preserve to get off."

"Bite me," he retorted.

My gaze bore into him. "Maybe we should find someplace else to hang out. This place has gotten crowded."

"Not so fast." He hopped off his car, eyes locked on Kira. "Where were you?"

"Messing around."

I'm not sure who looked more shocked by her statement, me or the guy from the mall. Kira went on.

"If you were hoping to watch, you're too late." She grabbed my hand. "Let's get out of here."

"Messing around?" I asked as we drove out of the forest preserve.

"It was the only thing I could think of that he wouldn't question."

"And *he's* a demon?"

"Yes."

"What is he doing with my sister's best friend?"

Kira froze, her hands halfway through pulling her hair away from her face. "That girl he was with is Ariana's friend?"

"Best friend." I floored it, putting as much distance between us and our unwanted company as I could. "Why is a demon dating her best friend?"

She shifted nervously in her seat. "Do you want the scary theory or the really scary theory?"

Chapter Twenty-Eight

Ariana

I was sitting on the couch doing homework when Logan got home. He looked as awful as I felt. He grabbed two sodas from the fridge and joined me in the family room.

"Your afternoon must have been as bad as mine." I closed my English book and set it on the coffee table. "I had a Blessed tell me we're screwed. You?"

"Three demons. Four if you count Kira. What's a 'blessed' or whatever you just said?"

"Four demons, no way!" I took the soda from him. "Did they say anything to you?"

"No. Kira and I hightailed it out of there. Blessed?"

"A servant of the angels, a.k.a Ben. Long story. Did Kira know there were other demons in town?" I asked.

"Nope." He popped the top on his can and chugged it.

"What'd they look like?" Even though I knew a demon who looked as human as I did, red skin, black eyes, and long discolored fingernails came to mind.

"The first two looked like typical power-hungry businesswomen." He paused, his mouth pulled down into a scowl. "The third was Becca's new boyfriend."

"What!" I jumped up, sprinting to the kitchen.

"Why didn't you call me the second you found that out?"

"I was a little busy at the time. Running, remember?"

I snatched my phone out of my purse and punched the number two to speed-dial Becca. "Why is a demon dating my best friend, Logan!"

He set his soda down on the coffee table—way too calmly, I might add. "Kira had a couple of theories. The scary one: to keep an eye on us. The really scary one: for leverage."

"You have got to be kidding me!" I'd never forgive myself if something happened to her. "First they messed up our lives, and now they plan on messing up our friends' lives? I'm so not going to let that happen."

One ring.

Logan swiveled so that he could see me. "Think about it. There's no way you'll say yes if they have Becca."

"How's *that* supposed to make me feel better?" I drummed my fingers on the counter. "Come on, Becca. Pick up."

"You can't tell her about the demons. Even if you did, she wouldn't believe you."

Five rings.

"I know." That didn't mean I couldn't try to look out for her.

"This ought to be good," he mumbled.

"Hey, Ariana." Becca sounded as if she was in a wind tunnel, like she was driving with the windows down.

"Hey, where are you?"

"Don't mention demons," Logan said from his seat

on the couch. His unruffled attitude was enough to make me want to throw the phone at his head just to get a reaction out of him.

I covered the receiver and retorted, "Duh!"

"With Justin," Becca practically squealed into the phone. "He surprised me! Isn't that cool?"

"Awesome." How was I supposed to get her away from him without sounding like I was trying to sabotage her happiness?

"We're grabbing dinner in the city." There was emphasis on the word *city*.

"No!" Darn it. What if he brought her to a nest or a den or whatever they called a place where demons gathered?

"Ariana, are you okay?" Becca asked.

Of course I wasn't okay. I wanted to shout into the receiver, *Your boyfriend's a monster—run!* Instead, I said, "We have that English paper due, and I really need your help with it."

"It's not due until next week."

"But we need to start it," I insisted. I didn't want her alone with him. "Please!" I begged.

"Smooth," Logan remarked. I turned my back to him.

"Ariana, seriously, is everything okay?" Becca's tone changed to one that emanated concern. The background noise disappeared, like she had rolled the windows up to hear me better. "Sweetie, are you and Ben on the outs again? Because you two make a cute couple. I know if you'd just talk to him—"

"I'm not on the outs with Ben." Not in the way she thought, at least. And I *had* talked to Ben, though what I'd learned hadn't been reassuring, not that I could tell her that. I bounced on the balls of my feet as I tried to think of something that would get her home.

"Ariana?" Logan took the phone from me. I didn't even know he had gotten up. He placed his hand over the receiver. "She'll be in more danger if Justin finds out we know what he is." To Becca, he said, "Hey, it's Logan." A pause. "Yeah. I just got home." Another pause. "It's my fault. The battery on my cell phone died, and I couldn't call her." Silence, and then, "Yeah. No problem." He flipped my phone shut. "She'll call you when she gets home."

Logan was right, although knowing that didn't make me feel any better. My legs were rubber. I went and sat back down on the couch. "If he hurts Becca…"

"I don't think he will. He's here to keep an eye on us."

Or use her for leverage. I wondered if Logan forgot he'd mentioned that. He sat next to me.

"How'd you know they were demons?" I asked.

"Kira recognized them. She was petrified. Said that her boss must be getting impatient if he sent them here. What happened with Ben?"

"He's sure the Fallen will find a way to get you to say yes." I told him what I'd seen when Ben kissed me, about how great things could be. "I've been thinking, maybe I should do it."

"No!" He swept a hand through his hair. "There's more to it than saying yes. Kira told me—"

"What she wants you to believe!" I snapped. "Have you stopped to think that she might be the one setting this trap you've been warned about? She made a deal with a Fallen Angel. She's bound to him, Logan. She's going to say whatever it takes to make you trust her."

"She's not the one pushing for me to complete the ceremony," he shot back. "If Kira can have fire sprouting out of the ground like a geyser by just wishing it to happen, think about what an army from Hell can do. We are *not* going to start this war."

Visions of Logan in the fiery Hell from my nightmares invaded my thoughts. Only now Becca and Justin were there, too, and I was alone to face what little future would be left once the war was over.

I drew my knees close to my chest, hugging them. "It's going to start eventually. If it's not us, it will be the next set of siblings. Think of the precautions the demons and angels will have added by then. Logan, we can't save the world, so I say we save ourselves. I was thinking that I should tell Ben I'll do my part as long as he promises to keep you and me and our friends safe."

Logan shook his head. "Ariana, Ben doesn't have the power to make a deal like that."

"We won't know unless we try."

"No. There's another way. There has to be." He placed a hand on my arm. "A united front, remember?"

I rested my chin on my knees and nodded. I admired my brother's optimism and determination, but I really felt he put way too much trust in what Kira had told him.

Everything that was happening to Logan and me was because of an argument between the angels. God's children having temper tantrums. God obviously had never heard of a timeout. Maybe if he had, his children wouldn't have pissed him off to the point he'd cast them out of Heaven and into Hell. We wouldn't be in this mess.

"Kira thinks the Fallen sent the other demons here

to make sure she's doing her job." Logan said, interrupting my meandering thoughts. He told me about the sigils on our childhood home, about the demons tricking our father into starting the fire that had taken his and our mom's lives, and about Kira's plan.

I sat in silence for a while, absorbing each word. In a way—although we'd never discussed it—I think we both realized something had trapped our parents in the house.

"You okay?" he finally asked. He had been reading one of the books we'd bought from the bookstore in Chicago.

I nodded. A tear slid down my cheek. "Logan, you do realize this incantation Kira mentioned could be *the* ceremony?"

"Yeah." He folded the top corner of a page to mark it.

"So we can't do it."

"I know, but we can let her help us trap the Angels in Grace."

Knowing that the Angels in Grace had tried to kill me and my brother right along with our parents made them a threat to us. It reinforced our need to disappear from all things supernatural.

"Then what?" I wanted to believe he would find a way out of this mess. That Ben was wrong. That it wouldn't come down to one of us agreeing to do our part in the ceremony. I could feel the tears welling up in my eyes. "Damn it! I'm sixteen years old! I should be worrying about the winter dance and after-parties and shopping, not avoiding some life-threatening war."

"I know, and I spent the last couple of hours thinking about this, and I came up with a plan of my own." Logan told me about it. "Are you with me?"

Chapter Twenty-Nine

Logan

If Kira was right about why the other demons were there, Ariana and I didn't have much time. Everything from that moment forward had to be planned and executed carefully. The first thing I did was call the shop in Chicago where I had gotten Ariana's pink bracelet and ordered two new ones: a light lavender one for her and a new tan one for me. The store owner agreed to overnight them to the apartment.

"Why do we need another bracelet?" Ariana asked from her perch on the kitchen counter.

"Variety."

She raised an eyebrow skeptically.

"Look, I don't know if this will work and I don't want to get your hopes up, but if the sigils in the grove can create a place to hide from demons, then maybe, if we were to draw them on the back of the bracelets, they will help us disappear."

"A shield we can wear." She gave a nod of approval as she studied her pale pink bracelet. "Couldn't we just do that now and run away?"

"If it doesn't work, then all we'll have done is let the Fallen know we are planning to run. He'll keep a closer eye on us than he already is. Maybe even—" I broke off, not wanting to think about the worst case scenario, but Ariana said it.

"Kidnap me and force you to cooperate."

"Yeah. Do you want to go over the plan again?" I asked.

"Not really."

We'd been over the plan several times in the past twelve hours, but we had to get it right. Hearing it one more time would do us both good. In theory, it was simple: trap the angels, evade the demons, and run. But I was still working on the logistics, like how we were going to get the angels together without the demons in town noticing.

"This is important." I leaned back against the counter across from her, a cup of coffee in hand.

She whined out a sigh. "I let Ben believe I'm considering agreeing to my role in everything. I try to get him to tell me more about the ceremony, specifically where it would be held."

"And whatever you do, don't kiss him."

The tips of her fingers touched her lips. "You know, if I think about it, I can still feel his lips on mine."

"I can identify with that." All I had to do was think about Kira's mouth pressed against mine and my lips warmed. I hadn't told Ariana that I'd kissed Kira since the day she'd shown me the images of Hell or that Kira could turn the visions on and off. "It's part of their powers. Kira chose to show me pure evil, and Ben chose to show you an unobtainable paradise."

She opened her mouth as if she was about to correct me but then closed it. When she didn't say anything, I voiced my concerns.

"If they can put images in our heads, what's to stop

them from putting thoughts in there, too? If they were to suggest we agree with them—"

"We could end up doing something we'd regret," she said. "I get it. It's like our power of suggestion celestialized."

And that wasn't a comforting thought. Ariana and I could get people to do things they normally wouldn't—steal, lie, walk into oncoming traffic—but we wouldn't. We didn't use our ability like that. Knowing that Ben and Kira had similar abilities was frightening knowledge. Not only could they make Ariana or me participate in the ceremony, they could turn us against each other. I guessed that the only reason they hadn't done exactly that was because they had to follow certain rules, a set of laws that kept them from using more of their powers on us.

I let Ariana drive to school. She did better that time. She remembered to stop at the stop sign on Middle Street and managed to avoid all the potholes. If she'd just taken the right-hand turns a little slower, my butt wouldn't have suction-cupped itself to the seat while she drove.

I didn't think our situation with the demons could get much worse, but as soon as I walked into fourth period, it did. The blonde-haired demon I'd seen at the mall sat at Mrs. Larson's desk. She wore a tan pantsuit. Her short blonde hair stuck out in all directions like she'd stuck her finger in an outlet, or maybe it was just the effects of centuries in Hell. A pair of mirrored sunglasses rested on the corner of her desk, and I suddenly remembered where we'd met—on the side of the road, only she wasn't a substitute teacher then; she was a cop pulling me over for speeding.

"Where's Mrs. Larson?" I asked.

"She had a family emergency," the demon replied without bothering to look up from the assignment notebook in front of her. I took my seat.

If I thought the demon had surprised me, it was nothing compared to Kira's reaction. She stopped in the doorway, looked over her shoulder as if thinking about leaving, took a step into the room and then a step back out, all before she squared her shoulders, raised her chin in the air, and marched over to our table.

"I take it you didn't know we have a sub today," I said when she sat down.

"No. I didn't." Kira quickly pulled her cell phone from her purse and sent me a text: *Careful what you say, she has incredible hearing. Did you tell Ariana?*

I nodded and texted back, *Is that Tess?*

The demon looked right at me, as if she could read my thoughts. Her eyes narrowed. I did my best not to squirm under her glare. Kira put on lip gloss, ignoring the scrutinizing eyes upon us. As soon as the demon turned her back to the class, Kira grabbed her phone.

No, that's Jazlyn.

If it had been Tess, I would have taken my chances and tried ramming my demon-killing dagger into her chest, to test its authenticity and avenge my parents' death in one shot. The demon—Jazlyn—scrawled a capital *M* on the board, making a loud grating noise with each curve and line. Several of our classmates chatted quietly amongst themselves.

Will you help me? Kira texted.

Yes.

That was the first time I lied to Kira. Considering I didn't know how much of what she had told me was true and how much was lies to get me to trust her, I wasn't sure how guilty I should feel about my own deceit. One thing I did know was that I needed Kira's assistance to trap the angels, and I didn't think I'd get it if I refused to help her.

Kira's fingers flew over the keyboard of her phone, stopping instantly when a stern *ahem* came from the front of the classroom. Jazlyn fixed Kira with a meaningful glare. "I'll take that phone."

Kira groaned and stood, but not before I saw her phone shutdown. She walked to the front of the classroom and placed it in Jazlyn's outstretched hand. I couldn't hear what they were saying, but from the way their eyes flicked my way I got the impression I was the topic of conversation.

I wondered if the other demon, Tess, was at school, too. Was she subbing in Ariana's classroom? Maybe the demons weren't going to take any chances on me not accepting what they deemed to be my destiny. I worried more for Ariana's safety than my own, because she was my weak spot. I'd do anything to keep her safe, and I had a feeling the Fallen knew that.

When Kira returned to her seat she barely looked at me. Jazlyn introduced herself to the class and instructed us to read chapter thirteen in our books.

"Let's study after school," I said a few minutes later, meaning, *You can tell me what that was all about, and then we'll plot against your superiors*. I was sure she understood the hidden agenda.

"I can't. I, um, need to do a little shopping. Let's do it tomorrow."

"The fate of"—I caught myself before I said "the world" and quickly changed my wording—"our grades are hanging on this, and you want to go to the mall?"

Even my fashion-conscious sister wouldn't think about shopping at a time like this.

In barely a whisper, she hissed, "There are things we're going to need. Trust me." She said the last two words in the same tone she'd used in the forest, only that time she had told me not to trust her. An unsettling chill slithered its way down my back, warning me that something wasn't right.

"Miss Rose, do you have a question on the assignment?" Jazlyn asked in a surly tone.

Kira shook her head.

"Then zip it and read."

Jazlyn paid closer attention to us after that. Kira's gaze remained fixed on the book in front of her for the rest of the class, but her eyes weren't moving from side to side, and she never turned the page.

Kira jumped up a moment before the bell rang, mumbled a hasty, "I'll catch up with you tomorrow," and was out the door before I had time to close my textbook.

****

After school, I parked by the football field and watched a parade of cars leave the student parking lot, looking for one person in particular. I saw Elaina Preble nearly back her car into John Kraft's SUV. Ariana got in a silver Scion tC, but not before she'd looked past the parking lot to where I waited. She gave me a discreet thumbs-up, which I took to mean our plan was on track. Finally, Kira's Eclipse filed in line with the rest of the cars. She took a left onto the main road. I followed at a distance, using traffic to keep my car hidden. When she turned down a small two-lane road, I lagged behind, keeping her taillights barely in view. The further we drove, the less traffic we passed.

We'd driven over an hour before Kira turned into a small dirt parking lot. A white brick building the size of a farmhouse stood there but looked abandoned. A faded sign in front of it told me it was once a church. It looked like something out of a Quentin Tarantino movie: a cold, square structure with no windows on the first floor and dirty, narrow windows on the second. The stairs leading to the weathered double doors in front of the building looked as if they should have been condemned.

There was nothing around us but prairie, tall weeds, and a dilapidated white bus with busted-out windows. I pulled off the road, hiding my car behind a large faded billboard for an auto repair shop in town. Kira parked next to a black Lincoln Navigator and got out. A moment later, the driver of the Lincoln got out, too. It only took a second to recognize Tess. They walked around to the front of their cars. If they weren't in an empty parking lot in the middle of nowhere, I might have thought they were old friends catching up with what was happening in each other's lives.

All Kira's talk about wanting to help me: lies. She'd been playing me for a fool. I cursed under my breath, anger seething in me. The weight of my talisman in my pocket became obvious. Kira's words, *This could kill a demon,* played over and over in my head like a bad recording. I opened my car door, cringing when the familiar creak of the old hinges pierced the silence. I watched Kira and Tess; neither looked in my direction.

When I was sure they hadn't heard me, I sprinted

through the tall weeds to the side of the church, coming to a stop just out of sight. I gripped the talisman in my right hand as I concentrated on slowing my ragged breathing.

"God, please let this work," I muttered as I pinched the body of the bone-angel. The blade extended with a soft *shhffttt* sound.

But did I have what it took to end another person's life?

The answer was simple: no, I didn't. But, then again, Tess wasn't human, and I could kill monsters.

Tess was the reason my parents were dead, I reminded myself. It was her fault Ariana and I had lost our family and had been forced to be alone. I'd ram the silver instrument into her back. The bittersweet taste of satisfaction rose within me just knowing I was about to avenge my parents' deaths. The glory of it was quickly choked out of me, however, when I looked at Kira. She wore a serious expression as she nodded at something Tess said.

Even now seeing Kira talking to the demon who had murdered my parents, I couldn't stop myself from believing she wasn't evil. That somewhere deep inside of her still lived the girl who had unknowingly sold her soul to save her brother. But if that were the case, she wouldn't have been talking to Tess, would she?

I fast-walked hunched over to the stairs near the front entrance and ducked behind them. I was about to run over to the Navigator when the skin on my wrist seared with excruciating pain. I clenched my teeth to keep from screaming. In the parking lot, Tess shifted her weight from one foot to the other, but she didn't turn around to face me. Kira shook her head at something Tess said. Both demons seemed unaware of my presence, so I looked around me, wondering if someone else was there. The air grew thin. Nonexistent. I dropped my only weapon and grabbed my throat, gasping for oxygen. This may have been my only chance to kill Tess, and I'd blown it. Ariana wouldn't know where I was or what had happened to me. My legs gave out, and I fell to the ground. My lungs burned, and my vision blurred. With no other choice, I gave in to the vertigo and passed out.

Chapter Thirty

Ariana

"Damn it, Logan! Where are you?" I slid my phone shut. My neighbors came and went, paying little attention to Ben and me. A frigid wind attacked the mild fall afternoon, bringing with it a growing sense of uncertainty.

"You shouldn't swear." Ben had his back against his car, almost looking bored, but I knew he was just giving me space while I tried to reach my brother.

My wrist still stung from the unexpected burning sensation I'd felt a few minutes ago. Ben and I had just reached my apartment complex when I'd screamed, clutching my wrist as if my hand had been chopped off. The pain had to mean Logan was in trouble.

I let out a string of cuss words and stuffed my cell phone into my back pocket. My wrist still felt as if it was on fire.

"I swear when I'm angry, okay!" With less of a bite, I added, "It's not like Logan to ignore my calls."

I paced aimlessly, blinded by worry. At one point, Ben's fingers wrapped around my arm, tugging me to the curb and out of the path of Jim Baker's sedan. Mr. Baker looked as if I'd just taken ten years off his life, face white and eyes wide. I offered an apologetic wave for wandering into the street as he drove by.

Ben took my chin in his hand and turned my face so that I was looking at him. "I'm sure Logan's fine." He'd already told me this.

"How can you be?" My mind kept going to the worst possible scenarios: Logan sliced open by the horned beasts of my dreams; Logan trapped in a burning building, his flesh bubbling off; Logan cornered at the edge of a cliff, wild dogs in front of him and jagged rocks below him.

"Ariana." Ben's fingers laced through mine. A calmness filled me, starting in my trembling hand and traveling swiftly to my toes. I knew the relief that flooded me was Ben's doing. I tightened my grip on his hands, afraid if I let go my legs would lose their strength and I'd crumble to the asphalt panic-stricken that Logan was dead. Ben stepped behind me, sliding me even closer until I was cradled in his arms. "I can still sense his presence," Ben said. "He's fine. Concentrate. You'll know I'm telling the truth."

I closed my eyes and focused on Logan, but he was too far away. I couldn't feel the tug of our connection. I let out a whimper.

"If something happened to him, it would feel like a piece of you is missing," Ben added, sending a new wave of calm through me with a tender squeeze.

I concentrated harder. I definitely felt whole. There had to be a logical explanation for why Logan wasn't answering my calls, one that didn't have him dead in a ditch at the feet of some monster.

He could have left his cell phone in the car, I reasoned with myself.

I shifted so that I could see Ben's eyes. "Are you sure you can still sense his presence?"

"Positive." Ben kept his arms around me as if he knew I'd have a full-blown panic attack if he let go. "I've been a Blessed for a long time. I know how to zero in on a Chosen."

I forced myself to trust that Ben could still sense Logan even though I couldn't. That didn't mean I was ready for him to let go of me and lose the angelic sedative he provided. Nor did it mean I wouldn't keep trying to reach Logan the way a normal human would—on his phone—every few minutes.

"How long have you been a Blessed?" I asked, surprised I hadn't thought to ask this sooner.

"A very, very long time."

An evasive half-answer; why didn't that surprise me? I tried Logan again. The call went straight to voicemail.

Before my birthmark had gone inferno hot on me, Ben and I had been discussing—not too calmly—the fact that he knew what Justin was and hadn't told me.

"I saw no point in worrying you needlessly," he had said, among other lame excuses. It seemed silly to go back to that argument now that I clung to him as if my life depended on it.

"If I do it, and that's a big *IF,* I want to know everything about the ceremony. What I'll have to do, where I have to do it, and what happens afterward."

"Wait, you'll do it?" He shifted so that he could see my eyes. "Why the sudden change of heart?"

"I *might,*" I reiterated.

He kept his arms around my waist, pumping in a continuous supply of angelic feel-good agent. Logan was right; with the slightest suggestion, Ben could easily make me want to help him. But that wasn't what this was about. I needed Ben to believe I was close to saying yes. It was part of Logan's and my plan, but what I hadn't discussed with Logan was Plan B. If it came down to Logan or me having to accept our destiny, I would make sure I was the one to participate in the ceremony. Not just because I didn't want to see what type of creatures would walk out of Hell's doors. "Logan's good. Better than I'll ever be. I don't want him being dragged to the pit. I won't let that happen."

Ben glanced down as he wet his lips. "I don't have the details. I'll get them. Will you be okay if I leave?"

I nodded. He slowly released me, making sure I didn't fall apart again. Satisfied, he got in his car. As soon as he left, I tried Logan again. Still no answer. I closed my eyes and concentrated. I still felt whole. I went upstairs and tried to keep busy with housework.

I must have called Logan another twenty times before he finally picked up, and, when he did, it sounded as if I'd woken him. I turned off the water in the kitchen so that I could hear him better.

"Logan, where are you!?" I blurted into the receiver.

"Um." There was a pause, broken only by a few grunts. Then he said, "At church."

I actually moved the phone away from my ear to make sure there was nothing covering the speaker part. "What?"

"It's a long story. What time is it?" I heard his car door close with its usual groan.

"Are you kidding me?" I placed the dish I'd been washing into the drying rack. "Logan, have you been drinking?"

"No." The Camaro's engine roared to life in the

background. "Just tell me what time it is."

I checked the clock on the microwave. "Nine thirty. I've been calling you for hours."

"I'm on my way home. I'll explain when I get there."

I had a cup of hot chocolate waiting for Logan when he walked in carrying an orange bag from the hardware store. He always made me hot chocolate when I'd had a bad day. "Hot cocoa fixes everything," he would say as he'd drop in extra marshmallows.

I wished it were true.

"Thanks." He smiled when he saw the small marshmallows floating at the top of the mug.

The right side of his face was scraped up, and he had dirt and dried blood in his hair. His clothes were dusty, as if he'd rolled around in the dirt. I rushed out of the room to get a washcloth. He was sitting on the couch when I got back, his mug held tight between his hands.

"What happened to you?" I lowered myself onto the cushion next to him and gently pressed the damp cloth to his forehead. He winced.

"I'm not sure." He took the washcloth from me, frowning when he saw the dirt and dried blood on it. "I got a bad feeling when I was talking to Kira today, so after school I decided to follow her. You know, to see what she was up to. She met up with Tess at this old, out-of-the-way church. I think she's been playing me."

That was something I'd considered days ago, but Logan was miserable enough without me pointing this out.

"Odd place for demons to meet, don't you think?" I myself liked the standard belief I got from movies. The

229

ones that led people to believe demons couldn't walk on hallowed ground, that they'd burst into flames. "What happened? Could you hear what they said? Did they see you?"

"No and no. Last thing I remember is getting ready to stab Tess—"

"You were going to do what!?" He could not have just said he'd tried to stab a powerful supernatural creature.

"She killed our parents, Ariana. She deserves to die."

"Logan, I have no problem with demons dying, but I'm sure killing one is not as easy as just stabbing it to death."

"They can't kill us, remember. We're protected."

"That doesn't mean we should provoke them. Geesh!" I scooped my bangs off my face and fell back against the couch. "What were you going to use?" Last I'd checked, Logan didn't carry a knife in his pocket.

He tossed the washcloth on the table. "The talisman you gave me."

My jaw dropped. "Have you completely lost your mind? Gone certifiably insane? What were you going to do, poke her eye out with the wings?"

"It's a dagger." He held up a hand in an I-know-what-you're-going-to-say manner. "I swear, the trigger is the body of the angel—"

"Don't you mean phoenix?"

"It's not a bird. Press the center and a long silver dagger shoots up between the wings. It's amazing and incredibly light and unbelievably strong."

"No way. Let me see!" I jumped to the edge of the couch, ready to see the impossible.

"Love to, but I lost it."

"How? Did Tess take it? Is that why you look like you lost a fight with a tree?" I picked a twig and dry leaf out of his hair.

He shook his head. "I don't know. One minute I was sneaking up on Tess and Kira, and the next I was struggling to breathe. Things went black. I don't remember anything after that until you called. Tess and Kira were gone, and so was the dagger."

I leaned forward, elbows on my knees and head cradled in my hands. "I knew something was wrong. I just knew it. My birthmark burned, and I couldn't reach you. I thought one of my dreams had come true."

"I'm sorry I worried you."

I nodded, knowing he'd never do it on purpose. "The talisman is really some demon-killing dagger?"

"That's what Kira said. It's not made out of a polished stone either. It's the bone of a Fallen Angel."

Okay, I had to let that one sink in a moment. My emotions sprinted through a state of utter awe to grossed out to elated in a matter of seconds. "If she's right, if it really is made out of the bone of a Fallen Angel, that means—"

"—they can die," Logan and I said at the same time.

He drank half his hot cocoa. "I still can't believe Kira met up with Tess. She seemed terrified of her at the mall." He tilted his mug, watching as the creamy chocolate got closer and closer to the edge. "I just don't get why she'd tell me what she is or about the prophecy if she was trying to trick me."

He didn't get it because he wasn't thinking like a girl. "She needed to gain your trust. You already knew something was up, and you had a pretty good idea she was involved somehow. So she admits it. Tells you she's having cold feet and that she wants to switch sides and help you. Who knows how much of what she said were lies."

"I really wanted to believe her."

"I know."

He rubbed the side of his head. "Damn, there's a bump."

"Wait here." I hopped off the couch. In the kitchen, I filled a baggie with ice. It was like Ben had said: the demons would find a way to make him participate. I handed the baggie to him as I sat back down.

I was feeling less and less confident that our plan would work. Who was to say there wasn't a higher power listening to us right then? Knowing that the only thing stopping them from dragging us off to this war of theirs was the rules of some prophecy was not comforting. Like angels and demons were so against bending the rules for the greater good.

"What do we do now?" I asked.

"We stick to the plan. Did Ben tell you where the ceremony would be?"

"He didn't know, but he's going to find out." I looked in the orange bag on the coffee table. "What's the black light for?"

"I'll show you." He snatched the book on sigils off the coffee table. "There are special markers in the bag, too. The ink can only be seen under the black light. Grab one, will you?"

I tore open the packaging and handed him the red marker. Next, I grabbed the black light and followed him into the hallway. He waited for Mrs. Harker, the old lady down the hall from us, to enter her apartment.

"Turn the light on and point it at the wall near the door."

"What are you doing?"

"Turning our apartment into our personal safe haven." He opened the book to the first dog-eared page. "These symbols are used for different types of protection." He pointed to a picture of an eye drawn inside of a triangle that was drawn inside of a circle. "This one protects against demonic spirits. When drawn on the door, demons can't enter."

I switched on the light, shining it on the door. "What does this one do?"

"What does—" He glanced up and his jaw dropped.

In the center of our cream-colored door was a sigil: four separate squiggly lines encased in a double circle. It was faint, like it had been there a long time.

"I didn't draw that," he said.

I moved my hand around, shining the purple-black glow on different parts of the wall. "How about the one above the door?"

His gaze moved upward. The symbol above the door resembled a fancy *M*. He shook his head. "I recognize that one, though." He flipped through the pages of the book. "Here! It keeps angels out. According to this, they can't walk under it." He flipped through a few more pages. "And the sigil on the door weakens a person's aura, making them hard for an angel to sense. I bet it counteracts our birthmarks and makes us harder to track."

"I doubt Ben would draw sigils on the door to keep the good guys out," I said as I checked the rest of the wall. There were no other markings. "Think it was Kira?"

"Maybe. Or Tess. This just confirms one thing."

"What's that?"

"Someone else believes these things work." He uncapped the marker and flipped back to one of the pages he had dog-eared. "Let's add a few more."

I held the light on the door as he drew two symbols to ward off demons and a sigil that was supposed to hide our presence from them.

An amazed giggle slipped through my lips. "Who would have thought you can stop an angel or a demon with a little ink and a few lines."

"Be thankful there is a way to stop them."

When we were done, Logan had drawn six symbols to protect against demons and four to protect against angels.

The symbol that someone else had drawn on our front door was also above the patio door and bedroom window. We added ours to these locations, too.

"What if you used the wrong symbols?" I asked as we stepped back inside. "What if some of them make us easy targets?"

"I thought about that." He tossed the book on the kitchen table. "Our birthmarks make us easy targets. There isn't much we can do to make that worse. And I drew enough symbols around our apartment that even if one or two are used for drawing a higher power nearer, the others would cancel it out."

"We're putting a lot of trust in the unknown these days. You realize that, don't you?"

He sat down. "I'm putting a lot of trust in you and me. I'd bet everything I had, even my life, that I'm making the right choice."

Seeing as we were up against higher powers, he *was* betting his life.

And mine, too.

Chapter Thirty-One

Logan

The next day, I was pissed at myself for believing Kira's lies, at Kira for playing me for a fool, and at the disembodied voice for waking me forty-seven minutes before the alarm was set to go off just to offer more garbled hints of what was to come: *"Desperate," "Things aren't right," "Careful."* No shit everyone was desperate. Things hadn't been right for as long as I could remember. And what did *careful* mean? Like Ariana and I weren't being careful. I imagined the next thing it was going to tell me was to stay away from the light. I decided the voice had to be my guardian angel. If there was such a thing as an Angel Hotline, I'd report mine as completely and utterly useless.

I wanted to be done with Tess, Jazlyn, and Kira's boss. The only way to do that was to follow the plan. Stage one, letting Ben believe Ariana was willing to go through with the ceremony, was complete. Stage two involved getting our affairs in order. First thing on my list was to take care of the bill for our storage unit. There wasn't much left there: my uncle's tools—now my tools—and boxes of memories I hadn't looked at in more than a year. Still, it was our stuff. I didn't want to lose it.

Then there was school. I had enough credits to

graduate in December. I'd do the work remotely, special arrangements like the school had done for Jimmy Armstrong after a car accident had left him in traction for three months. Ariana's schooling would be more difficult. If I talked to the right people though, I was sure I could figure out a way to get her enrolled in homeschooling.

Stage three was where it got tricky. We had to get Ben and his angel buddies together, trap them before they realized Ariana hadn't actually said yes, and get out of Dodge before the demons suspected anything. To make that more difficult, Kira was the only one who knew how to trap an angel, and Ariana and I hadn't told her about the plan, nor could we because, let's face it, she worked for demons.

I wasn't sure if I should confront Kira, tell her I saw her talking to Tess, and demand an explanation. But I didn't want to hear her excuses. I already had enough of her bullshit to sift through. I felt as if I was searching for a nugget of truth in the sea of lies.

In the end, I did what any mature male would do when he didn't know what to say to a member of the opposite sex. I avoided her.

And it worked, until school let out.

"You weren't in foods." Kira sat on the back bumper of my car. The sun reflected off her hair, making it look like curls of fire dancing in the breeze.

"I had something I needed to do." The storage unit was now mine for the next ten years. I'd figured since I'd been there telling the guy he wanted to show it as paid, I might as well cover it for as long as I could.

"I thought we were getting together today." She moved so I could put my backpack in the trunk.

"I can't."

"What?"

"I made plans." I slammed the trunk shut and continued in an acid tone, "Figured you'd be busy sneaking off to another top-secret meeting with the demon who killed my parents."

She lowered her voice. "You know, following me yesterday was about the dumbest thing you could have done."

"You knew?"

"Of course I knew. Your birthmark makes it so that I can track you. Duh!" She crossed her arms over her chest. "I could have kicked myself for thinking I didn't have to focus on your whereabouts for one afternoon. I was so frickin' nervous about what Tess wanted that I didn't realize you'd followed me until it was too late. I'd already pulled into the parking lot."

"Why didn't you just tell me you were meeting with her?" *Unless you had something to hide.*

"Because I was afraid you'd go and do something stupid. And guess what?" she asked in a sarcastic pitch. "You did."

"Whatever." I unlocked my door. "Kira, I don't have time for any more of your games, okay? I have somewhere I need to be."

In a movement faster than I could see, she snatched my keys from me. "You can spare ten minutes so I can explain. You owe me that."

"I don't owe you anything!" I grabbed for my keys and missed.

Her gaze moved to something behind me. When I started to turn around, she whispered. "Kiss me."

"What?" I shook my head. "I'm not going to—"

"We're being watched."

"I don't care." I tried to grab my keys again.

"Yes, you do," she said in a husky whisper. My mind went fuzzy, struggling with wanting to obey her and wanting to tell her to go to hell. The former won.

Her lips were way too warm, but instead of pushing her away, I pulled her closer, lifting her to her toes. Her fingers tangled in my hair, trapping me in front of her. Her kiss was intoxicating. One by one, my nerve endings came alive. I never wanted to stop kissing her. There was a small part of me that knew Kira was controlling my mind, but I didn't care.

This time, Kira showed me Tess's beady black eyes watching us from the glass doors that led to the auditorium. I took it as Kira's explanation for why she forced me to *want* to kiss her. Somehow I knew that Tess didn't just happen to be leaving school at the very moment Kira and I were talking. Kira was being kept on a very short leash. As we kissed, I began to feel like I *had* to hear what she wanted to tell me, yet that didn't stop me from thinking that it sucked to have someone controlling my thoughts.

Through all of this, I felt a familiar tug in my gut become increasingly stronger. Ariana was near.

"Uh hmm." Ariana stood behind me. Ben was next to her.

I let go of Kira, and she stepped to my side.

"What the hell, Logan," Ariana snapped as she pushed by me and threw her backpack into the car.

"It's not what it looks like." I had just told Ariana the day before not to kiss Ben because he was a Blessed and could mess with her head, and there I was making out with a demon. Kira grabbed my hand, and I forgot what I was about to say next.

Ben's eyes narrowed as he glared at Kira. "The Fallen know you're using mind control on one of the Chosen?"

Kira's eyes grew wide. "Shut up, Ben!" She walked over to the passenger door. "Shall we?"

"Mind—" Ariana started to say.

"We're going to grab something to eat," Ben said, interrupting her. He placed a hand on the small of her back.

I grabbed Ben's arm. I didn't want my kid sister going anywhere with him. Not with how effortlessly they could control our thoughts.

But before I could protest, Ben said, "She'll be fine. I promise. Let me go."

I did. Not because Ben promised Ariana would be safe with him or because Kira was waiting for me. I did it because Ben used his powers to make me want to let him go. It infuriated me. And Ben didn't just get me to release him; though I wanted to kick my tire in frustration or slam my hand down against the car, I couldn't. It was like Ben had also told me to remain calm.

Ariana looked at me, confused, but she let Ben lead her away.

Kira and I got in my car. I glanced next to me about to demand answers, starting with what she'd been doing with Tess at a church, but stopped myself. She had her hands in her lap, her fingers twisting nervously together. Her eyes were focused on the floorboard in front of her. I started the car instead and got in the line of others leaving for the day. Tess was just outside the doors to the auditorium, arms folded over her chest and a disapproving scowl on her face.

Once on the road, I asked, "Why's Tess watching you?"

"She doesn't believe I have the situation under control."

"The situation being me?" I asked for clarification.

"Yeah." Kira wiped her palms on her jeans. "She wants me pulled from the assignment."

I looked sideways at her, not sure if she should get an award for her acting abilities or if I should believe her.

"How much of what you've told me is true?" My fingers curled around the gearshift. Once again, Kira's fear of her superiors had shaken my hard exterior and thrown a wrench into my plans to forget I'd ever met her. The betrayal and hatred I'd harbored toward her since I'd seen her talking to Tess mixed with compassion and the desire to help her, and these emotions were all mine—no demon mind tricks involved. Even though I knew I *shouldn't* trust Kira, I did. I wanted so badly to believe that despite her situation, she was good. That despite everything she'd been through in Hell, evil hadn't seeped into her soul. I needed to believe that if things went south for Ariana and me and I was sent to the pit that I wouldn't turn into a heartless monster.

I turned right at the light, no destination in mind.

"Logan, I haven't lied to you."

I was sure she hadn't told me the whole truth either. "Why meet out in the middle of nowhere. Why not just talk at school or grab a cup of coffee?"

Kira let out a nervous laugh, the type someone does when they're busted. "Tess won't talk at school.

She swears the angels have spies there. I mean, besides Ben. What were you doing following me anyway?"

"Seeing if I could trust you."

"You have got to be kidding me!" She threw her hands up in the air. "That's great. Just great. I could be burned alive for all of eternity if they find out how much I've told you, and you don't even believe me."

I shrugged, not convinced she didn't have an ulterior motive behind everything she said.

"We're being followed," she announced without having to turn around to check.

I glanced in my rearview mirror. "Who?"

"Black Navigator, two cars back."

I slammed my foot down on the accelerator, blowing through a yellow light. The car behind me stopped, forcing the Navigator to stop, too.

Kira looked between the seats and out the rear window. "She'll just catch up again."

"Can she hear through metal and glass?"

"No," Kira replied, annoyance dripping from the word.

"Then let her." I drummed my fingers on the steering wheel. "What did Tess want yesterday?"

Kira sighed. "The Fallen is tired of waiting. He wants the ceremony performed the day after next. If I can't convince you to cooperate, Tess is to do it."

I looked at her. "Meaning?"

"If she has to hold a gun to your head to get you to perform the ceremony, she will."

"When were you going to tell me this?" I took another right. "Kira!"

"I've been trying to buy us more time!"

I hit my palm against the steering wheel. How were

Ariana and I going to slip out of town with all these demons showing up, and where the hell were the angels? "I'll die before I go through with the ceremony."

"Tess realizes that. You're not the one she'll hurt." Kira sat back in her seat. "Don't let Ariana go anywhere without either you or Ben as an escort."

Every muscle in my body tensed. "If anyone so much as lays a finger on her," I growled.

"Those in Hell can smell the impending war. They grow impatient, Logan. They want out, and, quite honestly, I think the Fallen wants them out."

"I could have killed Tess," I said, glancing in my rearview mirror. The only cars behind us were a Chevy Impala and a pickup truck. "If only—"

"You managed to sneak up on a senior demon?"

"Wait, that was you yesterday at the church? You're the reason I passed out?"

"Damn straight it was me. Tess thinks I'm wasting time, and she's not wrong. I've been stalling. She wanted me to bring you with me so that she could talk to you. I refused. So what do you do? You go and try to deliver yourself to her. Do you have any idea what she would have done if you'd managed to stab her?"

"Die," I said, offering her my guess.

"All you would have done was piss her off more than she already is."

"She'd be dead if I managed to hit her heart," I insisted.

"Big *if*. And if you failed, she would have used your weapon to carve you a new one. You don't have to be in one piece to participate in the ceremony."

I took a right at the next intersection, heading back

toward school.

"I'd just heal. The birthmark would see to that." My brash reply was all nerves talking. "Does she have my talisman?"

"No. She wasn't expecting you, so she wasn't paying that much attention to her surroundings."

I held out my hand. "Give it to me."

Kira shifted in her seat. "I don't have it in my back pocket."

I huffed, sure she wouldn't let it that far out of her sight. "Your boss put a deadline on this. In two days, right?"

She nodded.

"Will he be there for the ceremony?"

The Navigator was behind us again.

"He has to be. From what I understand, he's the only one who knows how to perform it."

"And this incantation of yours, you're sure it will send him back to Hell?"

"Yes."

"Kira, if you're screwing with me, if this is your way of tricking me into the ceremony—"

"I'm not. I swear. Logan, if my boss is trapped in Hell, then I'm free to stay here."

"Until he gets out."

"*If* he gets out."

We'd driven a full circle. I pulled into the student parking lot; most of the cars were gone. I parked next to Kira's Eclipse. Tess stopped at the corner and turned the opposite direction. I wondered if she thought she was being clever. Kira and I got out of my car, and I walked around to the passenger side.

"I want my talisman back," I said.

Kira slung her backpack over her shoulder and dug around in her purse. "If the demons find out you have this thing, they're going to barge into your apartment to get it. They don't take kindly to objects that can kill them."

"I'll be ready." I held out my hand. Besides, the sigils Ariana and I had drawn around our apartment would keep them out.

She glanced up at me. "What was your plan last night? Kill Tess and then what?" When I wouldn't meet her gaze, she asked, "Were you going to kill me, too?"

I thought about lying, but I didn't. "I wasn't sure what I was going to do with you."

She pulled the talisman from her purse, triggering the dagger. "Do it."

I glanced down at the silver dagger and then back up into her eyes. I couldn't move. My muscles froze as my mind whirled.

She pressed the bone handle into my hand and closed my fingers around it. "You'd be freeing me from my contract with the Fallen. My soul will finally be at rest." Her voice was soft. Tired. She raised her chin and closed her eyes. "Just make sure you hit my heart because I'm not going to promise getting stabbed isn't going to piss me off."

It wouldn't take much effort to kill Kira. She stood in front of me, half an arm's length away. I shouldn't trust her. She was too tuned in to my whereabouts for my own good. But killing her wouldn't end the war. It wouldn't make Tess and the other demons disappear. It wouldn't protect Ariana. I pressed the center, withdrawing the dagger. Kira's expression was a mix of relief and regret: half glad to be alive and half sorry I hadn't ended her eternity of servitude.

She opened her car door and turned to face me. "I wasn't lying when I told you I wished you were a jerk. It would make my job easier. Don't become one."

Chapter Thirty-Two

Ariana

Knowing that your boyfriend isn't human tends to put a damper on a spontaneous date to the mall or the movies or even a romantic walk along the river. Stinks even more when you know the reason he was interested in you in the first place was because you're Chosen. Like being Chosen isn't a totally sucky thing to be.

Logan was in the same sinking boat as I was. I couldn't believe he'd made out with Kira knowing what we did about her, and while Ben had said that Logan hadn't had a choice, it still burned me up inside.

Ben did say that he hadn't *had* to ask me out. He'd done that because he wanted to get to know me. As part of the whole angelic thing Blesseds have going is they can't lie, I believed him. But why did he want to get to know me? So we could spend eternity being the puppets of angels, creatures that were just as responsible for my parents' deaths as the demons.

The whole Chosen-demon-Blessed thing had my emotions more tangled than my hair gets on a windy day. *Chosen* sounds as if it should be a good thing, but it's not. Demons are bad, yet Kira wasn't. Not entirely anyway. Blesseds are the closest thing a human can get to becoming an angel, yet, as far as I could tell, the only thing that separated a Blessed from a demon was who they reported to. The Who's Who of the celestial world reminded me of the hierarchy at school. Only, I couldn't tell who made the better freaks, the Blesseds or the demons.

Ben dropped me off at my apartment complex just before five. I stopped at the mailboxes in the lobby, fumbling in my purse for my keys. The ability to move things with my mind would have been a nice power to have. I could have unlocked our slot with a wave of my hand instead of having to figure out how my keys always ended up buried under all my other crap.

"Ariana. How are you?"

I looked up to see my elderly neighbor. "Hi, Mrs. Harker. How's your leg?"

"Much better, thanks for asking." She unlocked her mailbox. "Quite a tasty dish you're seeing these days."

"Dish?" I giggled.

"Mr. Harker wasn't a bad dish." She smiled fondly.

My fingers wrapped around the miniature pen on my keychain. A moment later, I had my mail slot open. I yanked a white box out of it. It was for Logan.

I listened to Mrs. Harker tell me just how dashing her Wilber looked in a tie as we walked up the three flights of stairs together.

"You're such a sweet girl." Mrs. Harker patted my hand. "You make sure that boy treats you right."

"I will." If Logan's plan worked, I wouldn't be seeing him much longer, though.

"Stop by this weekend. I'm baking chocolate chip cookies. Lord knows my hips don't need me eating the entire batch by myself."

"Mrs. Harker, you still have the figure of a woman in her thirties."

She patted my hand. "Like I said, you're a sweet girl."

She continued down the hall to her apartment. I went inside mine.

Logan got home after six. He found me in the basement laundry room folding a pile of clothes.

"Hey," he said with a guarded expression.

"Did you and Kira get a room?" I hoped my anger rolled off me and crashed into him like a cartoon anvil.

"Not funny, Ariana." He walked over to the dryers and grabbed one of his T-shirts.

"'Don't kiss Ben,'" I said, my voice deeper to mock him. "'He might put thoughts in your head.' And then I see you and Kira are swapping spit in the parking lot."

"It wasn't like that."

I slammed the sweater I'd folded on top of a pile of laundry. "Then what was it like?" Despite what Ben had told me, I needed to hear it from Logan.

He ran a hand over his hair. "Imagine our mind control turned up ten notches."

I set another shirt on the pile. "Ben said she could get in a lot of trouble for using her powers on you."

He snorted. "Ben's a hypocrite."

I tilted my head to the side. "What do you mean?"

"He used his powers to get me to let go of his arm."

And to keep Logan from making a scene in front of the demons watching us; I was sure of that. Ben had been livid when we'd left school. "The rules are clear," he had mumbled. "No powers." He'd ranted something in Latin or Nordic or whatever language was spoken in Heaven. Then, in English: "Impulsive! Impossible! She doesn't think!" I'd been quiet. Unsure what to say and when he would be calm enough to answer my questions. It was clear he cared about Kira even if she was on the opposite team. For several minutes, I'd been convinced Ben had forgotten I was in the car with him.

I tossed the next load of laundry into the dryer. The smell of fabric softener filled the room.

"What did it feel like when she was controlling your mind? Ben swears he's never done that to me, but I wonder if I'd know."

"You would," Logan assured me. "Even though I knew she was controlling my thoughts, I couldn't get myself to care. And then when I was about to explain my actions to you, Kira touched my hand, and I couldn't remember what I was going to say."

He grabbed the laundry basket and told me about his conversation with Kira as we headed up to our apartment. "The Fallen has given Kira two days."

"Two days!?" I wasn't ready to say goodbye to my friends, but what choice did I have. Becca's Prince Charming was a demon, and it was my fault that he was in her life. The longer I stuck around, the longer she was in danger.

I unlocked the door to our apartment.

"So what now?" I asked, trying to sound brave, but I could hear the disappointment and doubt in my voice. I knew Logan could hear it, too.

"We beat them at their own game, starting with the angels." Logan set the laundry down on the kitchen table and picked up the book on sigils. "And we do it tomorrow."

"Why tomorrow?"

"Because I don't want to be in town when Kira's

boss shows up."

I totally, wholeheartedly agreed with that, but Logan had forgotten a couple of things. "What about the demons who *are* here?"

"I'll have them covered." His grin was all cunning determination with a hint that he had a few tricks up his sleeves. It made me smile.

"And how are you going to trap an angel?" I asked, going back to our original conversation. I pictured an angel caught in a gold net, feathers tangled in the holes.

"No clue," he admitted. "But Kira knows, and I told her I'd help her do it."

Whipped, I thought with a shake of my head, *by a demon with a pretty face.*

I wished I'd had half the faith in her that he did; maybe then I'd have felt better about working with a demon. I then reminded myself that Logan had managed to keep us safe for several years. He had good instincts. I trusted *him.* And we'd agreed on a united front.

That didn't mean I ditched my back-up plan, just in case things got ugly.

Before we went to sleep, we packed as much of our clothes as we could in duffle bags. In the morning, we stuffed the bags into the trunk of the Camaro along with a few boxes of personal possessions we didn't want to leave behind when we left. We had the black light, several markers, the book on sigils, and a few other items in a spare backpack on the floor behind the driver's seat.

We were running late for school, but since we always ran late, I doubted anyone would suspect we were planning to skip town. Logan parked in front of the student entrance.

I got out and bent down so that I could see him, one hand on the roof of the car and the other on the door. "Tell me again why I'm going to school and you're not."

"Because you have a biology test this morning, and I have something I need to do."

I pursed my lips. "Why should I take the test? I won't be around to find out how I did on it."

He had to think about that one a moment. I waited.

"If you're not in school, how are you going to talk to Ben?"

I frowned. He held out a silver permanent marker. "Here. Take this."

I grabbed it with two fingers. "Um. Thanks."

"Keep it on you."

"Right." I tucked it in my back pocket. "'Cause a marker is going to save my life."

I slammed the car door closed, but not before whining, "I *so* don't want to start my last day here taking a test."

He cranked down the passenger-side window. I thought he was going to tell me to get back in.

"Ariana. Don't leave school without Ben or me. Okay? Kira said you could be in danger."

I rolled my eyes. "Great. There goes ditching."

Chapter Thirty-Three

Logan

The grumpy cashier at the hardware store frowned at the cans of spray paint I set on the counter. She didn't look like she could tighten a screw, let alone tell the difference between a ratchet and a wrench.

"Planning to paint a mural somewhere?" she quipped.

Figures she'd think I was going to deface a wall. I glanced at my faded black jacket and jeans. There wasn't anything delinquent-looking about me besides my age, and there was nothing I could do about that.

"If I was, I'd buy the cheap stuff," I retorted.

"I can refuse to sell these to you." She glared at me as if I was a rodent. "ID."

If she had asked nicely, I might have showed it to her. I also figured that now was as good a time as any to drop off the grid.

"I already showed it to you." Her dull hazel eyes glazed over. Since I was destined for the fiery pits of Hell, I tossed a handful of candy bars and a bottle of water on the counter with the paint. "You already rang me up, remember? You were about to apologize for being a bitch."

"I'm sorry." Her unrelenting scowl softened. She bagged the cans of paint. "It's been such a bad week.

Husband lost his job. Kid needs braces." She put the candy and water in a separate bag. "You have a nice day."

I pulled my car around back to the delivery area. With a can of black paint and the book of sigils, I got out.

"Sorry, girl," I said to my car, the nozzle six inches from the hood. I paused, unable to mar my new paint job with symbols that would make it stand out like a gangbanger at choir practice. I tossed the paint back in the plastic bag and grabbed the black light and markers instead. Using the light to see what I was doing, I drew two symbols on my car. On the front corner of the hood, I drew the one Ariana and I had found on our front door to hide us from angels. On the back corner of the trunk, I drew the one I'd found in the book to hide us from demons.

Next, I used a Sharpie to draw the same symbols on the inside of the extra bracelets and tucked them in the front pocket of the backpack. Then I did something I hadn't done since our parents had died. I prayed. I didn't know who would hear me, if anyone. God. Those in Grace. The Fallen. I prayed they'd leave Ariana and me alone. That they'd keep their war amongst the higher powers and resolve their differences without us. I didn't expect my prayer to be answered.

I got back to school during the middle of third period and waited in the hall outside of Ariana's classroom. She was one of the first to leave after the bell rang.

"Have you seen Ben?" I asked.

"Yeah. We're all set for after school. Are you sure this is going to work?"

"Don't worry; he won't even know I'm following you." With our connections, I'd know which direction they were traveling even if I couldn't see Ben's car. We reached her fourth period class and stopped a few feet from the door. "Don't leave until you know I'm outside."

Ariana had led Ben to believe she was about to say yes, and, as we hoped, Ben was going to take her to meet Elise and her angel friends after the final bell. Kira and I would follow them at a safe distance. Once there, we'd set the trap, text Ariana when we were done, she'd claim to need some fresh air, and the three of us would leave. I was still playing it by ear when it came to Kira. If she had been telling me the truth, I'd drive her wherever she wanted to go. But if she had lied, I'd leave her ass to deal with Tess and the other demons. Then Ariana and I would swap our bracelets for the ones with the sigils drawn on them, drive west and disappear.

"Is Kira ready?" Ariana asked.

"I'll talk to her next period."

"I hope this works," she mumbled as she went into her classroom.

I hurried to foods class. Jazlyn—a.k.a. Mrs. Keane—was still subbing. Kira and I had to keep our conversation short and in writing. Kira was under the impression she'd be training me in angel combat, so she had what we needed in the trunk of her car. I was sure she'd help Ariana and me once she found out we managed to get the angels to gather in one place.

I grew anxious as the day edged on. Ariana and I were within hours of being rid of higher powers. We'd be able to start fresh somewhere new. Halfway through eighth period, I started to think of aliases. John Smith. Too plain. Kyle Reese, after one of the characters in my father's favorite movie. Not really me. Maybe I could keep my first name. Go by Logan Howlett or Godspeed or Johnson.

With a jarring snap, I felt my connection to Ariana break. She wouldn't have snuck off for a latte with everything going on. I dug my cell phone out of my pocket, not caring that Mr. Bannerman was addressing the class, and typed, *Where'd you go?* My screen flashed that I received a message before I could send mine.

Ben insisted we leave early. Three angels arrived. Ceremony's at dusk.

I reread Ariana's text before I slammed my civics book shut, grabbed my things, and raced out of the classroom, ignoring Mr. Bannerman's protests. How was I supposed to find Ariana now? Driving around town hoping I'd feel her pull was one option, but that could take hours, and she might not have been in South Elgin anymore.

I deleted my message and typed a reply as I hurried to my car. My finger lingered over the send button. What if she was being watched? I erased what I had and sent, *Hanging with Kira after schl. See u l8tr,* instead.

My car door opened with a groan. I tossed my things inside.

"Leaving without me?" Kira asked from my right, a large army-green duffle bag at her feet. I didn't bother to ask her if she'd ditched eighth period altogether and had been waiting outside or if she was that tuned in to my whereabouts that she'd known I'd left school.

"Ariana and Ben are gone," I said, trying to remain

calm. My plan had barely begun and it was already going all wrong.

Kira shook her head. "So?"

I had screwed up by thinking I could outsmart the angels. I hoped my gut feeling was right about Kira because I had no choice but to tell her the truth. "Ariana led Ben to believe she agreed to do her part in the prophecy. She told him it had to be today."

"She what?" Kira grabbed her cell phone from her purse. "When were you going to tell me this?"

Later. Never. When I had to. I snatched the phone from her.

"Hey!" She went to grab it, but I'd already tossed it on the ground and smashed it under the heel of my gym shoe.

"I have enough higher beings to worry about without you calling in reinforcements."

"I wasn't—"

"You said you've never lied to me." I stared at her, challenging her to admit she'd been lying that whole time. "Are you going to start now?"

She flipped her hair out of her eyes. Instead of answering my question, she said, "It wasn't a good idea to lead the angels into believing Ariana was ready to do her part. Do you have any idea how upset they're going to be when they find out she lied?" She cursed. "Logan. I don't even know if this stuff will work on the heavy hitters."

"Heavy hitters?" I repeated.

"The archangels, and I'm sure one will show up for the ceremony. Trust me, just because they're angels doesn't mean they won't smite first and ask questions later."

"Great!" I kicked the broken cell phone pieces across the parking lot.

"What's the plan?" Kira asked.

"Ariana brings the angels together in one place, you and I trap them, and we disappear."

"We, meaning you and Ariana?" Kira's expression grew solemn. She bent down to pick up the last few pieces of her phone as she asked in disbelief, "Do you have any idea what Tess and Jazlyn will do to me when they find out you're gone?"

I wished I trusted Kira enough to ask her to come with us, but I didn't. Yet that didn't mean I'd feed her to the sharks. "I'm not going to run out on you. Before we leave, I will make sure they can't get to you. You have my word."

She shook her head. "That's a big promise you won't be able to keep, and once they're done punishing me, they will find you."

"You're going to have to trust me." When the time was right, I'd let her know just how I planned to help her.

Kira took a deep breath and nodded her okay before picking up the duffle bag. "We'll just have to hope this stuff works on everyone there. Where are we going?"

I took the bag from her and shoved it into the backseat of the car before she could ask me to open the packed trunk.

"I don't know." I said and ignored the fire that flickered to life in the back of her eyes. She looked as if she was trying very hard not to turn into a human torch like she had the other day in the forest. "I was supposed to follow them."

"You have got to be kidding me!" Kira walked to the rear of the car and back. "Great. That's just great, Logan. Well thought-out plan."

"There has to be a way to find her." Then it hit me: maybe I didn't need to hope I would sense Ariana's presence. "Can't you track her?"

"Not if she's surrounded by angels. They'll cancel the signal I get."

My mouth fell open. "You mean to tell me if Ariana and I had left with the angels, you wouldn't have known where we went?"

She looked at me as if I'd just said the dumbest thing she'd ever heard. "Like you would have wanted to be held captive by the very creatures who not only stood by and did nothing while your parents burned alive but tried to get you and your sister to run back into the house to die right along with them." The bell rang. "It would serve you right if you lose Ariana." Kira walked around to the passenger side of the car and opened the door. "Let's get out of here."

I got in, started the car, and hurried out of the parking lot before more than a few students made it out of the building.

"What do you mean 'lose Ariana'?" I asked.

"I'm going to be skinned alive." She let out a shaky laugh. "This is what I get for going behind my boss's back and telling you the truth."

"Kira!" I snapped.

She frowned when she looked at me. "Logan, do you think Elise is going to let Ariana walk away once she's there? Elise will pressure her into saying yes and if Ariana goes through with the ceremony, she will seal your destinies. You guys will ascend. She'll become a servant of the angels, and you'll become a minion of the Fallen. Life as you know it will cease to exist. There. Is. No. Going. Back."

I floored it, heading north on Kenyon Road, not knowing where I was going. Before I could reply, my phone vibrated. I checked caller ID. It was Ariana. I quickly flipped it open.

"Where are you?"

"I don't know," Ariana whispered into the phone. "A small office, I think."

"What way did Ben drive when you left school?"

"I don't know," Ariana replied, her voice trembling. "One minute we were outside and then the next I'm in this room with a Sasquatch guarding the door."

"Son of a bitch!" I took a couple deep breaths, forcing myself to hold it together. "Are you hurt?"

"No. They're actually quite hospitable as long as I don't ask to leave the room. And I've met Ben's boss before. Remember the guy from the coffee house, the one who was immune to my powers? *He's* Ben's boss."

I raked my hand through my hair in frustration. "Look around you. Do you see letterhead or plaques on the wall, a nameplate? Anything?"

"Nothing." The sound of drawers sliding open and slamming shut rang out of the receiver. "The desk is basically empty, and the walls are bare. I don't think this place is used much. Logan, I'm scared. Ben's boss doesn't look like the type of person—angel—thing—whatever—you want to cross."

I swerved, nearly rear-ending the white Toyota hatchback of a driver who'd stopped abruptly at a yellow light. I sped through the intersection.

"Is there a window?" I asked. "Can you see a street sign or another building?"

"I've tried. The glass is too narrow to get a good view of anything but a field, a white bus, and some old sign, but I can't make out what it says."

A flicker of hope ignited in me. "Is the bus busted-up, and are most of the windows smashed?"

"Yeah. How'd you know?"

"Because I've been there. I'm on my way." I slammed on my brakes and took the first right, causing the minivan behind me to veer to the left to avoid hitting me.

"Logan, Ben promised nothing will happen to me. Maybe I should just—" Ariana paused. "Someone's coming, I gotta go."

"Ariana, Ben's not telling you the whole truth," I blurted into the phone. "Whatever you do, don't go through with the ceremony!"

The line went dead before I could find out if she'd heard me.

"Please tell me she's not at the church Tess and I met at." Kira held onto the door, her knuckles turning white from the death grip she had on the handle. It was hard to imagine that my erratic driving could frighten someone who was immortal.

"Why?" A church seemed like the perfect place for angels to gather. I looked at her, at the road, and back at her. I couldn't tell if she was breathing. "Kira! Why is that a bad thing?"

"Because the angels would never take Ariana to *that* church. It's not one of theirs."

Chapter Thirty-Four

Ariana

I quickly slipped my phone into the front pocket of my jeans and stepped away from the narrow window. Ben and Justin appeared in the doorway.

"What's he doing here?" I asked.

Justin cracked a wicked grin. He no longer looked like the likable college boy who dated my best friend. "I'm just seeing for myself if it's true. Lover Boy really got you to come with him."

"Shut up, Justin." Ben stepped into the room. "Ariana, do you need anything?"

"Maybe some company?" Justin quipped, ignoring the evil look Ben gave him. "Someone to gossip with while you wait?"

I decided not to give Justin the satisfaction of a response and instead looked around the small office. A filing cabinet sat along the same wall as a wooden bookshelf filled with ancient-looking books. There was a worn leather chair pushed under a nicked mahogany desk. A thick layer of dust covered everything.

"I need answers." Casually, like every internal warning alarm wasn't wailing excruciatingly loud in my head, I walked over to the bookshelf. "Ben, why's Demon Boy here?"

"To be witness to the ceremony," Justin replied

before Ben could. He leaned against the doorframe with an amused expression.

Ben shot him one of those looks that scolded, *Not another word from you.*

I nodded. Of course the other side would want proof I'd completed the ceremony. I looked at Ben. "Are you going to tell me where we are?" I had asked him this already, but he'd skirted the question.

"We're someplace safe."

And apparently he was going to keep skirting it.

"You still haven't told me what I have to do."

"It's not my place to."

He walked into the room, stopping when I took a step back. I didn't want him pulling any of his angelic, calming mojo on me. I needed my head clear.

"Are you always so spineless?" I asked. Ben winced. Justin snickered. "I want the details and then I'll say—"

"You'll get them," Ben reassured me.

I got the impression all this cloak-and-dagger stuff was to make sure I didn't back down. Or maybe it was too late. Maybe I didn't choose my words carefully enough, and I'd already said I'd do it. Maybe I'd already sealed my fate and all I had left was to save Logan.

I looked back toward the window. It didn't open. I had tried. It was also unbreakable. I'd found that out when I'd chucked the stone paperweight on the desk at it.

I squared my shoulders, refusing to let them know how scared I was. "I have a few conditions before I *choose* to help."

Ben slithered up next to me. I went to take another

step back but bumped into the wall. He regarded the books on the shelves with bored interest, and his chest brushed against my arm. "What are they?"

My conditions were simple. First, I wanted it in writing that both Logan and I would be safe. That once I did my part, we would be free to go. Second, they had to take their fight someplace where innocent people wouldn't get hurt. That way, I'd protect my friends and everyone else, too.

That was what I wanted to say, but when I opened my mouth, all that came out was, "I'm thirsty."

In my head, I cursed every foul word I'd ever heard because I knew Ben was keeping me from voicing my conditions.

Ben turned to Justin. "Get her something."

Justin hesitated at first but then left.

"What's going on?" I demanded as soon as we were alone. "Why aren't you letting me talk?"

"The angel will tell you more when the time is right." He pulled a copy of *Wuthering Heights* from the shelf. "In the meantime, try to relax." When I didn't move, he added, "I promised I wouldn't let anything happen to you. You're safe."

"But why did you—"

"I'm going to make sure Justin doesn't do anything to your drink."

He left before I could finish my sentence. The burly man I'd nicknamed Sasquatch was back guarding the door. I scanned the titles of some of the other books, thinking I was too nervous to sit and read. Then I realized there might be something useful in one of those volumes. Perhaps even the prophecy Logan and I had heard so much about. There were a few other classics, but most of the books were related to religion. One, a gray book with symbols I recognized as Nordic written down the spine, caught my eye. I shoved *Wuthering Heights* back on the shelf and grabbed the gray book instead.

"Have a rag?" I asked Sasquatch.

He just glared at me.

"Napkin? Paper towel? Your shirt will do."

To my surprise, he removed the flannel shirt he wore, revealing a linebacker physique beneath a tight black T-shirt. Knowing that my power of suggestion didn't work on Blesseds or angels, I guessed he did so to get me to shut up. I snatched the flannel, wiped the years of dust from the desk chair, and held it back out to him. "Thanks."

He just grunted and turned his back on me. I shrugged and dropped his shirt on the desk.

Once seated, I opened the book, expecting it to be written in Nordic. When I saw it wasn't, I tucked my hair behind my ear and got as comfortable as I could. The smell of weathered leather mixed with the musty pages of the book.

While Sasquatch guarded the door, I read. The first chapter talked about the Fallen. How they tried to reason with their brothers and sisters. The Fallen felt that their father had betrayed them by creating man—a flawed creature as the book often referred to us. The Fallen felt their father loved this creature more than his own children, whereas the Angels so-called in Grace believed their father loved us all equally. Chapter two talked about being cast into the bowels of eternity, which I took to mean Hell. I could barely read chapter three, which had long passages written in Nordic that claimed to summon a demon or angel. It was chapter four I found the most fascinating. It contained countless short phrases that did all sorts of things from protecting against spirits invading one's dreams to creating a barrier that celestial beings couldn't cross.

"I knew you'd like that book." Ben entered my makeshift prison cell. Sasquatch must have gone on break.

I quickly rested the book on my lap so that Ben wouldn't be able to see I wasn't reading the one he'd selected.

"I hope water's okay." He set a bottle on the desk in front of me.

"Where'd your dog go?" I asked, a bitter bite to my words.

He just watched me.

I didn't like how secretive Ben had become, and I didn't like being locked in a dinky, grimy room in the middle of nowhere. I would have expected better treatment from angels, something sanitary with nice furniture and maybe a television, at least.

"O-kay." I twisted off the cap to the water and drank. "Where have you been?"

"Talking to the angel, making sure my promise to you is kept."

I nodded. I'd been waiting to feel the tug in my gut that would tell me Logan had found me, but it wasn't there. I was alone.

There was a lesson in all of this. When scheming against higher powers, always have contingency plans. Ones that cover what to do when Plan A takes an unexpected detour, and you're not quite ready to invoke Plan B. I hoped to be alive long enough to remember that. Then I hoped to never need that newfound knowledge.

I tapped a finger on the book as I wondered if the Nordic sayings worked.

"Do you have anything to eat?" I asked, wanting to get him out of the room again.

"Yeah. Sure." He left.

I jumped up, snatched the permanent marker Logan had given me earlier that day out of my back pocket, and hoped Sasquatch didn't hurry back to resume guard duty.

Chapter Thirty-Five

Logan

Ariana and I had accepted the fact we were different a long time ago. Acceptance, after all, is the beginning to understanding. In our case, understanding why we were different blew. Being able to put thoughts into someone else's head does not make up for finding out you are the key to a war you want no part of. It does not make it okay that you have angels and demons on your ass.

I replayed the last few weeks in my head as I sped down the two-lane road toward the old church. I prayed I was wrong about where Ben had taken Ariana, because it would mean he was in league with the Fallen.

I'd been right to put my trust in Kira. She was the one who'd told me about the prophecy and what it meant for Ariana and me. It was Ben who'd been tight-lipped, providing nothing we hadn't already known, and pushing Ariana to believe her actions could make the world a better place.

"Are you sure the angels wouldn't go to that church?" I asked Kira. She dug through the backpack I'd brought.

"Positive." She took out the book on sigils and thumbed through it. "Why do you think Tess likes to meet there? It's not for the wonderful curb appeal or warm ambiance. It's because the Angels in Grace don't like to come within a thousand yards of it."

"Shit!" It was taking an eternity to get there.

"This book is good," Kira said as she returned it to the backpack and resumed her search. "Really good. Where'd you get it?"

"Downtown Chicago."

"Don't lose it. It will come in handy." She grabbed Ariana's rosary from the front pocket before shoving the backpack behind her and gathering half-empty bottles of water from the floor.

I'd taken to concentrating on my breathing. It had been Ariana and me for eight years. We were all each other had, the one thing solid in our messed-up lives. I'd promised her I wouldn't let anything happen to her. I'd promised I'd keep her safe. And I'd failed. I'd let her be a part of a plan that was destined to fall apart, only I hadn't been able to see how flawed it truly was until now.

Kira combined the bottles of water, ending up with three near-full ones. Next, she dangled the beads of the rosary in the water and recited something in what sounded like Latin.

"What are you doing?" I asked.

"Creating holy water. It won't kill a demon, but it will slow one down." She removed the beads from the first bottle and recapped it. "Although, you normally dangle the cross in the water, but the mouths of these bottles are too narrow, and we don't have time to stop at a store."

With the beads submerged in the water of the second bottle, she repeated her Latin incantation. When she finished, I asked, "What about the stuff you brought?" I tipped my head to the side to indicate the duffle bag in the backseat.

She did her thing with the last bottle and replied, "That stuff only works on angels who are still in Grace. We'll have to make do with what you brought. We'll need something to write with. Something that will work on any surface so that we can draw a few symbols near the exits. Lock the bastards inside."

"There's paint in the bag on the floor behind you."

She grabbed the bag and looked inside. For the first time since Ariana's phone call, she smiled. "This is perfect."

We were silent again. Each wrapped up in our own thoughts.

I touched my bracelet. Deep down, I had always known that someone powerful had to have marked us, but there was nothing special about our family. We weren't royalty. We didn't come from a prestigious bloodline. Our parents didn't even go to church. Why us? Why Kira and Ben for that matter? From the little I knew about their past, we had absolutely nothing in common outside of our birthdays.

I slowed down as I got closer to the church and pulled through the tall weeds behind the billboard. The square white building looked as unwelcoming as it had the other day. The pale blue sky and balmy breeze offered no comfort. There was a gray sedan, a red pickup truck, and a silver BMW in the parking lot. I couldn't feel Ariana's presence, though.

"There are at least four demons inside," Kira said.

"Ariana's not here," I said panic stricken.

"She's here." Kira rested her hand on my arm, and

my vision became sharper, like it had that day in the forest. There were markings around the door and windows that my human eyes couldn't see before. Written in the grime on one of the narrow windows was the word *jerk-face*. "I don't think a creature that has been around for centuries is going to write that on the windows."

I'd never been so happy to see the familiar curvy writing. "That's what Ariana calls me when we're messing around, but why can't I sense her?"

"My guess is that one of those symbols is blocking your link. Do you have that talisman of yours?"

I nodded.

"Good." Kira turned sideways in her seat. Her expression radiated doom. "Logan, you realize this is a trap to get you to cooperate. There's no way the Fallen will let Ariana be the one to complete the ceremony."

"I know." Like Kira had pointed out a long time ago, her boss knew my weakness. He knew exactly what strings to pull to get me to open the gates of Hell and start the war. There was one thing I didn't understand, though. "Why is Ben helping them? I thought he was supposed to be on the other side."

"He is. I don't get it either." She wet her lips nervously. "Logan, they'll know we're here. They'll be able to sense our presence. We have to hurry."

She opened her door. I reached over her and pulled it shut as quietly as I could.

"What are you doing?" she asked.

I grabbed the black light and shined it on the hood. The sigil I'd drawn that morning came into view.

"Omigod, I can't see it without the light." Kira chuckled. "That was pretty clever of you."

"I got the idea from you." I stared at the white building, trying to make sense of things. "Are you sure you and Ben aren't partners? That he's not a demon, and you guys aren't working together?"

"Puh-lease. He won't look at me, let alone talk to me. Not since I made the deal. And Blesseds and demons are never partners. It's in our nature to hate each other."

"Then why would he help the Fallen?" I mumbled, the question more for me than Kira. Ariana had been sure he couldn't lie and that his sole purpose for being there was to protect her, yet she'd also been sure he was still torn up about what had happened to Kira. Was guilt enough of a reason for Ben to betray the Angels in Grace?

I put myself in Ben's shoes and answered that question with a solid no. People didn't make deals with demons out of guilt. They did it out of love or greed. Since Ben wasn't hurting for anything material, I ruled greed out as an option.

"When Ben was human—a Chosen—was his role the same as mine?" I asked, beginning to realize that I had overlooked the obvious.

She gave a slight nod of her head, and, with it, all the pieces fell into place. Why Kira couldn't look Ben in the eye and why Ben didn't tell anyone that Kira had told me about the prophecy. I closed my eyes a moment. Now—at a time when Ariana and I were very close to losing our humanity—was not the time to pick a fight with Kira. Instead of demanding to know why she'd left out an important part of her and Ben's relationship, I shared my opinion on why Ben was here at this church.

"Maybe Ben's fulfilling his destiny. Maybe he's trying to set things right."

She shook her head. "He wouldn't put Ariana in harm's way like that."

"Not even for his sister?" I asked. I'd gotten it now. Ben and Kira were brother and sister. Kira had made the deal to save him, and when she became a demon he ascended and became a Blessed. The big brother in me understood why Ben was helping the Fallen. The scary part was that I was ninety-nine percent sure I would have done the same thing if I were in his shoes.

My understanding didn't mean I wasn't going to kill him for putting Ariana in danger.

"Ben wouldn't," she muttered, but she no longer sounded sure.

Silence stretched between us before her blank expression turned steely. Fire danced in the pupils of her eyes. "Did I tell you that my boss made an example of me? He strung me up on a pillar of bones while his obedient servants whipped and cut me in front of the damned until I'd passed out. When I woke, I'd be whole again, and the torture would start over with the first gash. Over and over until I lost track of how long I'd been there. Decades, Logan. It went on until there was someone else to take my place. After what I went through, the Fallen has no right to Ben's soul."

If Ben had made a deal with her boss, nothing Kira could say or do would change his future. No way was I going to point this out to her, though, when she looked as if she was about to combust. Instead, I gave a stiff nod of my head.

"I say we go in there and ask Ben what he's

doing." I was petrified of what we were about to face, but telling Kira that I thought we were all screwed wasn't going to help us, so that was one more thing I kept to myself.

Kira sucked in a lung-full of air. She made a soft raspy sound when she exhaled, which seemed to extinguish the flames in her eyes. "As soon as we get out of the car, they'll know we're here. They aren't going to give us time to have a heart-to-heart with Ben."

I grabbed the leather bracelets from the front pocket of the backpack, hoped I was doing the right thing by trusting Kira, and handed her the tan one. "Put this on your left wrist." I put the lavender one in the center console and swapped mine with the black one Ariana used to wear.

Kira ran her thumb over the symbols I'd drawn on the inside of the bracelet. Next to them, I had written, *To Kira, so you can disappear, too. Logan.*

"I was planning on giving it to you after we got away," I explained.

"Thanks." She put it on. "This might actually block our signatures long enough to get close."

"That's what I'm hoping." I grabbed the cans of spray paint Kira had left on the dashboard. She held the bottles of holy water. "Got any ideas on the best way to get Ariana out of there?"

"We go in the front door," she replied definitively. "I'll distract them while you get Ariana."

"What about Ben?"

"If he made a deal with the Fallen, I'll be seeing him soon enough. I'll talk to him then."

We got out of the car. This had to be the trap the

voice had been warning me about. If I ever met the person or thing behind that voice, I was going to slug him or it for being so freaking vague.

I tossed Kira a can of spray paint. At the same time, she tossed me one of the bottles of holy water. I shoved the water in my back pocket.

"Don't dawdle. Find your sister and get out of here."

I met her in front of the car. "I'm not going to leave you here to fight off several demons by yourself."

"Logan, if my boss finds out you're here, you'll never be allowed to leave. So you grab Ariana and run like hell. Got it?"

There was something sexy—and irresistible—about a pretty, petite girl taking charge. It also made me realize if things went south this could very well be the last time we saw each other.

I placed a finger under her chin, tilting her head up. "Kira, what kind of person would I be if I were to leave without you?"

She opened her mouth. Before she could continue to argue, I grabbed her around her waist, pulled her closer, and kissed her. Her muffled rebuttal quickly turned into a soft moan as my hand slid to the small of her back, crushing her against me. Her lips were soft and eager. We kissed as if it was our last day on Earth. Knowing what we were about to walk into, it probably was.

When our lips parted, I said, "I'm not going to leave without you."

Kira smiled a sad sort of grin. As if she didn't really believe me.

We'd taken a few steps toward the church when

my cell phone buzzed. I dug it out of my pocket and flipped it open. My insides went numb when I read the text from Ariana:

I'm sorry. There's no other choice. Stay away.

Chapter Thirty-Six

Ariana

Sasquatch and Justin stood just outside the office door, unable to step over the Nordic inscription I'd scrawled across the threshold. Ben stood inside the room staring back at them with his mouth hanging open.

I had carefully copied each letter from the book I'd been reading, purposely leaving the last one off so that I could trap Ben in the room with me. After stowing the book in my backpack, I'd waited next to the door, pretending to be bored. As soon as Ben had walked over the silver writing, I'd drawn the last letter. If he wanted my cooperation, he was going to have to start talking.

I capped my marker and slid it back into my pocket; a feeling of smug accomplishment filled me.

"Get her to remove it," Sasquatch growled a second before he stormed off down the hall.

"Told you we'd need backup," Justin said before following Sasquatch.

Ben rubbed his eyes with the palms of his hands. "Ariana, this is not going to help."

"We're doing this on my terms." I paced back and forth to keep him from seeing that my hands were trembling. Since Plan A wasn't going the way Logan and I had hoped, I needed to make sure Plan B didn't fall apart, too.

Ben sat on the corner of the desk and snorted. "It's not that simple."

I folded my arms over my chest. "I think it is."

"We're going to be here a while. Have a seat." He indicated with a nod at the desk chair.

Because my legs were shaking, I did. I hugged my knees. "Ben, I want your promise that Logan and I will be safe, and I want it in writing."

"I can't promise that." Ben stared at a spot on the floor in front of him instead of looking at me.

"Why?"

"I'm not at liberty to tell you that."

"If the angels need my help so badly, why are they keeping me locked up like a prisoner?"

He closed his eyes and remained silent.

"Damn it, Ben!"

I asked him question after question. He just kept shaking his head. It was infuriating. Our stare-down that came next was interrupted by a skinny lady with pitch-black hair, a tight burgundy dress, and shiny black stilettos.

"You're supposed to be getting her to cooperate," she said. In the dimming light of dusk, her eyes had a red glow to them.

"I'm working on it," Ben growled.

"Work faster," she retorted.

"She didn't do this on my watch!" Ben waved his hand toward the writing on the floor in front of the door.

No, I did it on Sasquatch's.

"If you would stop coddling her," the lady

snapped. Fire erupted on the desk in front of me. I gasped and pushed my chair backward, bumping into the wall.

"She's not to be hurt!" Ben jumped up. With a wave of his hand, the flames were smothered. "You don't need her downstairs right now!"

"It's almost time. Get her out of here."

"Five minutes." Ben glared at her. "Jazlyn, give me five minutes."

"Jazlyn?" The name had barely made it past my lips. "But you're a demon."

She wrinkled her nose like the little boy I babysat did whenever I caught him doing something he shouldn't have been. To Ben, she said, "Five minutes, but not a second longer or Asmodeus is going to burn this place down."

She turned on the balls of her feet and stormed off. The *click-click-click* of her heels on the wooden floor faded. A moment later, I felt a familiar tug in my gut.

"Logan," I whispered.

He barged into the room, hands folded into fists. He was a sight for sore eyes, and I was never in my entire life more grateful that he'd ignored my text. Ben had his arms crossed over his chest. Both guys looked pissed.

I uncoiled myself and went to stand. Ben held a hand up as if indicating for me to wait. Suddenly, his powers held me pinned to my seat. Before I could ask what was going on, Logan shoved Ben, sending him flying into the bookshelf.

"Did you get lost?" Logan spat.

Ben righted himself. "Watch yourself, Logan."

"Screw you." Logan held a hand out for me to join

him. "Ariana, come on."

"I can't." I tugged at my invisible bonds to demonstrate just how stuck in the chair I was.

Logan's gaze darted between me and the door, giving me the impression we didn't have time to chat. "Ben, you don't have to do this."

"Do what?" I tried again to get up and then sagged in the chair. "Will someone tell me what's going on?"

I was tired of being left in the dark, tired of being treated like a child, and most of all tired of the games.

Logan pinned Ben with a cold glare. "You want to tell her how you tricked her, that this is a House of the Fallen?" I took in the age old dirt and grime, the empty walls, and the lack of a single cross anywhere in the room. Logan went on. "He's Kira's brother, Ariana. She made the deal with the Fallen to save him."

A knot formed in my stomach. Things were happening exactly as Ben said they would. The Fallen would use me to force Logan to do his part. I never would have guessed Ben would help him do it. Furious and scared, I asked, "Why?"

Ben's fingers curled into fists. "Kira should never have made that deal. I had a plan!"

"That started with you saying yes." Logan inched closer to me. "You would have lifted the bonds that kept you safe."

Ben looked at me, but he spoke to Logan. "I've had to live with the guilt that I failed to protect her, knowing she went to Hell to save me. Now, I'm setting things straight. Her soul for mine." His expression turned icy as his attention slid to Logan. "And don't tell me you wouldn't do the same thing."

"Oh my God, Ben. What did you do?" I muttered

at the same time Logan said, "This is not what Kira wanted."

"And do you think I wanted her to sacrifice her life for me?!" Ben shot back. "When I first approached Asmodeus with my offer, he wouldn't even talk to me. The deal wasn't sweet enough. But then he said if I could get you to complete the ceremony, he'd accept my offer and there was only one way to ensure your cooperation." His gaze flicked to me.

"You bastard," I growled. Didn't he know that losing Logan would be worse than death? Knowing he was in Hell would make my life a living nightmare. I struggled harder to break free of Ben's power. "What happened to that perfect world you showed me?"

Ben wouldn't look at me now, let alone answer.

"You could have asked for our help," Logan said, eyeing me and the chair as if trying to determine if he could carry both of us out of there. "We could have worked together to find a way to save Kira."

Ben dragged a hand through his hair. "How? Run? She's bound to Asmodeus because of the deal she made. He would have been able to find her in a heartbeat. He knew!" Ben screamed. "He knew she wasn't even trying to convince you to do your part. Do you have any idea what he planned on doing to her for disobeying his orders?"

"So you offered up your soul for hers," I said, my eyes wide in horror. Had Ben been honest with me, had he trusted me, we wouldn't be in this situation.

"She wasn't supposed to go to Hell!" Ben snapped.

I wanted to hit him, but I still couldn't move.

Logan walked closer to the desk. To Ben, he said, "You drew the sigils on our front door and around our apartment."

I gaped at them, unable to believe I trusted Ben.

"I needed the Angels in Grace to feel they still had time," he confessed. "The sigils muted the signal your birthmarks give off."

Logan shook his head. "How do you think Kira will feel when she finds out that you offered up your soul? That her time in Hell was for nothing?"

"I promised her I'd find a way to save her." Ben's fingers unclenched and clenched, over and over. "This is how I can do that."

There was movement downstairs. Logan took another step closer to me. "It's not too late. We can help each other; just let Ariana go."

"And be stuck here to explain to a room full of demons how Ariana and you escaped. No, thank you." Ben held up a hand, palm facing Logan. A force of energy hit Logan in the chest, dragging him across the room and slamming him into the wall. The air in his lungs left in one excruciating grunt.

"Enough stalling," Ben said, his voice impatient. "We're doing this my way. Ariana, break the seal so that we can get this over with."

"No way." I rolled my chair further away from him.

Ben looked at Logan. "Then you do it."

It took Logan a moment to understand what Ben was talking about. Then his gaze fell on the inscription I'd written in silver permanent marker across the threshold of the door. For the first time, he took a good look around the small office and laughed. "You locked her in a room filled with information."

"You should see the books they have." I grinned

like a thief who had just stolen a million-dollar ruby. With a nod, I indicated to the writing on the floor. "It's Nordic. Higher powers can't cross over it."

Ben moved his hand forward. Logan gasped and grabbed his chest.

"Stop it!" I tried to get up. "You're hurting him!"

"Unseal the door," Ben said, his words unyielding.

Logan's face turned red. His eyes rolled to the back of his head.

"Release him or I'll say yes to the angels before Logan can say yes to the demons. What happens to you then?" I prayed it meant that his deal with the Fallen would become null and void. When Ben hesitated, I said, "Do it now, or I'll scream yes at the top of my lungs."

Ben lowered his arm. Logan's legs gave out, and he slid down the wall, crouched with his head in his hands as he took several quick, deep breaths. The relief that he was okay was cut short by an ear-piercing scream.

Chapter Thirty-Seven

Logan

Ben dropped his power-hold on Ariana as soon as he heard the scream. He ran toward the door, colliding into an invisible barrier he couldn't cross. He turned to face Ariana, who knelt next to me.

"Open this doorway or I'll kill him." Ben raised his hand, his fingers curling around air. My chest tightened as if someone squeezed my heart. With my head still pounding from earlier, I thought I'd pass out, only Ben didn't give the killing squeeze.

"H-he can't harm us," I stammered.

"What do you call what he's doing now, Logan?" Ariana spat.

I would have replied, *Holding back,* but the words didn't make it past my lips.

"Stop it!" Ariana yelled. Her arms tightened around me.

"That was Kira who screamed!" Ben twisted his hand around in the air, and I would have sworn my heart was going to burst.

Ariana stood and crossed the room. She used the heel of her shoe to smear away part of the inscription. "Now let him go!"

Her words fell on emptiness. Ben was gone. My heart was no longer being crushed. Ariana rushed over and helped me up.

I staggered, trying to get my strength back. "I promised Kira I wouldn't leave her."

Ariana grabbed her backpack, and we left the room, soundlessly descending the curved staircase at the front of the church. We stayed hidden in the entryway. I ran a hand over my face, hoping to wipe the last of my lightheadedness away. Ariana set her bag on the dull, dark wooden floor as she took in the modest entryway. White marble angels, their wings folded against their backs, crouched low on either side of the large double doors. Across from the stairway was a hallway. A white plaque above it read *Restrooms.* The sheet of dust on the floor showed signs of a struggle we'd missed.

I removed the talisman from my pocket and slid it up my sleeve for easy access.

"Are you okay?" Ariana whispered.

My chest felt as if a two-ton truck had been lifted off of it, and it still hurt to breathe, but I nodded anyway. "How many are there?"

"Five, including Ben. There might be more I didn't see."

"Let's hope no one else has joined the party." I took a deep breath, stifling a cough. "My car's out front, behind the billboard. Wait inside of it. You'll be safe."

"I'm not leaving you, Logan." I opened my mouth to protest, but she plunged on in a low hiss, "We can stand here and argue about it, or we can save your girlfriend and get out of here."

My foot hit a bottle of water, sending it rolling into the corner. I picked it up and handed it to Ariana.

"Splash it on anyone who gets too close," I said by way of explanation.

"Seriously? We're fighting with spring water?"

"Holy water," I corrected. "And I know how absurd that sounds."

"Insane is more like it." She shook her head as if she couldn't believe she was actually taking a bottle of water into a fight. "We doing this?"

I nodded and stepped into the opening that led to the church, Ariana at my side.

The church wasn't big. Twelve rows of pews faced a wooden altar covered by a black silk cloth. A pewter chalice, bowl, and several candles were among the items on top of it. Large paintings of angels in battle adorned the white walls between long maroon curtains. Like the rest of the building, it was in need of a good cleaning.

A rack made of bone had been erected in front of the altar. A man the size of a pro wrestler stood in front of it, his back to us. His arm moved in a quick jabbing motion, and a girl's scream pierced the silence. The man then moved aside, providing a clear view of the rack and Kira strung up in the middle of it. Steam rose from where thick rope wound around her wrists, each arm tied to a corner. Her head slumped forward, and blood stained her shirt and jeans. My gaze traveled to the man and the long hunting knife he clutched. A demon, I realized. An anger I hadn't known existed ignited within me.

As I surveyed the rest of the scene in front of me, I noticed Justin and Jazlyn to the right. Ben knelt between them, facing Kira.

Ariana's hand flew to her mouth.

"The floor," she whispered. I followed her gaze. An inscription similar to the one Ariana had used upstairs was written in red around the rack. I guessed this inscription only kept out Blesseds and Angels.

"Let her go." I took a couple of steps forward. Ariana followed my lead.

Kira opened her eyes and looked at me through a veil of red curls. She mouthed the word *go.*

If Ariana and I were to run as fast as we could, we'd have probably made it to my car. The sigils on the hood and trunk should have kept us safe, and we could have gotten away from the church and gone into hiding. It was a risk but our best option given the circumstances that faced us. Yet I couldn't leave Kira. I had promised her I wouldn't. Ariana grabbed my hand and gave a light squeeze as she took a step forward. Her way of saying she wasn't going anywhere.

Ben's glare met mine, and I felt his agony at not being able to help his sister ripple through me, causing me to stagger.

"*Stall,*" the disembodied voice said.

I had a good mind to snap back *screw you.* Where had this mysterious entity been when I'd needed it? Why bother to offer warnings if it wasn't going to stand by my side and fight?

Yet, since I knew it wouldn't answer my questions and I did need time, I took its advice and addressed one of the men. The guy was leaning against the front pew, legs crossed at his ankles and looking almost bored.

"You must be the Fallen I've heard so much about."

"You may call me Asmodeus. It's nice to finally meet you, Logan." He spread his arms like you might do when greeting a long-lost relative you've heard so much about.

"I can't say the same." I glanced around us. There were no windows behind the maroon silk cloths, but there was a door just past the altar on the left-hand side. I was pretty sure it was the one that led outside, the one Kira had sealed before we'd entered. Ariana and I were armed with two bottles of water—hers held loosely in her hand and mine still stuffed in my back pocket—and a seriously lacking-in-size angel dagger. I had to figure out how we could free Kira and get to my car without getting any of us killed.

"Prophecies are tricky things," Asmodeus said. "In this one, the Chosen must choose to accept their destiny, so if I could get you to step to the altar of your own free will we can begin."

"No," I replied without hesitation.

If I charged the burly demon near Kira, I might have been able to take him off-guard and sink my dagger into him, only I doubted he'd just stand there in shock, and his weapon was a lot bigger than mine. Even if I did surprise him, I'd have had to get by Asmodeus. Would it have been too much to ask for him to continue to lean against the pew while I killed one of his minions? I also had to worry about Ariana. Would she follow me? Try to fight with me? Would she attack Asmodeus?

"Cooperate and I promise that neither I nor anyone under my control will harm your sister."

I stepped protectively in front of Ariana. "I'm not making a deal with you. So you might as well let us go. The four of us," I said, motioning to Kira and, a bit reluctantly to, Ben. While it may have been one of the last things I ever did as a human, I would show him that he should have trusted me, that it would have been better if we had worked as a team.

"I'm sorry. I can't do that." Asmodeus didn't look the least bit sorry. "I think you'll change your mind, though." He snapped his fingers, and a second rack appeared next to the one holding Kira. He looked at Ariana. "You should have stayed locked in that room."

"Bite me!" Ariana went to move next to me, but I put my arm out to keep her partially sheltered behind me.

"You can't kill a Chosen," I replied in a tone that mirrored his monotone one. I knew he could harm us, though, and I wasn't going to give him a chance to torture my sister.

Asmodeus's eyes narrowed as he turned to glare at Kira. "You are a defiant little demon, aren't you? What else have you told them?"

She spit in his direction.

Asmodeus's gaze moved to the demon with the knife. He nodded. The demon then faced Kira, and in a movement quicker than my eyes could follow, he swiped the blade across her stomach. She screamed. Fresh blood stained her torn shirt.

Ben lunged forward, only to be knocked backward by the invisible wall in front of him. A new ripple of his anguish rolled off him and through me. Ariana shuddered, and I knew she felt it, too.

"Stop it!" Ariana screamed. She shoved my arm aside and ran halfway up the church, stopping abruptly when deep green vines sprouted from the floor in front of her and entwined themselves around each other until they'd formed what looked like a large birdcage with

Ariana trapped inside. I grabbed at the bars. They were as solid as steel.

"Ariana, he's not bluffing," Ben said, and I realized it was his cage that trapped her. "He will string you up next to Kira."

"Are you okay?" I asked her, glad Ben had protected her from Asmodeus's wrath.

She nodded.

"Ben, I'm hurt," Asmodeus said a hand over his heart. "I promised I wouldn't hurt Ariana and I keep my promises. Now Logan—"

"I won't do it." Even as the words left my mouth, I felt defeated.

Kira screamed again. Fresh blood trickled down her thigh. The demon with the knife smirked.

"I say you will." Asmodeus walked to the front of the altar. "It's quite simple. Since I doubt you read Latin, you'll have to repeat after me, bleed a few drops of blood into the bowl, and I'll do the rest. Ariana will ascend to her rightful place as a Blessed. She'll be safe. That is what you want, your sister's safety?"

"Logan, don't do it!" Ariana tugged at the bars. "We promised each other."

I looked at her. I couldn't save us all. Not without help and more time.

"You were willing to do the same thing to save me," I reminded her.

I guess in the end our willingness to accept our destiny if it saved others made both of us good. I wondered if saying yes would be considered self-sacrifice or suicide. There didn't seem to be much difference in the outcome.

I took a step toward the demon near Kira.

"Logan, don't you dare!" Ariana screamed, struggling harder to break free.

The demon rammed the knife into Kira's side. She screamed again, and her whole body jerked. It ignited a new wave of hatred in me that fueled my desire for revenge.

"Tell him to stop!" I demanded, stepping closer yet.

"He will," Asmodeus assured me, "as soon as the ceremony has been completed."

"Son of a bitch," I growled.

"It's not my mother that I'm angry with," Asmodeus said in an amused voice.

I glared at the demon. "Touch her with that thing one more time and I'll kill you myself."

He pressed the flat edge of his long serrated knife to Kira's cheekbone. His gray eyes never left mine as he dragged the tip down her cheek, leaving a bloody red line in its wake. Kira's breath came in short gasps. Her head lobbed forward.

"I meant what I said upstairs," I chided. Ben's afflicted gaze met mine. "You were a fool."

I hoped he understood the hidden meaning behind my words as I stepped even closer to Kira. The demon near her used his free hand to pin her head against the rack. He adjusted his grip on the knife.

Asmodeus studied the items on the altar. "What happened to the myrrh?"

"It was there." Jazlyn headed toward the altar, but Asmodeus held up a hand.

"I need you watching Ben."

"I got him." Justin placed a hand on Ben's shoulder, forcing him to his knees.

"Get your hand off me!" Ben elbowed Justin.

Jazlyn rushed back to her post on the other side of Ben, looking ready to place him in a headlock. Ben glared at her as if daring her to touch him. She straightened her too-tight dress instead.

Asmodeus regarded them disapprovingly. "Can the two of you handle one Blessed, or do I need to call in reinforcements?"

"We got him." Justin shoved Ben from behind. Ben planted a palm on the floor in front of him, breaking his fall.

"Good. I'll get the myrrh. You guys keep an eye on them." Asmodeus disappeared into the back room.

Ben's gaze met mine, and in them I saw a piercing light that hadn't been there a moment ago. His head moved a fraction of an inch down, then up. I didn't know if Ben had any weapons on him, but I sure as hell hoped he had something other than tricks up his angelic sleeves as I spun to face the demon near me.

Chapter Thirty-Eight

Ariana

Ben moved at preternatural speed. He went from a kneeling position at the edge of the inscription to being on his feet. He then crouched low as he did a three sixty, sweeping his leg under Justin and then Jazlyn. In the next instant, he held an iridescent spear of light in each hand. With his arms raised to the side, he dropped to one knee. The points of the spears sank into Justin's and Jazlyn's chests, piercing their hearts. Their bodies quivered, and an eerie red-orange light radiated from their mouths and eyes.

At the same time, Logan advanced on Sasquatch. Logan's movements weren't as fast as Ben's, but they were executed with the same determination; he shook his right arm, causing his talisman to slide out from under his sleeve and into his hand. Sasquatch turned to face him, his long hunting knife held loosely at his side. I screamed, and, armed with the talisman, Logan charged.

Sasquatch wrapped his bear-size paw around Logan's neck at the same time Logan rammed the dagger into Sasquatch's chest. Sasquatch's eyes grew wide as his gaze traveled to the dagger. Logan shoved it further into his chest, and a split-second of realization showed on Sasquatch's face. The same red-orange glow then erupted from his mouth and eyes as he lost his grip on Logan and crumbled to the floor. Logan cleaned his blade on his leg, smearing blood on his jeans.

I looked back at Ben. He stood between the demons he had killed, encased in a white, ethereal glow, looking very much like an angel. Logan knelt next to the dark red inscription separating Ben and Kira. Using the wing of his talisman, he scraped at one of the letters, breaking the invisible barrier. Once done, he touched the floor with the tips of his fingers, then held his hand in front of him, examining the red specks now on his fingers.

"It's blood," Ben said grimly from in front of him.

A sharp, brief scream came out of nowhere and bounced off the stone walls. A second later, the letter Logan had removed rewrote itself, completing the inscription once more with the glossy, curved *R* written in fresh blood.

"Justin didn't believe Ben could get Ariana here," Asmodeus said from the doorway of the back room. Logan and Ben quickly faced him. Holding a clear glass container in his hands, Asmodeus took in the scene in front of him. "He brought a little insurance, someone to make sure we'd get your cooperation." Asmodeus stalked forward, taking another look at Jazlyn's, Justin's, and Sasquatch's still bodies. "Those were three of my best demons." He set the glass jar on the altar. No true remorse showed in his expression.

"Glad to hear it," Logan replied. "Who did Justin bring?"

But I knew the answer to that question. There was only one person Justin would have brought. My stomach sank to my toes. I gripped the bars of my prison tighter for support.

"No, no, no," I muttered. "Please, no."

Asmodeus gave a flick of his wrist, and a person appeared tied to the second rack, a black rag stuffed in her mouth to keep her from screaming. There were dark red stains on the sleeves of her shirt and the palms of her hands. Her scared brown eyes found mine.

"Becca," I mumbled, numb all over.

"She has nothing to do with this," Logan barked, taking a step over the writing and closer to the Fallen.

"Picky inscription, that one is." Asmodeus pointed to the wording at Logan's feet. "It had to be written in the blood of an innocent. That she is a friend of yours makes it poetic, don't you think?"

"If you hurt her…" I growled.

"You'll what?" Asmodeus asked.

I hadn't figured out the *what* yet. In my silence, he peered at Becca out of the corner of his eye. A thin red line appeared on her cheek as fresh blood dripped down her face. She whimpered, unable to do much more with the gag in her mouth. I swiped at the warm tears trailing along the side of my nose.

"Now, Logan," Asmodeus continued, "you just have to accept your destiny and the girls will be free to go."

Ben moved so that he was behind Logan and stealthily removed the bottle of water Logan had shoved in his back pocket. Logan adjusted his grip on the talisman.

"Logan, don't do it!" I yanked and kicked at the bars in front of me with even more urgency.

Just as Asmodeus's arrogant gaze fell upon me, Logan and Ben charged. Logan plunged the dagger into

Asmodeus's rib cage. Ben doused him with holy water.

Asmodeus trembled, his eyes wide. "Where'd you get—"

Logan twisted the blade in response. Only, instead of screaming in pain, Asmodeus let out a bellowing laugh. Ben and Logan exchanged worried looks and took a colossal step back. Logan removed the dagger as he did so.

Asmodeus wiped water from his eyes. "Stings a little. Like sweat in your eyes."

He swept his hand to the side, sending Ben flying across the room without laying a finger on him. Ben landed on the front pew with a deafening *crack*. I screamed again and continued tugging on the vines.

"Now," Asmodeus said, the wound in his ribs already healed. His tone was so even and calm I knew we were in trouble, that before this day was over, Logan would be condemned to Hell and I would become a Blessed. Normal would be over for us. College, falling in love, a house with a white picket fence were things we'd never have; the only thing left for us to do was save our friends. Asmodeus continued, "I'll forget that you killed my most loyal demons. I'll even let you keep that blade of yours"—he motioned to the talisman in Logan's hand—"if you would be so kind as to step closer."

Asmodeus rearranged the items on the altar so that the pewter bowl sat in the center. He filled it with myrrh. The white candles ignited on their own.

"You will need to be able to reach the altar." Asmodeus glanced up at Logan. "I won't bite."

I wasn't so sure about that. I don't think Logan was either because he didn't move.

Asmodeus began to flip through a large book. Its pages, more gray than white, were edged in gold. Ben, still slumped on the front pew, looked at me and then at Becca and Kira. He mouthed, *Help them*, and the cage around me dissolved. I nodded. Slowly, one step at a time, I approached the racks. My heart raced uncontrollably as I pried the knife out of Sasquatch's dead grip.

"He can't help you," Asmodeus said. I froze.

"Who can't help me?" Logan asked. If he knew I'd been freed, he didn't let on.

Asmodeus gave a nod toward the front pew. "Ben's no match for me, and even if he were, he'd be a fool to cross me."

I heaved out a silent sigh of relief when I realized Asmodeus was talking to Logan and not me. Ben pushed himself up into a sitting position.

Asmodeus continued in the same level tone. "But you will have plenty of time to talk to him once we're done here." He added a pinch of some dark powder to the bowl.

I inched closer to Becca since she was in better shape than Kira, whose dark red curls clung to her forehead. Kira's eyes were unfocused, and tears and blood stained her cheeks. I was going to need help carrying her.

I brought a finger to my lips and gave Becca an unspoken *shh*. She nodded. I dragged the serrated knife over the rope, careful not to cut Becca in the process. I'd only sliced through half her bindings when Asmodeus's disapproving voice made me freeze mid-swipe.

"I can't allow you to do that," he said.

Asmodeus appeared busy reading. Praying he was talking to Logan or Ben, I continued to saw at the rope.

"Ariana." This time when I looked up, I found Asmodeus's perfect blue eyes drilling through me. "Your friends will be released when the ceremony is complete and not a minute sooner. If you don't want to find yourself in the same position as them, I suggest you drop the knife."

I did. Asmodeus's attention returned to the book. Logan took a step toward me.

"You will complete the ceremony," Asmodeus said.

"That will never happen," Logan spat.

Asmodeus smirked. "As it is written, so shall it be. You can't change your destiny."

"Ben and Kira did," Logan argued. "And so did the Chosen before them."

"Are you sure about that?" Asmodeus rubbed his thumb over his bottom lip as if trying to remember something. I didn't like the smile that followed. "Let me quote a few lines of the prophecy for you: 'The first to be Chosen shall meet their maker by their own doing. The second shall be separated by the brother's selflessness. The third shall switch places before either takes their last mortal breath. The fourth shall change the Fallens' lives forever.'"

Logan had told me about the siblings Chosen before us. The first had committed suicide. The brother of the second had sunk a dagger into his gut to get out of his role. Until recently, I had assumed that was Ben. Kira, the sister of the third set of siblings, had made a deal with a Fallen Angel that resulted in her going to Hell and Ben subsequently going to Heaven. So far, destiny had taken each set of siblings as it was written in the prophecy.

Logan hissed his reply, which was too soft for me to hear.

"My pocket," Kira whispered in a hoarse voice. Her eyes were narrow slits, and it looked as if it took a tremendous amount of effort to hold them open. "Quickly," she added when I didn't move.

I slid closer to her. With my body between Kira and the altar, I ran my finger inside Kira's front pocket and didn't feel anything.

"Back left," she mumbled.

I bit my bottom lip as I shifted so that I could check her back pocket. I palmed the piece of paper I found there.

"Now what?" I asked out of the side of my mouth.

Kira barely got a syllable out when an invisible force yanked me upward, forcing my arms out to the side and locking my ankles together as if they'd been bound. I quickly looked to both sides, thankful I didn't see my wrists pinned to a rack like Kira's and Becca's. I kept my fingers curled tightly around the paper.

Chapter Thirty-Nine

Logan

Ariana looked as if she'd been nailed to a cross suspended six feet in the air. She squirmed like a worm on a hook, and, just like a worm, her efforts were in vain.

"Put her down!" I demanded.

Asmodeus cocked his head to the side as he looked at Ariana. "She's fine."

"I am not—" The rest of her words were stifled by a red gag appearing out of nowhere.

"I don't need you and Kira plotting against me," Asmodeus said.

Ariana's rebuttal was too muffled by the gag to make any sense. Out of the corner of my eye, I saw Ben push himself to his feet and face Asmodeus, his right arm raised over his shoulder as if about to throw a baseball. A moment later, his fingers were curled around a spear made of light.

"Kira is half dead," I blurted, hoping to keep Asmodeus's attention off Ben. "She doesn't even have the strength to hold her head up, let alone plot against you. You don't have to keep them strung up like they're about to be sacrificed!"

Asmodeus's lips twisted into a wily grin, sending a chill through me. I got the unsettling feeling the reason the angels had kept the details of the ceremony a secret was because a sacrifice was exactly what it took to open or reinforce the gates of Hell. Before Asmodeus could reply, Ben hurled the iridescent spear at him. It sailed silently through the air, straight for the Fallen's head. Asmodeus spun the moment the spear was about to pierce his temple and snatched it from the air. The spear turned red and then black as it disintegrated to ash.

Asmodeus's expression became steely as he whipped a ball of fire at Ben, who dove over the pew to avoid being hit. They continued to battle, fire against light, each taking a beating that would have killed a mortal. It was a fight I didn't dare join.

But it was the distraction I needed. Ariana wiggled and bucked, trying to break loose of her invisible bonds. I rushed to help her, wrapping my hands around her ankles and tugging. On the other side of the church, Ben did more ducking than actual fighting. His eyes met mine briefly. With his left hand, he threw a white ball of energy at Asmodeus, and with his right, he threw an identical ball at Ariana—only, the one aimed at her hit an unseen force at her back. Ariana let out a grunt as she was thrown forward. I caught her, breaking her fall, and she yanked off the gag. We exchanged looks and rushed to Becca and Kira.

"Hurry," she whispered as she attempted to free Becca.

I glanced over my shoulder, fingers straining to work the knot holding Kira's left wrist to the rack loose. Several rows of pews had been reduced to kindling. Ben only had a few more pews to hide behind before he'd be left unprotected. "We need to work faster!"

The knots weren't budging, though. Ariana grabbed the long serrated knife from the ground and frantically sawed at the rope holding Becca to the rack. I'd just worked a finger under Kira's bindings when she screamed, "No!" I hadn't even known she had opened her eyes, which were focused on something just over my left shoulder.

I pivoted on my heels to see what she was hollering about. Ben hovered several feet over the last row of pews encased in a white glow, his chest to the ceiling and back arched.

"No!" she screamed again as Ben plummeted to the ground, landing with a thud on the unyielding backrest of the pew. Ariana and I were yanked away from the racks and dragged across the floor until our backs slammed into the rubble that used to be the front pew. The knife Ariana held skidded across the floor.

"Enough games!" Asmodeus roared. He tugged at the hem of his shirt as he returned to the altar.

"Are you okay?" I asked Ariana.

She peered at me through a veil of bangs. "I've been better."

We sat slumped against each other, catching our breath. Kira's gaze met mine, and she looked sincerely sorry that we had failed to save Ariana and ourselves. I had no doubt she had never wanted it to come to this. Becca stood on the ground, twisting her trapped wrist as she worked her hand free. Asmodeus glanced at her and went back to his work.

"Now, Logan," Asmodeus said, the pitch in his voice indicating he would no longer show any patience. "I will finish the preparations, and you will willingly add your blood to the incense, say the incantation, and ascend to a demon as is written in the prophecy."

"You don't need the girls. Let them go," I demanded. Just because I was damned didn't mean they had to be.

Asmodeus turned the page in the book and replied, "Think of them as insurance. You cooperate, they live. You resist, they die."

"Got any other ideas?" I whispered to Ariana, because *demon* was not an accomplishment I wanted on my college applications.

"Kira gave me this." She slipped me a crumpled piece of paper the size of a note card. At a quick glance, it looked like some type of prayer or spell. In the top corner, the word *salt* had been crossed out and *myrrh* written next to it.

"We can do this the easy way or the hard way," Asmodeus said. I quickly hid the paper behind my back before Asmodeus's gaze moved from the book to me. "You can willingly walk over and stand by my side, or—" Becca, who'd just managed to slip off the ropes, disappeared from near the racks and reappeared in front of Asmodeus; he pinned her back against his chest, one hand under her chin and the other around her waist. "Or I can kill your friend, and we can try this again."

Ariana gasped.

Did Becca even know why she'd been brought there? Why they had drained enough of her blood to write the incantation on the floor? What was at stake?

Refuse to cooperate; sacrifice one life to save thousands by avoiding war. It was the right decision, the one a soldier would make. I knew that.

But I wasn't a soldier, and this was Becca we were talking about. Sweet, caring Becca, who was the best friend Ariana had ever had and an extension of our little family. I looked at my sister. Ariana nodded, her eyes pleading with me to surrender and save Becca.

Fear and bewilderment showed in Becca's expression as tears ran freely down her face.

"Okay," I said, hands held in front of me. "Just let Becca go."

"Say the words," Asmodeus demanded. "Say you accept your destiny and will do your part in the ceremony."

But those words would lift the angelic bindings that protected Ariana and me. They would make Ariana just as vulnerable as Becca.

I took a cautious step forward. "I said okay. Now let her go."

"Not good enough." Asmodeus yanked Becca closer to him with one hand and put her chin in an ironclad hold with the other.

"No!" Ariana and I screamed in unison as he wrenched her head violently to the side.

A nauseating snap reverberated through the cavernous church. Becca went limp in his arms.

"You bastard!" Ariana screamed as she jumped to her feet and went to charge the altar. I barely managed to get an arm around her waist and struggled to hold her back as she continued to scream, "Becca wasn't a part of this!"

I blinked a few times, trying to keep the tears welling up in my own eyes from spilling over. Ariana was crying so hard her whole body trembled. We had one chance left, and I planned on risking it.

"You're going to have to trust me," I muttered into her hair.

Chapter Forty

Ariana

Becca was dead, and it was my fault. Experience had proved that the people who I loved died. I should have known it would happen to her, too. I was sure my legs would have given out if it wasn't for Logan, who had wrapped his arms around me. I forced myself to stop crying.

"What are you going to do?" I asked in a whimper.

"End this."

"And bring Becca back?"

But I knew he couldn't breathe life into my best friend. She hadn't stirred—not even a twitch—since Asmodeus had let her fall to the floor at his feet. I sniffed back more tears and glanced around us. Things were dismal. Kira's wounds weren't healing, and she looked as if she would pass out at any moment from the loss of blood. Ben was strewn over one of the pews like an unwanted rag doll chucked aside, eyes open but not seeing. Logan and I had nothing to fight with and no way to escape. But when I looked into Logan's citrine brown eyes, I saw a speck of hope.

"I'm going to let you go. Promise me you will stay here." When I didn't respond, he added, "Trust me."

I should have accepted my destiny and said yes to the Angels in Grace. They were good, right? If I yelled at the top of my lungs that I'd do it, would they hear me, or was I too late?

"What happens if—and it's a big if—I agree?" Logan asked Asmodeus.

"Logan, don't," I growled. Hate and anger turned my insides to ice. No way was I going to let Asmodeus win.

"Trust me," Logan whispered again and loosened his grip on me.

I did trust him with my life, but I feared he was about to do something stupid. I didn't want to become a Blessed, and I sure as hell didn't want the price of my immortality to be a one-way ticket to the pit for Logan.

Logan hastily scanned the piece of paper I'd given him while Asmodeus crouched and sprinkled a thick line of dark gray power around the altar, enclosing it in an oval of incense. "I'm a man of my word," Asmodeus said. "You will be safe—a new person—but I will not require you to fight. Ariana will become a Blessed, so she will be free to leave this church. Kira, too, under the terms Ben has set forth in our deal."

At the mention of Ben, I turned to the back of the church. He was still draped awkwardly across the pew, only there was something different about him. His eyes were no longer open and staring blindly at the cathedral ceiling. His form shimmered, appearing solid yet ethereal at the same time.

"And our friends?" Logan asked, returning my attention to the front of the church. He took a step forward, nonchalantly holding a hand up, motioning for me to stay where I was.

Asmodeus gave an exaggerated roll of his eyes as if the lives of hundreds of innocent people were of no concern to him. Yet something in Logan's determined expression made him frown. "You have my word I'll do what I can to steer my army south of your precious little town. I'm afraid that's the best I can do, as the enemy is not here to make the same offer."

The enemy—a.k.a. the Angels in Grace. If Ben was any example of how they worked, I doubted anyone would be safe during the battle.

"And Becca, you'll heal her." Logan said. There was nothing in his tone that indicated it was a question.

I held my breath, waiting to find out if Asmodeus had the power to save Becca. I didn't care if she came back too scared to ever talk to me again, as long as she was alive.

"That is beyond my power."

Logan immediately faced me. *Sorry* was written all over his face, and I knew he was upset about her death, too. He mouthed the words *Trust me* again as if he knew I was thinking about clawing Asmodeus's eyes out. I gave a reluctant nod; I wouldn't have done much damage to Asmodeus anyway. I hoped Kira's little spell would work.

Asmodeus set the empty myrrh jar on the altar. "Does the fact that you haven't tried to leave mean you've chosen the path of least resistance?"

"Something like that." Logan stuffed his hands into the front pocket of his jeans and moved closer to the altar, carefully stepping over the line Asmodeus had just laid.

Asmodeus held up a gold dagger. His sharp gaze met mine, and I hated that I couldn't look away. I choked back a scream, praying Logan knew what he was doing. A large ruby gleamed from the hilt of the dagger as Asmodeus wrapped his fingers around its blade and, with no emotion showing on his face, pulled the dagger from his fist. He held his hand over the bowl, allowing several drops of blood to trickle into it. He then flipped the dagger around and held the handle toward Logan. "It only stings for a moment."

The muscles in Logan's jaw twitched as he pulled his talisman out of his pocket and armed it. Smart move on Logan's part, I thought. Kira had sealed her deal in blood, and Asmodeus's blood was on the dagger.

Asmodeus shrugged. "Suit yourself."

Logan took a deep breath, holding it while he ran his blade's tip over his palm. His gaze found mine as he allowed a few drops of blood to land in the bowl. I bit my bottom lip to keep from begging him not to do this. He hadn't actually said yes, though. That had to mean something.

Logan snatched a black cloth from the altar and wrapped it around his hand. "In this circle, it shall end…" he said.

Ben appeared behind Asmodeus, a thin, foggy image of himself. I blinked, wondering if my eyes were playing tricks on me and I just imagined him there. He held one finger to his lips, and I forced myself to look at Logan so that I wouldn't give Ben's position away to Asmodeus.

Logan continued, "…from here to Hell. Are you ready for that?" His tone oozed cockiness.

I recognized most of those words from the piece of paper I'd taken from Kira. Logan had added the last sentence, though. Hope edged its way through me.

"I was ready for this day centuries ago." Asmodeus raised his hands. The incense around them ignited, creating a ring of fire. His next few words were in Latin, but Logan's words drowned him out.

"Through air to fire, from Earth to Hell, as penance for your sins…" Logan paused, looking past Asmodeus at Ben. Ben's hazy image solidified. He grabbed Asmodeus by his arms, holding them behind his back as Logan drove the dagger into Asmodeus's chest.

"That defiant little demon!" Asmodeus growled. Like nails on a blackboard, his tone sent horrible shivers through me. The fire that surrounded him, Ben, and Logan vanished, leaving a ring of smoke rising from the myrrh. In the next instant, a white light covered the incense like a protective barrier. The air around them grew thick in a crimson fog that swirled as if a storm stirred it.

Ben, encased in the same ethereal glow as when he'd killed Justin and Jazlyn, tightened his grip. I picked up the serrated hunting knife and ran to Kira, fiercely sawing at the ropes that held her to the rack.

"Finish it!" Ben ordered.

"…shall Hell hold you bound for eternity!" Logan screamed.

Blinding scarlet light erupted within the circle. When the glow subsided, Logan was the only one who remained, Becca's lifeless body not far from him.

"What just happened?" I asked. "Where's Ben?"

Logan lifted Becca into his harm and carried her closer to me. "I bought us some time."

With one last downward slice, the rope fell away. I staggered as I caught Kira, keeping all her weight from hanging on her one arm still tied to the rack. Logan set Becca down.

"We can't leave Becca," I said. She deserved a

proper burial, and her parents deserved closure, even if they would never know what had happened.

"We aren't leaving her." Logan grabbed the hunting knife from me, freed Kira's other wrist, and then scooped Becca up again. I ducked under Kira's arm and held onto her wrist with one hand and her waist with the other to keep her from stumbling. For such a petite person, she was heavy. "You're going to have to help me get you out of here. Can you do that?"

She nodded.

Logan jogged to the entrance of the church, and Kira and I followed as quickly as we could. Once near the door, I tightened my grip on Kira's waist and snatched my backpack from the floor. With it slung over one shoulder, we went to follow Logan outside, only we hit an invisible barrier. I pushed my shoulder against it. It was like a sheet of glass stood between us and freedom.

"We're trapped!" I exclaimed, kicking at the air in front of me without a problem, yet Kira and I still couldn't walk outside.

"Crap!" Logan dropped to one knee, lying Becca down on the wooden steps. "Kira and I sealed the door."

He dug the talisman out of his pocket and used it to scrape at the black sigil painted on the landing. As soon as the seal was broken, he ran toward the billboard. I could just make out the nose of the Camaro.

Kira and I had made it out to the parking lot when Logan returned with the car. He hopped out and helped me get her into the backseat. Next, he lifted Becca from the steps and placed her in the front passenger seat.

"Where's Ben?" Kira asked, her words strained.

I looked back at the church, hoping to see Ben burst through the door.

"He'll meet us," Logan said. Kira's eyes closed from exhaustion and probably shock from the torture she'd been through.

"We can't leave him," I said.

Logan practically shoved me into the backseat. I had to push a green duffle bag onto the small ledge under the back window to fit.

"He'd want us to get Kira somewhere safe." Logan got in, started the car, and put it in reverse. His worried eyes stared back at me in the rearview mirror. "I'm sorry; we can't wait around to see if he's okay," he said.

"What do you mean *if*?" When Logan quickly glanced away, I asked, "What did you do?"

Instead of answering, he threw the car into drive.

"We can't leave him!" I screamed. Ben was egotistical and righteous and, well, infuriating half the time, but we wouldn't have been sitting in the Camaro having this conversation if he hadn't held Asmodeus so that Logan could finish the incantation. Logan locked the doors as if he feared I'd climb over Becca from the backseat to get out of the car.

He floored it. We barreled forward.

"Logan!" I hollered.

"We can't help Ben right now, okay! And Tess wasn't in that church, which means we have to get out of here before she decides to show up."

I fell back against the seat. Logan was right; we had to get as far away from the church as we could. I scooped my hair away from my face and stopped arguing. That didn't mean I liked it.

311

Logan reached into the center console and grabbed the violet bracelet. He held it over his shoulder for me to take. "Put this one on or they'll be able to follow us."

It only took me a moment to see he'd drawn the sigils on the inside. "What if it doesn't work?"

"The ones at the church did. There's no reason these shouldn't."

I couldn't get myself to look directly at Becca, as if by not facing her it would make this whole afternoon a dream. I'd wake up in my bed and speed-dial her number. She'd answer in her normal cheerful voice. Everything would be all right.

But nothing was okay. Becca was dead. Kira was barely hanging on to her immortality. And Logan and I were fugitives, running from forces we couldn't see. I swiped at a tear with the back of my hand.

"Where do we take Becca?" I asked.

"I'm hoping her car is still at school."

It was. The driver's side door was ajar, and her purse and backpack were on the passenger seat. Logan guessed that Justin had surprised her, only this time he hadn't brought flowers, nor had he asked her if she'd wanted to come with him. I had a small amount of satisfaction knowing he was dead.

But it didn't make up for the gigantic hole inside of me, and, despite how hard I tried to hold it together, I couldn't stop my tears long enough to help Logan get Becca into her car. As upset as I knew Logan also was on the inside, though, he refused to let it show on the outside. He not only took care of Becca, he guided me into the passenger seat of the Camaro. While I curled into a ball and cried, he got us out of there.

Once we were several miles from school, Logan

placed an anonymous call to the police about there being a suspicious car in the student parking lot so that Becca wouldn't be left there long.

We drove in silence for a while. Finally, after about an hour on the road as we headed west on the expressway, I dried my eyes with my sleeves and asked, "Where are we going, and how will Ben know where to find us?"

"I'm not sure yet, and Ben will call if he can."

There was that word again, *if.*

Logan glanced in the rearview mirror. "Shit!"

I looked behind us. Several cars back, behind an older sedan, a black SUV erratically switched lanes. It swallowed the distance between us at an alarming rate.

Chapter Forty-One

Logan

A knot formed in my stomach when I saw the Navigator. Either the sigils were worthless, or we had picked up a tail when we'd left the school. I should have known the Fallen would have lookouts. Escaping wouldn't be as easy as driving off into the sunset.

"Who do you think that is?" Ariana asked, her voice several octaves higher than normal.

"Probably Tess." I slammed my hand into the steering wheel and cursed again. There was nowhere for me to go. I was trapped behind a grandpa in a Cadillac and sandwiched between two semi trucks.

Kira moaned. In the rearview mirror I saw her eyes flutter open before rolling back in her head.

"She's going to bleed to death." Ariana shoved half her body between the seats, placing her hands over the stab wound in Kira's side. "Shouldn't she be healing faster than this?"

"How am I supposed to know?" I laid on the horn, trying to get the driver of the Cadillac to grow a set of balls and drive.

"Maybe we should take her to the hospital," Ariana said as she crawled into the backseat with Kira.

"Don't you think they'll notice she's not human?"

"Right. I need something I can press against her

wound, then." Blood seeped through Ariana's fingers.

"Hang on; let me grab the first aid kit." I laid on the horn again. "Oh, wait! We don't have one."

"You don't have to get snippy!" Ariana took off her sweatshirt and balled it up. Kira yelped when Ariana pressed it into her side. "Sorry," Ariana mumbled.

The Navigator swerved, nearly clipping the back of my car as it squeezed in behind me. A small amount of relief washed over me, though, when I saw a middle-aged man driving. He was alone. It wasn't Tess. That was good, I thought a moment before I realized it could have been another demon.

I glanced at Kira; she was deathly white. I couldn't tell if she was breathing.

"Kira! Don't you dare die!"

To my relief, the Navigator got off at the next exit.

Ariana continued to apply pressure to Kira's wounds and occasionally offered her a sip of water. We drove for another hour, ending up in the quaint town of Galena not far from the Mississippi River. I was able to get us a room at a small bed and breakfast. Ariana distracted the middle-aged woman working at the front desk while I carried Kira through the elegantly decorated lobby and up the stairs. Ariana didn't take long to catch up to us. Our room had two full-size beds, both with girly bedspreads and a ton of pillows. I laid Kira down on the one furthest from the door.

There was a cast iron radiator, an ornate wood fireplace, and a television in our room. We also had a private bath complete with brass accessories, vintage sink, and one of those old-fashioned clawfoot bathtubs. My favorite feature in the room was the very solid, very heavy wooden door—the kind that makes a statement when slammed. Ariana stood next to it, hugging herself.

"Are you trying to attract attention?" I asked.

She closed the door. Her eyes were still red and swollen, but having to take care of Kira seemed to stifle the tears.

"Nothing went like we had planned it," she said. "Becca's gone. Kira's not much better. Please tell me that something went right. Tell me Kira's spell sent Asmodeus to a fiery prison."

"It appears to have worked." If it had failed, I doubted we would have made it out of the church.

She nodded as if she'd already figured that much out and had only asked to be sure. "What happened to Ben?"

I ran a hand over my hair as I lowered myself onto the corner of the bed. "Ariana, he—" I heaved out a sigh. "The incantation works on all higher powers, not just demons."

She stumbled to a chair. "You sent him to Hell? He wasn't a good guy, but he didn't deserve that. No one deserves that."

"He morphed into the circle before it was sealed. He knew what he was doing. I'm sorry."

She remained silent for a long time. When she finally moved, it was to grab her purse. "I need some air."

"Ariana—"

She held up a hand. "I just need a few minutes by myself."

While Ariana was gone, I cleaned the worst of Kira's wounds. She was bloody and unconscious but breathing. I pulled a pillow out of one of the pillowcases, tore it into long strips, and used them to secure towels over the deep gashes in her waist and thigh. She had burn marks around her wrist where the ropes had held her pinned to the bone rack. I pictured the steam rising from her bound arms and realized the rope had been soaked in holy water. I rinsed the abrasions with water from the tap.

Over an hour later, Ariana returned with a change of clothes for all of us, a hot meal, and enough snacks and drinks to last a few days. I didn't ask where she'd gotten the money for everything she'd bought. She didn't want to talk about Becca or Ben, and I respected her wishes.

****

Two days passed.

Becca's death had made the news, and her parents were offering a reward for any leads that would provide answers. Ariana and I had made the news, too, something we weren't too happy about. We were sure Becca's parents had been the ones to report us missing, which was "sweet" as Ariana pointed out, but the last thing we needed was to be spotted by a Good Samaritan.

"The cuts on her legs and arms are almost healed," Ariana commented as she changed Kira's bandages. Kira's breathing was slow and steady. She hadn't woken up yet, though. "Her side is looking better, too."

"Good." I looked out the window. In the distance, tourists could be seen strolling up and down the old-fashioned streets, occasionally disappearing into one of the small boutiques. No one looked as if they were searching for three teenagers. I closed the velvet drapes.

Ariana tossed the dirty bandages into the trash can

before checking her cell phone; I knew better than to say I didn't think our mobile provider had service in Hell. Ariana hadn't given up hope that the spell I'd read hadn't cast Ben into the bowels of eternity. She'd spent hours analyzing the words to the incantation, hoping to prove it merely sent a higher power back to where it came from. Even if she was wrong, she clung to the belief that a Blessed couldn't be held prisoner in a place so evil.

By day four, I felt like a caged rat. I hated the tiny flowers on the wallpaper, the frilly bed skirt, and the doilies under the lamps. If I never saw another sheer lace curtain, it'd be too soon. And when it came time to get coffee and other necessities, Ariana and I would flip a coin to see who'd get to leave the room. I even sank to a new low, suggesting that people give me cash. I wasn't proud of using my ability to steal from them, but there were things we needed that we couldn't get for a suggested discounted price, like new cell phones and take-out food.

That evening, Ariana sat at the small table in our room, mapping out a route for when we left the bed and breakfast. I sat on the second bed, dealing out a new hand of solitaire. We hated that we couldn't attend Becca's funeral, but our appearance would bring on a slew of questions we couldn't answer. Besides, I was sure Tess would be there, waiting for us.

"Is that pizza I smell?"

"Kira!" I rushed to her side and helped her sit up.

Ariana hurried over and checked her bandages. After a minute, she said, "Her wounds have healed."

Kira ran her hand over her smooth stomach. Only a few red lines remained where there had been deep gashes and a stab wound. "How long was I out?"

"Four days." Ariana got up and piled cold pizza on a plate while Kira took a long drink of water from the glass on the bedside table.

"Damn." Kira took the plate from her.

I used my fingers to comb Kira's hair away from her face. "You had us pretty worried."

She looked at Ariana. "I'm so sorry about your friend."

"You didn't kill her." Ariana managed a weak smile. "Um"—Ariana grabbed her purse—"I'm going out for hot chocolate."

"That's not necessary," I said, wondering if she was trying to give Kira and me a few minutes alone or running away to avoid talking about Becca.

"Sure it is. Hot chocolate fixes all illnesses, remember?" She was out the door before I could say anything else.

"How are you feeling?" I asked Kira.

"Weak." She set the plate on the table. "Have I really been out for four days?"

"Yeah. I was starting to worry you'd never wake up."

She looked around the well lived-in room. "Where's Ben?"

I took her hand in mine. "He entered the circle before I sealed it. He helped me weaken Asmodeus long enough to finish. If there was another way…"

Kira shook her head as she mumbled, "No," over and over. *Sorry* seemed too small a word for sending someone's brother to Hell, so I squeezed her fingers to let her know I was there for her.

"He'll get out." She worried her lip between her

teeth. "Elise, the angel I told you about, won't let a Blessed of hers rot in Hell. Right?"

"That's Ariana's theory." Although I wasn't so sure if the Angels in Grace would take sympathy on a Blessed who had made a deal with a Fallen Angel, even if the deal fell through; two souls for his sister's freedom didn't seem to fit in with what Heaven stood for, if you asked me.

"He'll get out. I know he will." Kira rested her forehead against mine. After several long seconds, she said, "You should have left as soon as you had Ariana, but thank you for keeping your promise and not leaving me."

"I'd be no better than the demons in that church if I had."

She chuckled. "I told you, you're not evil. Did Ben say why he was working with Asmodeus?"

"For you. Asmodeus promised to release you from your contract if Ben got me to do my part in starting the war."

"He shouldn't have done that." She looked at me. "I'm sorry that he put you and Ariana in danger."

"He was trying to save you." I shrugged. I'd given this a lot of thought. "I'd love to hate him, but the truth is I would have done the same thing for Ariana."

She smoothed the sheet over her lap. After a few seconds, she said, "I wish we had met under different circumstances. You know, because I really do like you."

"Yeah, me too," I admitted.

"Now that I'm up, you don't have to stay. You and Ariana can leave. Start a new life. I promise I won't follow you."

I could feel her sadness flowing off her like heat from the sun. The fact that she'd survived the torture and managed to heal was proof she hadn't been freed from her contract and was still a demon. I didn't care what she was, though.

I ran my hand through her hair, entwining my fingers in red curls at the back of her head. My gaze moved to her ruby-red lips. She was the one who closed the distance between us. Our lips met, saying everything that our words had failed to.

The knock on the door had the same moment-ruining effect as being caught by parents. Ariana peeked in cautiously.

"Come in," I said.

Kira picked up the plate of cold pizza and plucked off a piece of sausage. Ariana handed me a paper cup of hot chocolate from the lobby and then set one on the nightstand for Kira.

"Are you coming with us?" Ariana asked, her tone filled with sincerity. I could tell she wouldn't mind if Kira tagged along.

While I believed Ariana and I had fulfilled our part in the prophecy when we sent Asmodeus back to Hell, we still had the ability to sway the minds of the people we came across. That led me to believe we still needed to be careful and to cover our tracks.

Even so, I'd had plenty of time to weigh the pros and cons of Kira coming with us. In the pros list, she had never lied to me and, as twisted as it may be—seeing as she *was* a demon—I liked her. Another plus was the sigils drawn on the inside of the bracelets we wore seemed to work. In the cons list, though, Asmodeus wasn't the only Fallen Angel out there. I suspected that others would look for us—they might already be looking for us—and if Kira could sense the presence of demons, what was to stop them from sensing her presence should she get too close to one. Traveling with her could be like traveling with a neon sign that said *Demon on Board.* Just repeating those cons in my head made me cringe.

Still, each time I went over the list, my decision was the same.

"We'd love to have you," I said.

Kira shook her head. "Hell doesn't take kindly to deserters. Every Fallen Angel and demon on the planet will know what I look like. You guys, too, probably. We stand a better chance if we separate."

"But you'll be alone," Ariana said. When Kira didn't say anything, Ariana looked at me. "Logan, tell her she's coming with us."

I took Kira's hand in mine. "We can alter our appearance. No one will recognize us."

"Don't you think three teenagers on a road trip in a vintage Chevy Camaro will stand out?"

"Not necessarily," Ariana quickly chimed in.

Kira cocked her head to the side and gave Ariana a look that said, *Oh, puh-lease.* They both then looked at me like I should be the one to make the final decision. I closed my eyes so that I could think without seeing their expectant faces. The silence stretched on.

When the quiet started to scream at us, I replied, "As much as I hate to admit it, I agree with Kira. We can't leave here together."

Ariana sank into one of the chairs. She didn't talk to me for the rest of the night. Kira ate her pizza, although she looked sort of robotic. Not exactly how I would have liked to spend our last evening together.

****

"Are you sure you'll be okay?" I asked Kira. She had her purse slung over one shoulder and her duffle bag over the other. "Let us at least drive you to the bus stop."

Ariana leaned against the rear bumper of my car looking depressed, like she had just said goodbye to her sister and not a demon.

"I'll be fine." Kira hitched the duffle bag higher onto her shoulder.

"You have the phone I gave you?"

She tapped her purse with her hand. I gave her a hug, hating to leave her, but we had to get moving.

"Call if you need anything." Ariana hugged her, then got in the car.

I kissed Kira one last time, memorizing the feel of her lips on mine and the taste of her mouth. "I programmed our numbers into your phone. Call once you get settled."

"Stop worrying about me." Her smile fell short of reaching her eyes.

She turned and walked away, never once looking back, though I did see her hand brush her cheek before she wiped it on her jeans. I was sure she was crying.

"This is wrong," Ariana said as soon as I got in the car.

I could have named a few things that were wrong about our lives, but I was curious to know what Ariana would say. "What is?"

"We should be sticking together."

"Like Kira said, three teens in a vintage car driving across the country would be easy to spot."

She crossed her arms over her chest. "Not with the sigils we found."

We had already had this argument. Ariana had lost two-to-one.

I started the car and put it in gear and headed in the opposite direction as Kira.

Chapter Forty-Two

Ariana ~ One month later

Logan lowered the radio to a murmur and came to a stop in front of the chain-link security gate. He peered through his recently dyed black bangs and glanced cautiously up and down the desolate two-lane road. Logan looked good with darker hair, like it could be his natural color. It was the reflection of the girl with bright topaz eyes and raven-black hair that stared back at me each time I looked in a mirror that I was still trying to get used to.

"Dude, we've spent the last month driving in circles. We weren't followed." I handed him the credit card security key.

"Better safe than sorry."

I was pretty sure if we played it any safer we'd be living in a cave, but I kept that thought to myself because Logan might have decided that was an awesome idea.

I gave a nod to the small metal box outside his window. "Let's get this over with before you change your mind."

He swiped the card, and the gates slowly slid open. Logan pulled through the entrance, taking the first right. We followed the road through a maze of storage units until we reached number sixty-eight. A large orange door glared back at us. Logan looked a little green.

"You sure you're going to survive without your baby?" I asked.

He gave me a sideways glance but said nothing.

"It's not goodbye, you know," I teased.

His fingers tightened around the steering wheel as he checked the rearview mirror. "Shut up and open the door, will you?"

A chuckle escaped my lips as I got out of the Camaro. I leaned in the open window, planning on jibing Logan one more time, but he really did look like he was going to be sick. Instead, I said, "This was your idea."

"I know." He stared straight ahead. He had a white-knuckle grip on the steering wheel. "The door."

The storage unit had white cinderblock walls and seriously bright tangerine doors. I guessed the colors were supposed to make the place look cheery, but there was nothing chipper about having to rent a storage unit. It announced we didn't have a home to warehouse our stuff.

I slid the silver key in the lock and turned the handle. A metallic grinding noise pierced the air as the door went up. Logan parked and met me at the back of the car.

"Seriously, she'll be safe here," I said, knowing it was taking a lot for Logan to leave the Camaro behind. It wasn't just a car. It was the last thing he had of our dad's. "Shouldn't our ride be here?" I asked, hoping to get his mind off the fact that he had just parked his most prize possession in a cold eight-by-ten cement box.

"We're early," he said.

But we weren't. Not even by one minute. Logan

had taken the side streets to make sure of that. He handed me a backpack and my purple plaid duffle bag and tossed his own backpack and duffle bag on the ground behind him before slamming the trunk closed and stuffing the keys into his jacket pocket. He'd just secured the storage unit when a black four-door with tinted windows snaked around the corner. Logan stepped protectively in front of me as the car came to a stop next to us. We bent down to get a look at the driver.

Kira pushed a pair of rose-colored sunglasses up to the top of her head. Slowly, one side of her mouth turned upward. "Need a lift?"

She hopped out of the car before we could answer.

I ran around the other side and gave her a hug. "It's great to see you."

"You too." She stole a glance at Logan, who stared at the car with his mouth hanging open.

"Out of all the cars you could have chosen, you picked a Ford," he said.

"Beggars can't be choosers, Logan." Kira pressed a button on the clicker and popped the trunk.

"But it's a Ford."

I dropped my things in the trunk. "It's less conspicuous than your car," I reminded him.

With one last groan, Logan shoved his bags in next to mine and Kira's. I got in back and let them have a moment to play smoochie-face. None of us had heard from Ben, not that I'd have kissed him hello if we did see him. But after everything we'd been through and knowing why he had done what he had, I didn't think he deserved an eternity in Hell.

"Any sign of trouble?" Logan asked Kira after they

got in.

"Nothing I couldn't handle." She started the car. "Where to?"

"West," Logan and I replied at the same time.

"We should drive to Hollywood!" Kira exclaimed as she pulled away. "Or maybe Disneyland. Have some fun."

"I vote for Disneyland," I chimed in. I'd always wanted to meet Tigger.

"We need to keep a low profile," Logan reminded us in a very fun-killing tone.

Our lives would never be normal, I knew that, but hiding wasn't living, and we were too young to become hermits. Kira and I exchanged sly smiles.

"Sorry, dude," I said.

"You're outnumbered two-to-one," Kira added.

So Disneyland it was. From there, we'd have to see.

A word about the author...

Cherie believes there's a little magic in everyone. She also believes in following her dreams and never giving up. Her books are proof of that.

Besides writing, Cherie enjoys spending time with family and friends, reading, the great outdoors, and she loves a challenge. While she has had many great experiences, what she finds most satisfying is seeing her children and her stories grow into their own exciting and distinct entities.

Cherie lives in Illinois with her family. To learn more about Cherie and her novels visit:

CherieColyer.com

http://cheriecolyer.com/

Thank you for purchasing
this publication of The Wild Rose Press, Inc.
For other wonderful stories of romance,
please visit our on-line bookstore at
www.thewildrosepress.com.

For questions or more information
contact us at
info@thewildrosepress.com.

The Wild Rose Press, Inc.
www.thewildrosepress.com

To visit with authors of
The Wild Rose Press, Inc.
join our yahoo loop at
http://groups.yahoo.com/group/thewildrosepress/

www.ingramcontent.com/pod-product-compliance
Lightning Source LLC
Chambersburg PA
CBHW071525260626
47170CB00002B/508